ON HIS TERMS

IONA ROSE

Publisher: Some Books
ISBN- 978-1-913990-39-8

AUTHOR'S NOTE

Hey there!

Thank you for choosing my book. I sure hope that you love it. I'd hate to part ways once you're done though. So how about we stay in touch?

My newsletter is a great way to discover more about me and my books. Where you'll find frequent exclusive giveaways, sneak previews of new releases and be first to see new cover reveals.

And as a HUGE thank you for joining, you'll receive a FREE book on me!

With love,

Iona

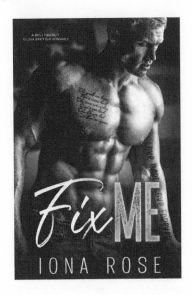

Get Your FREE Book Here:
https://dl.bookfunnel.com/v9yit8b3f7

PROLOGUE

OLIVIA

Eight Years Ago

There were very few things that made me nervous.

Or rather, there were very few things I allowed myself to feel nervous about, especially given how particularly ungracious life has been to me thus far.

However, standing close to the men's locker room at Emerson High makes my palms sweat.

For the better part of the last half hour, I had been waiting a little distance away, hoping my best friend would remember we agreed to meet up here after school so I could retrieve my biology notebook back.

I tried calling him once again, antsy, especially because I was running late for my volunteer gig at the animal shelter. He was well aware of this commitment and I was beyond aggravated.

He still didn't pick up. I frowned down at my phone. Perhaps his battery died again and he left it charging somewhere and isn't able to hear it ringing. I looked towards the door and imagined he's probably engaged in some sort of conversation with his teammates and had completely forgotten about our agreement.

"Don't ever ask me for my notes again!" I angrily typed out yet another message to him, anger simmered in the pit of my stomach.

The door swung open once again with a few of the guys heading out, but of course he wasn't amongst them.

My heart sunk when I moved a bit further toward the door. Maybe one of them would help me find him.

I truly hoped I wouldn't have to talk to any of the guys, but it became apparent now it's my only option. I began to inch closer, but made sure to stop a few steps away so it wouldn't appear as though I was outright trying to ogle them or something. The accusation, and the subsequent infamy it would bestow on me, is not particularly one I had any interest whatsoever in.

Another few minutes passed and the door swung open again.

My heart lurched into my throat when I stepped forward, ready to plead for some assistance in locating Danny, however, when I saw who it was my plan was immediately aborted. Because there was no way in hell I was going to speak to Xander King. He's super popular and for all the right reasons... smart, handsome, easy going, athletic, and so much more. I raised him up on such a pedestal that speaking to him was out of the question.

I turned to walk away, my eyes clenched shut as I cursed underneath my breath.

A few seconds later, I found the courage to open my eyes again, swearing to murder Danny, and turned back toward the locker room praying I had waited long enough for Xander to have moved on.

I'm not that lucky though and freeze because Xander hadn't moved and is staring right at me.

"Hey," he smiled over at me.

There was no hope of a response coming from me as my brain short circuited and I'm frozen in place staring back at him.

His smile widens to show his perfect white teeth. I could only imagine what he thought of me standing there. I tried to smile back but it came as more of a grimace.

He jerked his head toward the locker room door. "Do you need something?"

I opened my mouth and nothing came out. Could I be anymore lame? I'm tempted to look behind me to see if he was actually speaking to me or if someone walked up behind me.

But my brain slowly started working, reminding me the only thing behind me was a wall.

I'm tempted to turn once more to face it just so he'll hopefully walk away. Granted he would probably forever label me as mental but I could live with that. Anything was better than just staring at him like I'm mute.

At my continued stupor he held his perfect smile and a gleam in his icy blue eyes. They were usually cold… he has always seemed cold. He's never even looked in my direction, which makes it all the more jarring he's smiling at me now.

His hair's all over the place… raven black, thick, wavy, unruly. I'd fantasized about what it would feel like to run my fingers through it more times than I would ever admit, and now that I'm this close to it, the fantasies returned.

His gaze once again returned to the locker room door as it swung open.

"Are you looking for your friend?" he asked, looking back at me.

This startled me. *Friend? What friend?*

At my widened gaze, he responded. "I've seen you both around together."

I wondered if I would ever be able to speak again. He'd seen us around. I mean, it made sense he knew Danny, they played on the same team… but he knew *I* existed?

"Hello?" he waved again, and my throat had closed up. What in the hell is wrong with

Me?

My lips parted again as I tried to remember how to speak. At some point I backed up against the wall and I leaned more of my weight onto it.

An apology for my silence was on the tip of my tongue, but suddenly I heard my name.

"Olivia?"

I turned instantly to see Danny coming out the door, his phone pressed to his ear.

Just then mine began to ring and I looked down at my hand still clutching my phone.

Before I could stop myself the curse shot out of my mouth. "You piece of shit!"

The shock that followed from everyone, including myself, seemed to turn the entire corridor into a graveyard.

I'm not shocked I exploded, and neither is Danny, but the over six foot tall Adonis before me I had previously appeared mute to, is startled.

My gaze swept back over to him and met his widened eyes.

My lips parted again, but this time around it's with the intention to explain my outburst.

He however began to laugh, softly and shook his head.

"At least I know your name now," he chuckled and with a salute to Danny turned around to continue on his way, a satchel slung over his shoulder. "See you around... Olivia."

I couldn't breathe... I almost forgot all about Danny still standing there.

At least I know your name now? What did he mean? Why did he want to know my name?

"Livvy I'm so sorry, I completely forgot," I heard the afore-mentioned piece of shit say as he hurried over to me.

"Here," he held out my notebook but I couldn't look away from Xander King as he strolled confidently and unhurriedly away from us.

Just like every other girl in Emerson High who crushes on Xander my heart raced away in my chest, and I knew without a shadow of a doubt I would be replaying this scene in my heart and mind forever.

And his words- *see you around, Olivia?* What on earth could he possibly mean?

My palms were sweaty again.

On my drive here my steering wheel had received the brunt of my anxiety, but now it was the woven strap of my purse.

I looked down to inspect it as the elevator began to climb the floors. I loved this purse, it was a gift from my mother about two years ago when I had gotten my first job ever at Charter Middle School. The strap was woven in red and blue while the purse itself was a creamy, textured leather.

The last thing I wanted was for it to be sweat soaked so I considered unhooking it and instead use the short handle attached to the top.

I'd just gotten used to wearing it with the strap.

My gaze lifted to the floor display as the elevator stopped to let out and let in a few people.

It was a few seconds of shuffling about to make room, and then the car resumed its ascent.

7

My mind returned to the strap as my eyes glanced back to the display ahead showing we were now passing the 52nd floor.

My heart was racing, and I reckon it was going to be the case for the next hour or longer. Just as we reached the 58th floor, with three floors more to go, I began to unhook the strap from the corners.

It all came off just as the elevator came to a stop again. I lifted my gaze and watched as the entire car emptied out. However, I still had one more floor to go, the final floor.

I tried, but failed to swallow the lump in my throat so I gave up altogether and tucked the strap into the purse.

I arrived with a ding, the shiny steel doors parted but it took a few seconds for my legs to work.

I'm not exactly sure the exact moment life returned to them, but soon enough I'm heading into his reception area.

I was expected since I was already cleared from the ground floor, which gave me a bit of hope that perhaps this trip wouldn't be completely futile.

I hoped this meeting would produce the result I'm hoping for, otherwise my heart would be broken. This was my last resort, and one I would have never even seen as an option if my entire family's life wasn't hanging in the balance.

So although I wasn't expecting much, I needed to at least try so no matter what I could live with myself.

"Miss Rose?" the gorgeous receptionist called and I nodded in response.

"Please take a seat. Mr. King is on a conference call right now. He'll be with you shortly."

"Alright" I replied and headed over to one of the space's leather sofas.

Afterwards, I watched her leave, my gaze on her tasteful dark pumps and tailored pink pantsuit. She was gorgeous… hair blonde, slicked back into a neat bun at the back of her head. Behind the desk, was a man also dressed sharply in a suit and as our eyes met, he sent me a polite smile.

I settled in to wait, and once again assessed my appearance.

I wasn't over dressed, although I had been quite tempted to go that route but the last thing I wanted was to impress him. So I had chosen a simple pair of dark jeans, a lacy camisole underneath and a tailored camel blazer.

My wavy brown hair was arranged into a neat half up and half down style, my makeup simple, and on my feet were my usual low heeled work pumps.

I look decent, pretty even but I didn't expect him to think that.

In fact, I didn't expect him to think about me in any positive light whatsoever but still I had to try.

This is for your conscience, I had managed to convince myself before making the ultimate decision to come over.

The call was made almost two weeks prior but it was just the previous day I had received a response, relaying his approval and available meeting time.

And so here I was, in the midst of his extreme wealth and success.

I wasn't surprised... at his animosity towards me or his success so far. He was just twenty four, and as far as I'd heard, King Industries was now worth a billion dollars. The ultimate unicorn. Everyone in the media called him an ultimate success but only I knew how long he'd had this dream of developing the smartphone his company produced, and how he had begun working on it right from high school.

He deserved every ounce of his victory, and even though I was slightly jealous I had reminded myself time and time again I too was in the exact place I wanted to be. I'd always wanted to be a teacher, and I'd worked towards it from the time we'd both left high school.

That was one of the things I'd so loved about us... how clear we'd been about where we wanted to go. And how we both strived to achieve it. However the downside to knowing the exact directions we wanted had led to paths that had taken us away from each other. He had gone to San Francisco, while I'd remained here in LA.

But he had returned as expected, but it was too late. A lot of things were now too late but I had no regrets.

In the present I waited another half hour before I was called.

"Mr. King's ready for you," the receptionist said, and I rose to my feet.

I went with her down the elegant hallway, which was lined on both sides with what I was certain were original pieces of gorgeous art.

Soon we arrived at the wide double doors to his office and she turned to me with a smile.

"What would you like to drink?"

"Um... "

"Water? Tea? Coffee?"

I smiled because this wasn't that kind of meeting.

"Nothing," I replied. "Thank you." She nodded and went on her way.

I stood before the heavy mahogany doors and took several deep breaths. And my hand rose to knock. I hesitated for a little bit because it wasn't too late. I mean I could turn back right now.

With a sigh I knocked on it, and heard the response from within.

"Come in."

With my heart in my throat, I turned the handle down and walked in.

XANDER

I couldn't believe she was here.

It had been two weeks and I still couldn't believe she had contacted me.

The first time Laura had informed me of the call, I'd been in the middle of a meeting in my office.

It had taken a little while for the name to register, and all the blood drained from my face.

"She wants to speak to me?" I'd asked.

"Yes sir."

My immediate response had been a no.

"Tell her to book an appointment and come in."

The call had ended, but my silence had continued on. It was such a contrast to my much more lighthearted mood from the minutes prior, and so the men before me were quite taken aback.

They allowed me the time to recover... to think... and to make a decision. And then I'd call Laura back.

"Wait to call her back for at least two week to make the appointment."

"Yes sir." had been Laura's quick reply.

It should have been more, I should make her wait forever... if possible. But I had no clue about what she wanted, and dragging things out any longer might have resulted in her not needing to contact me again.

I didn't necessarily want to see her but I needed the confrontation. I'd waited for it and almost even hoped for it for too long.

And now she was here, and it was a hard pill to swallow.

A part of me had imagined she wouldn't show up. That she would find an excuse at the last minute and cancel the appointment but she had made it. I was truly surprised. It made me all the more curious now as to what she needed.

I knew her, and was aware she wouldn't be here if it wasn't a matter of importance. It made me just a little worried. *Was she alright?*

I pointed to one of the seats before me and with a nod, she headed over, her head lowered to watch her steps.

I was glad because it meant I could watch her.

And what surprised me the most was not much had changed about her.

She was no longer the same fifteen year old teenager that had kept to herself back in Emerson. She was a woman now, a bit taller, a bit more curvaceous. My gaze couldn't help going to the lacy camisole that covered her chest and how it stretched across her breasts.

I felt the immediate and responding tug in my groin.

It had been so long, but I remembered. My heart remembered… as well as my body.

I suddenly began to feel heated, but didn't even bother examining the ventilation of the room. Because the air conditioner was running and all the heat was emanating from the pit of my stomach and spreading out to the rest of my body.

I watched as she took her seat, cautiously and she was arranging her purse on her lap. She took her time, but I watched and waited until she was finally ready to look up at me.

She soon did, a soft smile on her face but her gaze… was guarded.

What stunned me the most was she had become even more beautiful. Sixteen year old me wouldn't have thought it was possible but yet here we were.

I gazed unashamedly at her brown eyes, warm and beguiling… the gentle slope of her nose and down to her full peachy lips.

I had kissed them, more times than I could remember but at the time was sure it would never be enough. That I would never get enough. I wondered now if it would be the case if I tasted her once again.

Perhaps we had outgrown each other or perhaps it was all still the same as back then. I felt like a moth drawn to a flame when it came to her.

"It's been a while," she spoke, and I didn't miss the slight tremble of her voice. She was nervous and it showed. I was too, somewhat, but I was able to conceal it well. I was already liking the direction of things.

She looked around the office when I didn't give a response. "You've done really great, Xander. I'm so proud of you."

I straightened in my seat. "Why are you here?"

I could no longer wait. I needed to know why she had set aside her pride and come all the way here to see me. She wasn't shameless as far as I knew, or perhaps she was or had become so? It had been almost four years now since we had been separated.

More than enough time for people to change, especially for her.

Bile instantly rose up in my throat at the reminder.

"Straight to the point," she smiled, nervous once again. "I won't waste your time. I just… I wanted to at least try."

Her gaze lifted to mine, and I didn't miss the slight sheen in them.

"My mom, um… she was diagnosed with breast cancer, about two years ago," she began. "She got treatment for it… a mastectomy, and then chemo. She started getting better, but we found out a few weeks ago it's back."

She smiled, but my heart squeezed at her words.

"We're still in debt from bearing all the costs from the first time around but now…" she sighed, smiling again.

15

"I couldn't help but come to you… to ask if perhaps you could help us out. It's alright if you refuse. I would understand. You have no obligation to help me out or anything. It was just… right now… it's a sort of last resort. Maybe another way will open up in the future soon. We're hopeful."

I looked at her, and had absolutely no idea of what to say.

I knew her mother, Linda. The sweetest woman to probably ever exist, she took me in like I was a part of her family for years. So hearing this hurt me deeply. But I couldn't let it show because her daughter on the other hand was a thorn in my side. A thorn I was still unable to pull out. And as I stared at her now, I wondered if I would ever want to.

A long silence ensued between us, and that was because I didn't particularly know what to say. Simply handing over whatever funds she needed for the surgery was no particular hardship for me, but as I looked at her I wondered if I was willing to just simply do this for her. I was willing to help her mother but her…

"I understand if you're not willing to do this, or if you need a bit more time to process it," she suddenly began to rise to her feet. "I'm grateful already that you were willing to have a meeting with me."

At this and without a second look at me, or even waiting for my response she turned around and began to walk away. I knew then what I wanted to say.

"What are you willing to exchange?" I leaned back in my chair. "For these needed funds."

She stopped in her tracks.

OLIVIA

I heard his words, but couldn't understand them.

What was I willing to exchange?

What could I possibly exchange?

Perplexed, I slowly turned around to face him but still couldn't find anything to say.

"What do you mean?"

He was leaned back in his chair, comfortably, and it gave me the perception perhaps his intent with this was to torture me. If it was the case then I was unsurprised as it was well deserved. Perhaps afterwards and even though I left with nothing, we would both be able to come to some sort of closure with each other.

"Well, you weren't expecting me to just hand the money over, were you?"

I smiled. "I wasn't, but I didn't think you'd be asking me what I could exchange for it either. I mean if I had anything worth exchanging, I wouldn't be here."

The smile left his face as he stared at me, intently, but I couldn't help but notice that despite the antagonism between us he didn't seem hostile.

Just withdrawn and with an obvious chip on his shoulder, but the intent of cruelty wasn't as present as I had expected.

"Have sex with me," he said and my brain scrambled to a halt.

At first I was certain I had heard him wrong.

"What?"

"Have sex with me," he repeated. "In exchange for the complete coverage of your mother's treatment expenses. I care about her, but not so much about you, so I can't help but hesitate in just handing the money over. In exchange it needs to bring some sort of discomfort to you for me to be consoled."

My eyes popped open, especially at how casual he sounded, as though we were discussing the weather. I turned more fully to face him, more than willing to unpack this.

"Why would you want to have sex with me?"

"Do you want to have sex with me?" he asked, and once again I was stumped, and a bit taken aback because in the past he always spoke kindly. Currently however, and with this conversation it felt as though he was throwing knives. They didn't hurt, at least not yet, but I still felt them lodge into me. Perhaps with time the resulting wounds would begin to fester.

"No, I do not," I responded, and his smile was mocking.

"Exactly."

I guess it was beginning to make sense but as I took another good look at him, I wondered if he truly believed this narrative he was championing. He believed we wanted nothing to do with each other, and having sex together would be torture for us both. But for me it absolutely wouldn't be. I had once loved him and till now, I was certain a part of me always would. I had never been able to forget him even after all the years that had passed, and it had made me come to terms with the fact he would always be a part of me.

There was no way he could know this, especially given my actions in the past so it wasn't surprising to see he expected it to be the utmost punishment to me that I would have to have sex with him.

Still however, I was going to refuse, because from the moment he touched me, I had no doubt I would be exposed. He would see and feel the truth of how much I had missed him… and of how much I had to sacrifice so he could be free enough to soar.

"No," I replied, and his shoulders lifted in a shrug.

"Okay then," he replied. "I guess this concludes our meeting. You can see yourself out."

I stared at him, dumbfounded.

And I called his name out loud for the first time in almost four years.

"Xander," his hand froze midway reaching for his pen.

"I know we didn't end things on the best of terms but…" I didn't know what else to say.

"But what?" he asked.

I sighed and reminded myself what was at stake. "I'll be honest with you. It won't actually be unpleasant for me to have sex with you at all. We were together for a while and in love so I reckon returning to it won't be too hard?"

He frowned, no doubt surprised.

"My point is, let's be civil with each other. I know what I'm asking for is completely ludicrous given our history but I also know you are not unkind. So if you do want me to exchange something for it I'm willing to. But I don't think my body will be the right exchange. It sends the wrong message that perhaps you're still interested in me which I don't think is the case at all. I mean look at all you have. You can't possibly be without a line of women ready to take you up on that offer, and for nothing in return I'm sure."

He smiled, and it eerily reminded me once again of the afternoon in the hallway where we had come face to face for the first time. After I had cursed at Danny, Xander had looked as though he was seeing me for the very first time. I knew now this was the look he wore when he was particularly pleased with my wit, although and especially in this case, it was unintentional. My mother's life was at stake and this was not the time to play hanky- panky with my high school sweetheart.

"I don't want them," he replied. "I want you."

I was even more confused. "I don't understand."

"Do you want me, Olivia?"

This felt like a trick of some sort, but what made it the most frustrating was I couldn't tell if he was serious or not. Regardless, I was certain the end goal was to ensure I was thoroughly humiliated.

And so I just decided to put an end to it altogether.

"No Xander," I replied. "I do not want you."

"Then this would be the ideal exchange for us."

I was even more confused. "Why would you be with a woman you dislike?"

"I didn't say I disliked you," he corrected and I felt a bit dizzy. "I've only said so far I want you."

"I might enjoy this," I warned him, and he smiled.

"I hope you do."

And at this I realized the entire trip was futile. I had absolutely wasted my time by coming here and things would just spiral downhill if I stayed any longer.

I was tempted to just walk away, and not even give him the pleasure of completing this most torturous exchange, however I was certain I was the one it would haunt the most.

"I can't do this," I said to him. "So, no thank you. I'll just have to figure out some other way. Thank you for your time."

"You're welcome," he said with a small self-satisfied smile, and I suddenly felt a surge of anger shoot through me or perhaps it was humiliation. I couldn't tell the difference. I no longer wanted anything to do with him, even in my memories, and it hurt. Truly. Perhaps this was what he meant by, he hoped I enjoyed it if indeed we got together to have sex. Was this his ploy to break my heart just as I had broken his?

"I wish you the best," I said to him, genuinely and truly and watched as the smile completely disappeared from his face.

With that said I walked away from Xander King for the last time and the hurt in my heart intensified even more.

XANDER

I *wish you the best?*

I stared at the door as it shut behind her, anger beginning to boil in my veins.

What aggravated me the most was the fact I knew she had truly meant it. I knew her at least this much... knew about her genuinely good nature, and kindness. Sure she had made a grave mistake four years ago, and I didn't think I could ever forgive her for it but back then it was because she hadn't seemed to care that she had devastated me. She'd instead come off as complacent, as though her mistake couldn't have been helped. But now... she was genuinely wishing me well?

I wanted to throw something at the door. But instead, I forced myself to take deep calming breaths and turned away from the door altogether.

Behind me was the entire glass to ceiling wall looking over the downtown skyline, and although my gaze was on the quite beautiful day beyond, my brain could barely process it.

All I could see in my mind's eye was the true sadness that had appeared on her face at the exchange we'd just had. It had been four years, and sure, I had always wondered how things would go if we ever met again, but I hadn't expected it to be this torturous.

My nerves tightened in worry as her mother's health came to mind and it made me wonder all the more why I was so affected by this.

She was the one who hurt you, my head reminded me, but all I could think about was her mother's life was truly at stake, and no matter how terrible our history, this was not a thing to mock or use to my advantage. It made me feel like a dick, and left a foul taste in my mouth. Perhaps the problem was that too many unnecessary words had been exchanged, because all I needed was to actually handle her mother's expenses and she would automatically feel indebted to me, eager to do what was needed to ensure she didn't feel like she owed me. It was one of the reasons I'd fallen so deeply in love with her in the first place, the fact that in all things she always strived to give more than she received.

So perhaps the exchange for sex had been the wrong approach, but how else was I going to get her back into my life and still keep my pride intact?

I had no clue.

My only hope was as a result of this conversation, she wouldn't reject the help I was still willing to give to her mother. No matter what, I couldn't look away, even though my actions showed I was only willing to help in exchange for using her body. I didn't believe it, and now I couldn't help but wonder if she did. If the latter was the case then perhaps this was why she had thrown our relationship away, but I couldn't help but remain sour at the fact every fiber of my being had hoped she would accept it.

OLIVIA

It took me quite a while to convince myself not to dwell on the exchange in Xander's office.

It had been confusing at best, and downright degrading at worst, and the more I thought about it the more upset it made me. Thankfully midway through the week, work had been more than enough to distract me and when the weekend came, I drove over to my mother's place so we could spend the day together.

When I arrived at her apartment complex however, I couldn't help but remain in my car, once again deep in thought as I replayed all of what was said in my mind once again.

What exactly had he wanted? To fuck me and leave me humiliated, or to fuck me and leave me heartbroken?

Neither of those options were appealing to me, but I couldn't help but think perhaps I was wrong in walking in there and outright demanding a handout. I'd expected to be rejected, but maybe if I'd asked for his help as a loan, which I would pay back with time, he would've been more willing to cooperate with me.

Instead, my outright request had only allowed him a vindictive option for me.

With a sigh, I got out of the car and began to head over to Mom's apartment.

I see the living room is empty as usual, so I headed straight to her bedroom and found her in bed with her puppy, Izzie, by her side.

The television was on some talk show rerun, and it was a delight to see the smile on her face as I walked in.

My heart however couldn't help but ache at how frail she looked.

"Hey, I thought you were going to come by later?" she greeted me.

"Yeah," I replied and immediately got into bed with her, sliding underneath the covers. "I thought so too."

I suddenly felt even more broody and although it hadn't been the plan, I huddled up close to her and threw an arm around her midriff. She accepted the embrace, her own hand going behind to stroke the back of my head.

And that was how we stayed for the minutes that followed as we both mindlessly watched the show.

Nothing in particular stood out since I wasn't paying attention. Instead my mind was on a pair of icy blue eyes whose owner I had once been convinced I would love forever.

Now however, I didn't know how to feel or even how I felt. Disappointment? Anger? Regret?

Perhaps I had been too harsh back then in ending things with him... too abrupt... too hurtful. But if I didn't do what I did, then I doubted he would have heeded my request for us to end things. But what haunted me even further till this day and perhaps till my last breath was if I made a mistake in ending our relationship. I had asked myself this question countless times in the past at this point, but his success I realized now in a way had consoled me. By letting him go we had both been able to chase our own paths without being an obstruction to each other, and look at just how much glory it had brought him at his age. In the entire country few others were worth as much as he was, and despite our antagonism towards each other I couldn't help but feel quite consoled. Perhaps if he hadn't turned out as well and our parting had been more of a stumbling block to him than a boost, then perhaps I would have been regretful.

I sighed, and felt my mother move. She turned to gaze at me, a small smile playing at the corners of my lips.

"What's wrong?" she asked, and I instantly shook my head, unwilling to ever bother her with any issues especially at such a delicate time in her life.

"Nothing. I'm just a bit tired."

"You should have slept in."

"You should move in with me so I can always have you in sight and won't have to worry about sleeping in."

She ignored me and returned her gaze to the TV, her response as always, a refusal.

"I don't want to encroach on your life," she had told me when I had first suggested the idea before she had begun chemo.

I'd fought with her on this for a little while, but eventually gave up because I'd realized what would have been even worse to her than this illness was her thinking in any way she was hindering me from living an unrestrained life.

I sighed again, and hugged her even harder.

"Work troubles?" she pressed on and I smiled, shaking my head. I did however remember there was one thing I could talk to her about so she wouldn't worry I wasn't sharing my own troubles with her.

"Caleb's parents might be moving soon. If all happens as planned the little devil will be out of my class."

She smiled.

"You'll miss him."

"I know," I replied, but yet again a pair of icy blue eyes came to mind. "All the other kids will be better behaved after he leaves."

"Isn't that what you wanted?" she asked.

Was it truly?

Was all of what he had achieved on his own truly better than what we could have been if I had allowed us to remain together? Perhaps we would have broken up somewhere along the way but had I thrown in the towel too soon?

I was exhausted from asking the same questions all over again, and so I finally rose up from her arms. Izzie came up to me, her tail wagging and I let her onto my lap.

"Your book club is checking out a new restaurant this afternoon right?"

"Yeah," she replied. However, at her tone I knew something was definitely wrong.

"But…?" I added.

"I'm not going. I'll join them next week."

My concern rose. "You canceled on them the week before."

"I went last week."

At my gaze she explained. "I feel especially tired. I just want to rest."

I understood she was more than entitled to this, but the fact the book club had been such a source of entertainment and activity to her had consoled me for so long. Especially because even during the worst of times the first time around when she'd been first diagnosed, she'd still managed to make her meetings. But this recurrence had dampened her spirit and it scared me. I was worried she would give up… she was becoming too exhausted to fight.

"I'll go with you," I told her. "I can be out of the way while you all eat together, and afterwards we could do a bit of shopping?"

"Don't you have a date or something fun to do today? It's Saturday, and you're twenty-three. You should go out."

"That'll be in the evening. Betsy will be over by then to take over."

"I don't need to be watched twenty-four seven Olivia, I'm not an invalid. I'm just ill."

Her words made me ache but as always, I didn't know what I could say to console her.

But soon an idea came to mind.

"I'll go out tonight, if you go to the restaurant with your friends. Then I'll be calm, knowing you've gotten a bit of socializing in for the week."

She looked at me, saw the earnest plea in my eyes not to fight me on this and nodded.

Later that evening, I returned home to my own apartment and collapsed onto the couch. The day thus far had been enjoyable, with my only wish still being that I could spend the entire weekend with her, but I was aware she would never agree to this. It would only fill her with the concern I was giving up too much of my life to be with her, but at this point, I had gotten tired of reminding her she was my mother and she was a huge part of my life. A huge part I didn't know if I would ever be able to function without if this illness did indeed take her. But at the very least, I needed to know I spent as much time as was possible with her, if ever the day came.

I could never share any of this pessimism with her, so maybe this was why she still remained somewhat guarded about fully moving in with me.

I had instructed her caretaker Betsy to make some chicken soup for her as I'd left, but now I was back in my own apartment and I realized I was the one that had forgotten to make any dinner plans for myself. I had barely had lunch, only nibbling from time to time on the ham sandwiches we had gotten from the grocery store.

I was thankful at least I had gotten some groceries for myself, so after resting a bit further, and in order to avoid some unwanted memories stirring up to the surface of my mind, I rose to my feet.

The meal for tonight was going to be spaghetti carbonara, quick and simple.

And *yes* I had indeed told her I would go out for the night, but there was truly nowhere to head to. Unless I called up Elise and made a plan? But it was already too late and the last thing I wanted was to stay up late.

I headed over to the kitchen and got started. As I went along though and even though I tried, I couldn't stop thinking about him, and what he had asked for and how it would bring my mom out of this hell. This was a recurrence and she was exhausted, completely worn out from fighting the initial diagnosis from a year ago and I was terrified.

Terrified this time around if we waited too long, she might truly come to the end of her strength.

So... I stopped, my hand stilling on the pot as I wondered about what truly would be so bad about having sex with him.

If my mom's strength and life depended on it, then why was it too much of a price to pay. I recalled her exhaustion once again from the day we'd had together, and how hard she'd tried to hide it all, and it reminded me of what had pushed me to even go ahead to see him in the first place. I was desperate and that made me a beggar, so truly what grounds did I have to maintain my pride with.

Especially when it came to her life.

And moreover, this was Xander.

Granted, the both of us weren't the best of friends but doing what he was requesting of me would truly not kill me. Perhaps it would hurt my heart, especially if our exchange in his office was any indication but it wasn't anything I hadn't done with him before, and loved.

With a sigh, I picked the spoon back up and resolved to call him after giving this a bit more thought.

However I eventually decided I wasn't going to wait, otherwise the gravity of the choice I was about to make right now would sink in, and I'd change my mind.

If I allowed myself a goodnight's sleep, and a call from my mother the next day feigning she was fine, I would once again become all too willing to believe it… because it was easier, and because it made my heart calm for a moment.

But at the back of my mind I knew we were all just waiting, or perhaps wasting time.

And so I turned the stove off and went into my room. I knew what I was looking for, it was tucked in a box at the back of my closet that I hadn't touched in years.

I headed over to it and settled down on the floor. A few minutes later and after shuffling through a few of my old journals I finally found it.

I'd stopped writing in my journals years ago. For one, I no longer found the time to since I finished college and then went job hunting, but also I hadn't wanted to give myself such a self-indulgent outlet to nurse my broken heart with.

More than anything, it had been making me wallow rather than helping me to actually heal, and so I had made the difficult decision to do my best in completely putting him

33

out of my mind. It had worked and I had been able to move on.

I looked at the scratched leather, one of the presents he had given to me when I had turned eighteen. It was still... beautiful... aged but beautiful, and it made me also think about the intimacy and depth of feeling we had shared. It was now aged but would it ever somehow return to ever being beautiful? Or was it simply just doomed to remain hidden away in a box?

I pulled it open and on the front page was the information I needed, two phone numbers.

Mine remained the same especially since I had never moved. As for his however... well I guess we were going to find out.

I took the note with me because although at one time I had known his number by heart, I could no longer recall it.

I returned to my couch, picked up my phone and began to dial.

I gave myself no time to think this through especially because I didn't expect the number to work.

I placed the phone against my ear, my heart rate picking up as it began to ring. Perhaps it had been changed?

A few rings after and the number was picked up.

My heart jumped.

"Hello..." I called, but there was no response.

I pulled the phone away from my ear to gaze at it and... my heart slammed against my chest. "Um... I'm sorry but I think I got the wrong number."

"Did you?"

I froze. Something cold began to slither down my spine, but at the same time, I felt a burning heat begin to gather in my chest. That voice… slightly hoarse but calm... chillingly calm.

Immediately I pictured the man in my mind's eyes and felt something akin to being in a stupor.

Perhaps it was because of how shocked I was that this number had remained his, and all this time I probably could have easily reached out to him.

Or perhaps it was the fact he had instantly known who I was. Which meant he had saved my number. Or did he just recognize my voice?

I felt a headache begin to come on.

"Hey," I greeted going the path of politeness.

He didn't respond, just as I expected and I almost smiled. I knew what the question was. 'Why the hell are you calling me?'

And so I cleared my throat and began, wishing I had picked up a bottle of wine at the store. I had eyed a 2012 Merlot that would have been more than enough to calm me and boost my courage to say the things I was about to but instead I was stark sober and exhausted to boot.

My impending and inevitable defeat at the end of this call settled on me.

"I was hoping to revisit what we talked about earlier." I said.

He remained quiet and so I went on. It wasn't the most encouraging of responses but at least he hadn't hung up.

"What um… what exactly would it entail?" I questioned, nervous for his response.

"What do you want it to entail?" he asked, and I almost groaned out in frustration, especially because this particular question could carry two different connotations. I chose not to address the more risqué one.

"If I… if we do this… all of my mother's medical expenses will be covered?" I felt so ashamed as my face burned and eyes stung with tears but I needed to press on.

It didn't help that once again he took his damn time in responding.

"Where do you live?" he asked, and my heart once again slammed against my chest.

My gaze lifted to the front door of my apartment and I gave him the address.

"Text me your address. I'll come over and we can discuss this in person."

My immediate reaction was to refuse because I wasn't sure I wanted him in my space. Even if we were truly going to do this, it wouldn't be here because I was scared that if I let him in once again, it would be too difficult and excruciating to purge him out. I looked around again… I really liked this apartment because although it was a bit old, I had done quite a lot of work on it and turned it into my home.

Xander at one point in my life used to be my home and the last thing I wanted was for the two to once again entangle themselves and become inseparable.

"I'll come out to meet you," I said and untucked my feet from underneath me ready to move. However, his response stopped me.

"No," he said. "If we are to proceed then it will solely be on my terms. If you can't accept this then don't waste my time," there was a short pause, "again." he released on a sigh.

XANDER

The moment the word left my mouth, I knew I had made a mistake. I had said too much... had revealed too much. With just one word... *again.*

She knew I'd cracked back then, but I didn't necessarily want to remember and neither did I want to bring it up in the present. I ran my hand through my hair and it was only then I realized I was beginning to pace.

I was currently in the lobby of a downtown hotel, and had stepped out of the bar and meeting just moments earlier to take the call. I knew the moment it was her, not even because her contact info had always remained on my phone but because I knew the numbers by heart. It had indeed been years since I'd used it but I doubted my mind and heart would ever unlearn it.

"Alright," she said. "I'll text it to you."

Silence.

"Can you let me know when you intend to come over? I'll make sure I'm available."

I already knew the response to this because from the moment she'd walked out of my office, my heart had been in a special kind of turmoil. I could focus as I usually did and needed to, however the distraction that was Olivia had lodged itself into my mind, and I'd been unable to get it out. To stop thinking about her in the moments I had nothing urgent to attend to in the office.

In the morning when I got up for the day, in the shower, on my commute... I recalled it all. Her scent from back then, and how I had been nearly addicted to it... what it had felt like to possess her body, at least for the time I thought I completely did.

Seeing her again now made me realize more than ever just how intensely in love with her I'd been.

Her calling it quits back then had nearly shattered me, but I had convinced myself she wasn't worth a second more of my wallowing and I'd gone on to achieve what I wanted.

I'd moved on, but it was clear to me I'd simply gone around in a circle because once again I was back here.

"I'll be there later tonight."

I ended the call and slipped the phone back into my pocket.

I still had at least forty-five minute left before the end of my meeting, and although I had begun to feel slightly tired, I realized now I was going to be a bit more patient and let it run its course, because the last thing I wanted was to run to her whenever she wanted. This needed to be on my terms or I risked getting hurt... again.

It took an hour and a half for me to eventually leave the bar, but I didn't put any haste to my movements. I took my time and it was already almost midnight by the time I pulled in front of her apartment.

I knew it was already quite late and I was borderline now acting like a dick but I didn't care.

Or at least I tried not to. I steeled my heart against any ingrained courtesy that protested and got out of the car.

I took my time strolling over to her apartment building and up to her door.

I knocked once… and waited.

When after a few seconds there was no response I knocked again.

Perhaps she had gone to bed? But I had told her I would be coming tonight and judging by her character, I knew she wouldn't be able to go to bed.

I was right because a few seconds later, the door was pulled open.

She was barefaced and it had been so long since I'd last seen her this way I couldn't help but be startled.

There wasn't much of a difference to how she appeared when she had makeup on, but when she was like this it was as if no time had passed and it truly affected me. It made me want to grab her and shake her. To demand why she had regarded what we had so carelessly.

It was so special… was still so special it haunted me as to if I would ever feel as connected to anyone in my life as I had been to her.

"Hey," she greeted, but I didn't want to acknowledge her. Instead my gaze perused the rest of her appearance.

She was dressed comfortably and not at all provocatively, and it made me wonder if she had gone out of her way to do this.

She was in long cotton pajama pants and a massive t-shirt. Her hair was pulled messily at the top of her head and she had her glasses on.

I couldn't help but smile. It was as though she was doing everything possible to dim my desire for her, but it had the opposite effect because underneath the clothes, I knew how she tasted and what it felt like to be plastered to her... skin to skin.

"Come in," she said and stepped to the side.

Afterwards she closed the door behind me and followed me into a quaint living room.

"Do you want anything to drink? I have water... tea."

I shook my head, as my gaze ran across the cozy and neutral toned space.

It wasn't huge by any significant measure but it was neat and smelled of jasmine.

I almost never wanted to leave.

"Have a seat," she said. "I'll get you some water."

She started to walk away from me but instead I caught her hand, and pulled her towards me. She was startled, and to an extent so was I because I hadn't expected her to be so light, but I no longer wanted to talk or needlessly torment myself.

What I wanted was to fuck her hard and to put myself out of this misery. Perhaps all I needed was to do it once for some sort of closure my mind had convinced me I never got but deserved.

And most importantly, I needed to do this so a clear exchange for her mother's medical care expenses would be in place. Otherwise she might be inclined to think I'd done it because I cared and this was the absolute last thing I would ever want her to think.

I stared down into her warm brown eyes, now widened slightly at my sudden grip and every other thought left my head.

I leaned down, and latched my lips onto hers.

She was taken aback and unguarded, so I was even able to taste her. I pulled away as the kiss broke apart with a small almost impossible smack.

Her eyes fluttered open, and all she could do was stare. I imagined she felt as I did, shaken, and immediately desperate for more, however she didn't make any further moves or even speak. She just stared at me and I couldn't read her... not like I used to anyway.

But then she surprised me. Her hand suddenly lifted and my gaze followed it, wondering what she intended.

I almost became amused when it occurred to me that perhaps she was going to hit me, but her hand curved around the back of my head and she pulled me down towards her.

Now it was my turn to be startled. She kissed me, hard and then her tongue slid into my mouth. I briefly became unaware of myself and could only process the heated taste of her.

Her tongue slid into my mouth, stroking against mine and the lushness made me stagger. Fortunately it was forward and towards her so my arms wrapped around her waist.

For one it was truly to regain my balance but then it was also incontestable because I needed her body pressed up against mine. My heart was racing so hard it could nearly no longer be contained within my chest.

My head slanted to take the kiss even deeper and before long we were grinding wildly against each other. I felt the softness of her breasts against my chest, as my hands slid down from around her waist to grab onto her ass and lifted her.

I was already hard, excruciatingly so, and as her crotch rubbed against mine, the resulting relief took me back to a time when I couldn't get enough of her. As she threw her arms around my neck it felt as though absolutely no time whatsoever had passed. The intensity however had escalated.

"Xander," she moaned into my mouth and emotion tightened my throat.

Kissing her felt like nothing else. In the past I had suspected this but now and after going around the circle I could confirm it now to be true. I needed a surface... any surface to press her against.

Wrenching my lips from her was excruciating, but one look behind me I decided on the wall. Her legs wrapped around me and soon she was pressed against it, her back slamming just a bit aggressively. Her eyes came open and I could see the accusation in them. I tried to control my smile but she caught on and annoyance flashed. She smacked me across the arm, and my smile progressed into a beam.

I kissed her again, before she could attack me any further and she melted into the kiss like butter, her chest heaving at the exertion as she tried to catch her breath.

We kissed for I would never know how long and she became restless. I pulled away to see her hands had gripped the bottom of her shirt, and it was coming over her head. She flung it aside and I looked down.

It was very clear to me her breasts had doubled in size from the last time I had touched them and I couldn't look away.

"*Damn*," I said and she laughed, as though we were old friends but we weren't. My gaze returned to hers and for a moment I felt them soften but the ache returned to my heart.

So I glared at her and heard her sigh in response. It was almost as though she surrendered to whatever I wanted of her.

"Where's your bedroom?" I asked and it took her too long to look away from me. Then she pointed her chin behind me. "Down the hallway. The first door on the left."

OLIVIA

I still couldn't believe this was happening. It was all going so fast, which was not at all what I had expected when he had informed me he would be coming over. I had imagined we would speak a bit, argue a bit, as was usual and somehow manage to come to an agreement as to when and where.

I'd expected everything else but this, and I was powerless to stop it.

I needed it I realized, wholeheartedly and this had only dawned on me after he had kissed me and every cell in my body had awakened.

This effect I knew but hadn't felt in so long and so easily... almost too easily I was falling back into it and into him.

This would only happen once and so I was prepared to completely give myself to it in any way he wanted. Perhaps in this way, we would both be able to take care of the dust that had remained from our time together in the past.

"Let go," he said as he lowered me, and I did so bouncing onto the bed.

He straightened to watch me and my eyes couldn't help but follow his hand as it cupped his dick through his pants.

He was dressed tonight in a white dress shirt, tucked in, but with the collar unbuttoned and his sleeves rolled up to his elbows. He was much more casual than the way I'd found him in the office, still in a dress shirt like this but in a tailored waistcoat and tie.

He had become oh so handsome. When we were younger, he was beautiful to me, but now… *my God, I couldn't breathe*. His hair had always been wild, thick, unruly, but now it was longer, still thick but tamed. For one it was brushed away from his face, falling down in mesmerizing effortless waves and stopping just shy of his shoulders.

I could stare at him forever I realized, and almost wished he would slow down as he unbuttoned his pants and pulled the zipper down.

"Are you just going to watch?" he asked and it truly was a feat for me to return my gaze to his.

"What do you want me to do?" I asked, embarrassed getting caught ogling him.

I almost licked my lips as his hands hooked into the waist of his pants and he started pulling them down his hips. He took his briefs along with them and in no time he was fully exposed. My breathing stuttered to a halt.

"Fuck," I couldn't help but mutter under my breath as I took in his hardness. He had always been well endowed from what

I could remember but back then we were still together. Now however…

"Fuck," I cursed again and at his laugh, my gaze returned to his. I moved almost unaware of my actions, driven by my now inflamed desire to carefully inspect him as strangely as that sounded. I crawled over and he waited, definitely curious as to what I would do.

Immediately I reached for his erection, thick and veined but he took a step back. A sound akin to a cry escaped from the back of my throat.

"Take off your bra," he said and I did so in seconds. I flung it aside, absolutely not caring where it eventually landed. I reached for him once again but he stepped even further back, until I was almost falling off the bed.

"Xander!" I called out and looked up to see the smirk on his face.

"Fondle your breasts," he said but I was completely unwilling to put on a show for him, and so I leaned back on my heels.

I considered things for a moment and scooted back across the bed till I was back against my pillows. Hooking my hand into the waistband of my pants I pulled the material down my legs, and those too were flung across the room. I had on a thong, lacy, skimpy, and as my hand went over it to grab onto my mound I watched as his pupils dilated.

"You've already forgotten what I said?" his voice sounded quite strained.

"Hmm?" I mumbled as my middle finger began a lazy trail up my slit.

His gaze returned to mine. "That you should only do what I say."

I smiled. "Xander you of all people should know I do what I want."

"Well in this instance you don't have a choice."

I considered this… and agreed.

"Okay," I said and in the moments that followed the thong was joining the rest of the discarded clothing on the floor. I was fully naked before him now and I felt somewhat light-headed, but that only lasted for a little bit before I recognized the illicit appreciation in his eyes. I had seen it too many times in the past to be unable to instantly recognize it, and it filled me with a confidence and thrill that was near over-whelming.

With my left hand I inch up my stomach and cupped my breast. My legs parted as the right lowered to palm myself once again, spreading the slickness all over. I watched the bob of his larynx up and down his throat as he watched and then the slight parting of his lips as I slid a finger into me.

A harsh breath escaped me and I slid another in.

The pad of my thumb soon joined, and my head was falling backwards. I tried my best to keep my eyes open so I could watch him but it was too much of a feat. I finger fucked myself, pinching my nipple as soft moans fell from my lips, the intensity of my thrill coming from my awareness he had his eyes and focus completely on me. I recalled he used to love it so much when I did this, he would watch and groan and drool and I would be on top of the moon.

Oh how I'd loved him, and probably still did but I quickly pushed the thought out of my mind. This was a onetime thing and although I was trying my best not to enjoy it, to remind myself this was for a cause, I still couldn't stop myself from leaking and throbbing with effervescent anticipation for when he would finally have his hands and mouth on me.

All of this made me realize it had been quite a while since I'd been intimate with anybody. Because being this way… before him… sent emotions coursing through my body I had almost forgotten existed.

After him I had dated one other guy, Josh, and it didn't even last a year. For the first half things had been okay but to my frustration, thoughts of Xander began to slip in. Those little memories left me weak. The emotions were uncontrollable but it made me accept the relationship I was in with Josh was barely passable as one.

We'd broken up mostly because I had eventually stopped bothering to hide my disinterest, and this was mostly because I no longer had the ability to.

To pretend I didn't know what it felt like to be touched and feel as though my whole being had been set on fire from the inside. To pretend I didn't know what it felt like to be so connected to another human being I felt it to the depths of my soul.

Currently I didn't necessarily feel connected to Xander, but it was too hard not to remember how it'd once felt, and with his presence currently, not to feel it all again. And so too quickly I was coming.

My thighs clenched, my body spasming, my feet digging into the bed as I tried to contain the tumult of sensations that were wreaking through my body.

A corner of my mind recorded how shameful this seemed especially as I was so wanton before him, but as my hands dug into my hair to grip it by the roots, I truly couldn't find the strength to care. Until a few seconds later when coherence began to return to me.

My eyes came open and what they met was the ceiling.

I was almost too afraid to lower my gaze in order to watch him and somehow he realized this.

I sensed his smile as the bed lowered in acceptance of his weight.

I felt his hands close around my legs and pull them open. Suddenly and immensely self-conscious, I tried to pull them shut but when his lips pressed against the heated, damp skin of my inner thigh I whimpered, my breathing still somewhat haggard from my release. However my heartrate was picking up all over again as he began to trace damp, heated kisses upwards.

Soon he arrived at my sex and I stopped breathing.

I couldn't help but recall he had been the first one to ever touch me so intimately there. And at the time I'd been so nervous. Eventually I'd learned to relax in his arms, willing and able to take as I received but now it was as though we were beginning all over again from scratch.

I tried to convince myself he wasn't a stranger so I could relax, but this was quite difficult to do because the truth was he was. We were different people and so my legs couldn't help but tightened even further around him.

But once again his grip hardened and they were jerked apart, giving him all the access he wanted.

His lips connected with my clit and the resulting sensations sent an almost violent shudder through my body. His hands rested with a firm grip on my hips, ensuring I remained in place even though I was now wanting to bolt off the bed.

"Xander," I breathed but he just sucked and licked me even harder.

He lapped up my release, the flat of his tongue devouring me like some delicacy he couldn't get enough of and it made me wonder if he too remembered.

Xander eating me out back then had been my favorite thing and as he did it all over again I was vividly reminded of why. Goosebumps broke out across my skin as his tongue slid up my slit and then his lips were closing around my throbbing clit.

I cried out, my back completely arching off the bed.

He moved down and started slowly fucking me with his tongue. My hands found their way to his hair and I grabbed a handful trying to get him to move faster, but my grip was too hard and so with a small laugh that seemed quite distant, his hand closed around my wrist.

He pulled the limb away and this pulled my eyes open amidst the barrage of ecstasy.

"W-what is it?" I panted, nearly unable to catch my breath.

He didn't respond but instead held my hand down to the side and began to loom over me.

He was now completely naked, and at the broadness of his shoulders this up close, the swells and dips of muscles beneath his skin, my heart raced even faster.

He had become so handsome. So breathtaking in every single way.

Our eyes met and for seconds after my gaze was trapped in his ice blue ones.

We didn't say a word to each other but I was certain he felt what I felt. The gnawing feeling of loss and hurt for everything we could have been and for what we weren't.

"Kiss me," I pleaded, wanting no longer to think. All I wanted was to drown myself in this moment and in him.

He obliged me, lowering to capture my lips in his but I didn't miss the heavy expression that came over his face.

However every thought on that soon disappeared as I was once again immersed in his unique taste mingling with mine on his lips.

Eventually he pulled away from me, his body now pressed against mine

"Protection?" he asked and my mind began to race. I suspected somewhere in the cabinets in my house I could probably find some condoms, however any will whatsoever to find them was quite the feat.

I sighed and before I could stop myself eased forward to kiss him once again. As though a reward he reached down between us and lodged his slicked cock between my sex. The stimulation was maddening.

His brow cocked but as his warm breath brushed all over me I felt myself quiver. "Protection," he urged again and I managed to gather my mental faculties so I could respond.

"Mmn," was all that left my lips as my hips began to writhe, trying to grind into him. I leaned forward once again to kiss him and he somewhat pulled away, a slight smile curving his lips.

I realized then and accepted what I truly wanted. We always used protection in the past. If this was to be our last time I didn't want any barrier between us.

"I don't think I have any." I felt him go still above me. "I'll handle it," I told him. "Tomorrow."

But as the words left my mouth, I felt so incredibly vulnerable and exposed before him.

I wondered if he would believe me and suspected he wouldn't agree, but to my surprise he did, and now I was near drowning in his kisses.

My legs parted further without any fanfare and the lush head of his cock was nudging into me.

The feeling was exquisite and oh so achingly familiar.

His width was something I had always appreciated and been nearly driven crazy by on several occasions. His length had impressed me from the first moment I'd seen it but the girth… I had missed it like nothing else.

He pushed further into me, not necessarily taking his time but yet not too quickly either.

He'd always known just the right pace to go, and as the satiny smoothness of his dick grazed my pulsing inner walls, I felt myself begin to transcend.

I loved fucking Xander, more than anything else I now had to admit it, as over the years I had somehow been successful at convincing myself otherwise just so I could survive the hurt.

The head of his dick soon reached the very depths of me, and at his complete sheathing I felt the slight shudder of his frame. I wrapped my arms around him as though in a cradle but suddenly and once again, his hands closed around my wrists.

He pulled them away and pinned them above my head with one hand. Then he lifted till he was poised over me… staring into my eyes.

My perception of whatever bliss was contained in this moment was shattered then.

I could see the veins straining against the sides of his temple and how I wished I could reach out to smoothen them. However he didn't let me.

In his eyes I could see the struggle between wanting to somehow punish me with this, but yet unable to contain his enjoyment of it.

My gaze softened as I watched him as once again, I thought of if I regretted what I'd done… what I'd thought was the best thing for us at the time. I still didn't know because what if we had stayed together and eventually grown apart. I couldn't help but think it would be worse than this because at least now, even though whatever affection left was solely on my part and non-existent on his, the memories of the good times had still lingered enough for him to find the desire to revisit.

I should have minded this... minded the fact he was just using me to perhaps revisit the past, but I didn't... couldn't because I was once again with the only man I'd truly ever loved.

I didn't know if I would ever get him back, and thanks to his antagonism I didn't know if I'd ever get the will to try but right now, I allowed myself to admit I was content.

His eyes fluttered shut as he started to slide out of me, and then he shoved back in. Mercilessly... ruthlessly.

I relished it... it was just as sweet but the downside was perhaps we wouldn't last as long... and it was exactly the case.

He fucked me till I was writhing and twisting under him. My heels dug into his ass urging him harder, until eventually his own coherence faltered and his grip around my wrists loosened.

I threw my hands around him and held on tight as he rocked me further and further towards the headboard.

I had a sturdy bed and thus couldn't help but be appreciative of my decisions to not go the cheaper route on the purchase, but truly I didn't think I would have minded if illicit creaking had ensued and resounded across the room at our copulation.

Currently the sounds were slick, illicit squelches from our joining down below and from our gathered breath.

The air conditioning hadn't been turned on and I couldn't seem to mind because it left us damp and sweaty all over, and how I loved his skin being plastered to mine.

I was overheating and so was he. What I wanted currently, was a release, but I also wanted this to go on forever because I was certain it would be the last time for us.

He came before I did, but at the burst of his release inside me, and the near animalistic groan that erupted from the back of his throat I succumbed and was thrown over the edge.

For the first few seconds after, very little registered, my entire body briefly numbed and the pleasure was wreaking through me like a storm. I almost couldn't contain it, one hand gripping the root of my hair while the other grabbed onto his ass. He kept fucking into me, unable to stop and with the sole desire to wring every bit of ecstasy out of the both of us until we both couldn't stand anymore.

It too unfortunately came to this and so our hips stilled, but my arms around him tightened refusing to let go. A knowing burn gathered at the base of my throat as an overwhelming emotion of nostalgic love and bliss swept through me like a wave. I tried my very best to hold back but could feel the heated moisture as it filled my eyes and trickled down my face, and so I hid in the crook of his neck and willed myself to retrieve the reins of my control.

If he turned to see I was falling apart in his arms, I was certain I wouldn't be able to survive the embarrassment and so I held on, taking deep breaths until he began to pull away, I let him go and quickly turned away to the side. Suddenly a cool blast of air hit my naked, now cooling body and it was just the excuse I needed to grab onto the covers and pull them over me.

I hoped he would stay… that he would reach out to me and demand we spend the night together just as he had demanded he fuck my brains out. However all I heard was him getting off the bed. And then I heard the shuffling of feet and clothing as he began tugging it on.

The moment the clinking of his belt followed, I felt my heart begin to fragment into pieces.

At least say something to me, I implored him in my heart, however there was nothing.

I buried my face in the pillow, and held onto my tears. A few seconds later I heard the door to my bedroom open and shut behind him.

The tears broke free then and they didn't stop until slumber pulled me under.

XANDER

Walking away from her home that night had to be one of the hardest things I'd ever done. And even after days had passed it still amazed me that I had.

However I'd been burned by her, and in a way no one or anything else ever had done to me and I was quite certain I would never fully recover from it. And so even in the midst of the absolute bliss that was being sheathed bare inside of her, and still recovering from what had to be the most earth shattering orgasm ever, that alarm had sounded internally, reminding me any affection whatsoever between us was unacceptable.

Her turning away and hiding from me had made it just a bit easier, because if things had gone more smoothly, like if she had gazed up at me with those beguiling brown eyes and requested for me to stay, then perhaps I would have completely lost my head and succumbed.

As the days went by however, I found myself wishing I had.

That I had succumbed to those emotions that up till today I'd never felt with anyone else.

For the longest time I'd judged it to be a fluke. A figment of my overactive imagination especially in the aftermath of our separation.

But that night... I was reminded it wasn't. The real connection between us had rendered me unable at times to even speak.

It hadn't felt like sex. At the beginning fucking her wildly had been my sole intent but somewhere through the middle I'd lost myself in her.

"Sir?"

"Mr. King?"

As the sudden call pierced through my mind, startling and returning me to the present, I looked up at the executive that had been giving a presentation.

His gaze was on mine, expectant, and as my eyes also went across the others seated in the room, awaiting my input I realized I would have to tell him to repeat himself.

I hated this as it more than showed just how distracted I'd been. And what was worse was it wasn't my first time. And so I decided to do something about it.

The moment I returned to my office, I thought of what I was going to say and how exactly I was going to spin this, but absolutely nothing came to mind.

'I haven't been able to stop thinking about you' was one route, but I was convinced I would most definitely rather swallow gravel.

And so I decided to take the straightforward route.

My goal wasn't to purposely be bitter towards her, but I couldn't help it.

I couldn't help the fact after all these years and even with what she did to me, I still couldn't move past her, and it infuriated me even further because I'd never wanted to.

And so I picked up the phone and gave myself permission to demand what I wanted from her until I was satisfied.

She didn't pick up. I could do nothing but stare at the phone with incredulity. Annoyance began to boil within me but thankfully before it could escalate into anything further, she called me back.

I was tempted to be dismissive, but I knew it would only go to show just how affected I was because otherwise she was well aware enough to know I never resorted to cheap games like this.

And so I picked up.

It took a few seconds but soon her soft tone came through the receiver.

"Hello?"

I couldn't help but exhale out in relief.

"Have you contacted the accountant?" I asked.

I didn't need to ask her this because I had already received the report from said accountant. He had established contact with her and had relayed the process of obtaining whatever amount she needed.

I could have just sent her a lump sum, but at the time I had no clue what it was and had decided perhaps it would be better to allow her mother continuous coverage of all of her needs at least for the first few years post recovery.

"I have," came her reply, but at this point I had nearly forgotten what I'd asked her. I eventually decided it didn't matter.

"I want to see you," I went straight to the point. "Where can we meet up?"

And then a long silence followed.

I waited, not saying a word but slowly becoming aggravated at the fact once again it seemed as though she was emotionally manipulating me.

Eventually however she responded.

"Um… I didn't know… w-why do we have to meet up?"

I scoffed.

"Why else?" I responded straight forwardly. "To fuck you again, of course."

My heart slightly jumped in response, even though my tone remained calm, but whether it was due to anticipation or nerves, I couldn't tell. I didn't want to examine it either and so I waited for her response.

"I don't-" she began again, but then stopped. "I didn't know we would do that… more than once."

I laughed, again, mockingly… dryly. "I've granted you unlimited financial access to the funds you will need for your mother's treatment. Is a few minutes of fucking you once a fair exchange for that?"

She went silent again and I couldn't help but to rise to my feet, somewhat nervous. I didn't want to have to resort to any drastic measures like cut off her access to the funds if she refused me, but I also didn't want to be slapped in the face at the resulting shame if she did and I remained unable to revoke it.

"I… how many more times then?" she asked. "How many more times are we talking about?"

My heart stopped pounding so hard, and so it was only then I was able to realize there was the background noise of children around her.

Despite our antagonism, I was content to see she truly had become a teacher just as she'd always hoped to be when she was younger. It had always made me so jealous then how clear she was in what she wanted to do in the future and how she had gone after the pursuit so single-mindedly. In many ways, I couldn't help but admit this had also shaped my own direction and fostered my zeal.

"We'll see," I said and waited for a response.

"Can I refuse?" she asked and for a moment I was sure I heard her voice crack.

And suddenly I wanted to withdraw.

I couldn't tell her yes.

But at the same time I also couldn't tell her no.

And so… I brought the call to an end.

I couldn't remember the last time I'd been at a nightclub.

During my early years in college they'd been quite the delight but mostly because being so unrestrained was such a new experience.

It had only taken my freshman year however for all that delight and excitement to wash out of my system.

I'd focused solely on my studies, dabbled slightly in dating and indulged in other more conservative forms of entertainment.

Xander to my knowledge wasn't the partying type either and as I searched my memories, I didn't even think I'd ever gone to a club with him. This was quite peculiar given just how young we had both been but it only just made me realize now just how much time we had spent in each other's presence rather than attending fun events.

I sighed as I made my way into the dim room, the walls thundering from the boom of the deafening music.

I thought of getting a drink first, so I could at least be a little less rigid and find a way to get past this meeting he'd called for with a little less hostility. I figured if I could somehow find even a bit of humor in whatever would be happening, then perhaps things wouldn't be too bad and perhaps I wouldn't feel so heartbroken.

The last three days... ever since he left had to have been the hardest I had encountered so far.

I'd forgotten what it felt like, to be so connected to someone but then to experience the aftermath of severing it.

I didn't think I was connected in the same way to Xander any longer, or perhaps I was. Perhaps I'd been all along and just couldn't bring myself to admit it.

Because if I wasn't then why had it felt as though my heart had been about to rip out of my chest after he'd left.

Then why was I here?

For anyone else I was certain I would have rejected this... even with the desperation to save my mother. Or perhaps I wouldn't have... I just couldn't tell. I couldn't tell anything anymore especially when it came to Xander and this I recall now was one of the major reasons why I had broken up with him.

His influence on me was too strong, and the spark between us was as alive as ever, and I had chickened out. For fear of completely losing myself.

I received a call as soon as I got in and a few minutes later I was making my way up to the second floor. I still couldn't understand why he wanted us to meet here. Perhaps it was because there were no other options. I mean besides here anywhere else would be either too personal or intimate. Like a restaurant for instance or perhaps my home, once again.

I sighed as I arrived at the stairs leading to the VIP floor and after confirming my identity, was led in.

The booth he had arranged for us was in a private room, encased in glass and overlooking the dance floor of the club. It was truly private I realized because I understood why I hadn't really noticed it from the ground floor. And that was because no one could see it from that angle so it simply seemed like a tinted reflective wall that revealed nothing.

From within however, the entire dance floor was displayed almost like a painting. The sounds were muted and so it was such a sharp contrast to the booming ambience of the club. It felt almost peaceful but could also have been due to the fact it was unoccupied.

It however looked like that was just temporary because there were drinks on the table… and used glasses.

Which meant there had already been people here. Perhaps this gave the answer of why he had suggested we meet here. He had a meeting and I was the afterthought. I couldn't help but feel somewhat sour. I didn't expect to be a priority in his life or anything but the hostility and disrespect was beginning to reach preposterous heights.

Perhaps he was trying to make me feel as bad as possible in order to compensate him for the hurt I had caused him in the past, and the benefit he was accruing to me now despite that, but I had already paid for it. And so I decided to bring it up. I went over to the window to watch the bubbly crowd below, and almost began to consider perhaps what I also needed was to dance.

To just get a little bit more tipsy and to let loose. Perhaps I would stop feeling as stressed and forlorn. An eerie feeling in my mind however told me in order to get to this state, I would have to be quite buzzed because looming over my every thought and deed recently was the man that had invited me here in the first place.

And so I turned towards the table and spotted what looked to be a bottle of wine amidst the other hard liquor.

I didn't peg Xander for a hard liquor kind of guy but perhaps those he had been entertaining were and he'd wanted to give them a good time?

I couldn't find a wine glass but I did find a clean tumbler, so I uncorked the already opened bottle and poured myself a generous drink.

I lifted it to my lips and as the dry but fruity taste of the liquid swirled in my mouth and slid down my throat, I felt something akin to relief begin to wash through me but that was until the door suddenly opened.

My heart immediately jumped in my chest, as I turned to it and indeed saw it was Xander who had arrived.

He looked… gorgeous. There were a myriad of other words that came to mind in that moment but beyond it all I couldn't look away from the fact he was stunning.

He was still somewhat formally dressed, but presently he didn't have a jacket on. Instead he had his white dress shirt still tucked into his tailored pants. The collar was loosened, giving an attractive glimpse of his olive skin beneath while the sleeves were folded up to his elbows.

My gaze lingered on the strain of veins bulging down said arms, and at the memory that came to me of how he had held me down just a few days earlier on the bed, I couldn't help but find myself already salivating.

I didn't want to feel this attracted to him, especially because I had issues to settle with him and so I looked away without even as much as eye contact to acknowledge him.

I hoped this ticked him off immensely, since I didn't know yet if I had been punished enough to be outright rude and dismissive to him without feeling any guilt whatsoever.

My gaze remained on the dance floor below as I continued to drink my wine, but I could feel and was very aware of his focus on me.

He slid into one of the booth chairs without saying a word, and I had no qualms whatsoever with that. However for how long we would be able to keep up this silent game of torture with each other, I had absolutely no clue.

So I continued to stare down at the dance floor, however, and in his presence I could no longer taste the drink. Soon I emptied it without even realizing it, and had to turn for a refill.

My eyes couldn't help but to rove over to him and I found him boldly watching me. I couldn't look away, my pride wouldn't let me but he didn't say a word either. His arms were folded across his chest as though he was studying me but not in any positive way whatsoever.

I couldn't help but to speak. "Are we going to discuss what I'm doing here?"

He didn't respond and instead continued to watch me, and my entire body began to feel squeamish. His arms were folded across his chest and his gaze intense until finally I was done with this.

"If you're not going to speak then I'm going to leave," I said.

But instead of even bothering to respond to the threat, he smiled and picked up a tumbler. He poured in a sizable amount of liquor for himself, and lifted it to his lips. His gaze turned to focus on the dance floor below and it made me realize what he was doing. He was daring me to leave and I wished I hadn't said a word because no doubt leaving would also bring an end to the access to the funds he'd granted me on behalf of my mother.

I could do nothing but wait until he was ready to speak. With a sigh, I returned my attention to the dance floor, since it didn't seem like he was going to offer me a seat anytime soon.

I stayed there... knowing whatever happened from then onward would be humiliating to me.

Eventually he spoke.

"You're not leaving anymore?"

I remained silent, but the longer I did, the more I realized we could both play this game. By reaching out to me yet again, it was more than obvious to me he had enjoyed our time from the other night.

His groan came to mind from the moment he had released his load into me and I couldn't help but feel aroused.

It had been a special moment, with me also clinging onto him… passion nearly driving me out of my mind.

"You said on the phone…" I began. "That you wanted to fuck me again?" I smiled. "I thought you just did that to punish me, and afterwards you wouldn't want anything whatsoever to do with me?" My heart was pounding so hard in my chest I was certain we could both hear it in the room.

He didn't respond and so a few seconds later, I summoned up the courage to look at him. However when I glanced over my shoulder I found he wasn't even paying any attention to me. Instead he was leaning comfortably against the seat with his phone in hand. I watched as he scrolled through it for a little bit and then turned around to face him fully.

"Xander?" I called and he lifted his face to meet mine.

"Are you hungry?" he suddenly asked and I was taken aback.

I watched him, almost expecting him to say the question was a joke but when instead nothing came I couldn't help but sigh.

"Sure," I replied.

XANDER

I placed the order for her automatically and without thought.

When we were together in the past, she was the one usually set in her ways and so I was left to order whatever I felt would be good for her to try.

And now... I'd done it again, without even realizing it. The waiter came over to take the order and then he left. I looked up, to watch her especially since she didn't say a word about it and it all made me truly wonder where I wanted things to go.

My goal with inviting her here was to induce some objectivity into the way I was handling her. I wanted to see her in a more public and general setting, nothing that was too personal to either of us like my office or her apartment.

Plus there was also the fact I didn't want to go to her like the last time. I wanted her to be the one to go through the trouble and come to me.

"I don't know when I'll be in the mood," I told her. "But when I am, I'll let you know. And then you have to come meet me, just like now."

She turned around to face me, her frame leaning against the glass.

"And so you're in the mood… now?"

"Not yet," I leaned forward and picked my glass up. "I'll let you know."

It was a few seconds later before she spoke again.

"You… you want to have sex here?"

That wasn't the plan but I couldn't help but notice the tremble in her tone. However I couldn't exactly tell if it was because the prospect excited her, or if she thought it was too out of left field. We'd always both been quite conservative people, myself more to my association and connection with her than anything else. But now... I couldn't help but wonder if there were aspects of her I hadn't ever had the chance to discover back then.

"How many partners have you had?" I asked, and her eyes slightly widened. Then her expression turned into a frown.

She turned away, her gaze returning to the glass wall and I couldn't help but be amused. I rose to my feet and walked over to her, my eyes unable to keep from admiring the outline of her frame. She was petite at about 5'4" while I was over 6'. I'd always loved this height difference between us, especially during the times when it didn't deter her from showing her annoyance at me when we would get into little fights in the past. I walked until I reached her but I didn't want to hold her from behind… it was too romantic. So instead I went to her side staring down at the crowd beneath us.

"You're not going to respond?" I asked, and couldn't help but to turn my gaze to her.

She had her hair in a ponytail, however tendrils of escaped curls from her temples framed her face, softening her look so immensely.

Currently it was as though she hadn't changed a single bit from the past. Her features were still soft… delicate… sweet, befitting the heart of the person I thought I knew. Which is why I still remained so confused as to why things had turned out the way they had for us.

"Pick whatever number you want," she said and I couldn't help but smile.

I thought about *him*… as I was sure she did too, but I refused to bring him up. However just the mere mention had now immensely soured the mood between us.

She turned to me.

"I have to get back home at a decent time so I can take my mother to the hospital tomorrow. So whatever's going to happen, we should get it over with."

I turned to her and stared into her eyes. And with my hand hooking into the band of her jeans, I pulled her to me. It was rough and so she stumbled, her hands shooting out to flatten against my chest. We stared at each other and despite how badly I wanted to kiss her I held myself back. Instead I began to unbutton her jeans.

She watched me, her pupils dilating.

I could hear from time to time the tiny gasps escaping her lips as my fingers grazed against her crotch. She tried her best to hide it... to pretend she felt nothing but it was too much of a feat.

Slowly, I pulled her zipper down and leaned in all the way till I could almost make out the specs of gold in her eyes.

My hand slid deeper in to grab her, my fingers splaying over her sex and digging into her slit. She was immensely wet, her underwear soaked through, and as the dampness stained my fingers, I couldn't help but curve my lips at her.

Her chest slightly heaved, and although she tried her best to control her reactions, the shortness of her breath and the dilation of her pupils were unmistakable.

"Next time," I breathed as my middle finger began to stroke the engorged bud of her clit. Her lashes however began to flutter close and for a moment I was mesmerized, so I lost my train of thought. Eventually though, she managed to catch herself, her eyes opening wide once again to stare into mine in defiance. I couldn't help but smile, and leaned in even further to catch her plump bottom lip between my teeth. I was tempted to hurt her just a bit, and at the sting, her eyes flashed at mine in indignation. Before she could pull away though, I slanted my head and kissed her.

Her taste, sweet and wet, met with mine and my knees weakened.

It was as though my heart had long since registered it as her taste and couldn't help but leave me nearly clutching onto her for balance. I staggered, my free hand reaching out to grab onto the side of her arm.

She moaned into my mouth, and although she was reluctant at first, in no time we both melted into the kiss.

We burned for each other, so much so that her arms which she had kept by her sides were now wrapping around my shoulders as she lifted herself onto the tips of her toes to delve further into the kiss. My hand was displaced as a result so it circled around her waist, while the other within her pants pushed the fabric of her underwear aside and slid a finger inside her.

"*Xander*," she gasped into my mouth, and the thrill that shot through me at the call made my whole body shiver. She was very aware of who was doing this to her, of how we were both unraveling each other.

We kissed even more deeply, her hips rocking into the thrusts of my finger until eventually I couldn't deal with the barriers. I needed to be inside of her.

The plan had never been to fuck her here, but I could no longer control myself.

Wrenching my lips from hers was borderline excruciating, especially since she didn't even want to let go. Our breathing was labored, hearts set ablaze, so when I turned her towards the glass wall. She had no complaints. Her hands shot out to flatten against the surface as mine hooked into her tight-waisted pants and began to pull the fabric down.

Suddenly there was a knock on the door. I stilled, but she was still overtaken by the intensity of the sensations, and so her body was writhing against mine, in search of some sort of relief from the pleasure that was coiling through her and winding her tight.

I kissed her, on the side of her cheek, almost apologetic because we had to stop. It hadn't been my intention to be so affectionate, but in response, I felt her body instantly go still as the softness of the kiss registered. With a sigh and reluctance to let go of her, I moved away and then I was heading towards the door.

"Make yourself decent," I said, my voice hoarse and almost unrecognizable to me. I almost even regretted that I had even bothered to order the meal.

The waiter greeted me with a smile as the door came open, which I unfortunately was unable to return. I gave one last look at the woman behind me who was still facing the glass wall but with her pants now once again securely fastened around her waist.

Her hands were by her sides, but I could very clearly see she had bunched them into fists.

I allowed the waiter in, and took the opportunity to clear my head, and to reclaim the reins on my libido by watching as the attendant neatly arranged the food on the table.

There were sandwiches, and a platter of creamy camembert and cured meats. There was also cheese, and other nut and fruit assortments.

I settled on a slice of ham and tried my best to ignore her presence, but this proved to be especially difficult. And so I gave in, and headed into the booth to take my seat.

I wondered for how long she would stand there watching the crowd, and was almost even roused enough to want to find out.

But eventually, she turned around and settled her gaze on me.

"Why are you eating here?" she asked.

I didn't plan to respond, but I couldn't help but notice the concern in her tone.

"What else am I supposed to do? Go to a restaurant? With you?"

My intention wasn't entirely to sound sarcastic but it was quite difficult for these sets of words not to come off as such. In response, her brows furrowed into her forehead in mild annoyance and I couldn't help my amusement. She returned to staring out at the dance floor and I truly wished for once, she would set down the antagonism between us and take a seat. That we could be honest and open with each other for just a moment, but it didn't seem to be the time yet. We were still both too guarded… too haunted. But at that moment though, there was one question I wanted to ask her.

"Do you regret it?" I asked.

I didn't expect her to respond immediately, and doubted she would even respond at all but then she surprised me and spoke.

"I don't know."

At that, I completely lost my appetite and I wasn't even sure why. I guess perhaps I was expecting her to remain unrepentant at her mistake, but then here she was telling me she didn't know. Anger surged through me but I tried all I could to control myself.

"You don't know?" I bit out. "You broke my heart without a second thought and yet you don't know?"

She turned around to face me.

I felt weak all over.

At first it was due to his touch and at how my bones had melted in response, but now it was due to a myriad of emotions that were tangling me into an emotional mess.

It all culminated into one singular and incontestable belief which was the fact I missed him... with all of my heart. I missed how calm he could be when I would be chaotic and uneasy, and I even missed his temper when I allowed the most inconsequential things and words from others to hurt me.

It frustrated him to no end that sometimes I would succumb to these and punish myself for it, but he would always bring me out of the sourness. I couldn't help but recall nights with us in my bed together... quiet... and with me wrapped up in his arms and being consoled.

Chemistry had been an especially difficult subject for me in high school despite my prowess at everything else, and he'd taken it upon himself countless times and mostly overnight before tests to pull me through when I would call him feigning tears.

He never fell for it, but he would always take it upon himself to tutor me and subsequently swat me awake whenever I began to feel drowsy.

He was the best boyfriend I'd ever had.

The best love I'd ever been gifted.

And perhaps because of this, I hadn't wanted him to be hindered in any way. For me to be a source of distraction to the goals that were so clear and set in his mind, and so I had allowed things to happen the way they had.

I also had to admit to myself though I hadn't been able to shake away my insecurities. And even till now, I still couldn't, and so I had taken the cowardly route and chosen instead to be the bad guy so it would be impossible for him to take that title in my heart.

Because if he had, I was certain it would have forever broken my belief in love.

At the time though, I hadn't expected him to so easily believe the story I had given to him. I had expected him to be relentless, until the truth had been pried out of me but instead he had listened, accepted my words, and walked away.

I was certain he'd been in shock, and perhaps his understanding of me had made him believe I would never have been silly enough to utter the words if they weren't true, and if I didn't plan on breaking him or hurting him.

He knew me well and although because of this, our parting had been without a single iota of fuss, it had filled me with regret and questions.

And now, I couldn't help but think perhaps this was a good thing because now we could seek some sort of closure and perhaps even stumble onto the truth?

Perhaps this time around he would pay attention enough and know to pull the truth out of me.

But still, I didn't know if I was ready… to be so consumed by that type and intensity of love again.

My hands folded across my midriff but still, I couldn't find the courage to look into his eyes.

"Olivia," he called, and I could feel myself tremble from the impending tears. I knew if I didn't take back control I was going to crumble into pieces right before him.

And so I summoned the courage I had left, and lifted my gaze up to his.

"This wasn't our agreement," I said. "We're meant to… "

I couldn't however bring myself to complete the words.

"We're meant to what?" he asked, face completely void of expression.

I steeled my resolve and tried again. "We're meant to fuck."

He stared at me, and it made me hurt even more till I could no longer hold his gaze.

"Tell me you regret it Olivia," he said to me. "Or tell me you don't. But don't tell me you don't know. Isn't that an insult… to what we had? Did it truly mean absolutely nothing to you?"

Annoyance began to burn in my heart. "Why are you asking me these questions now? Why didn't you ask me back then? You just walked away. I informed you and that was it. I never saw you again."

"What did you expect?"

I wanted to rage that he should have fought for us… for me, but somehow I was able to hold myself back. "I no longer expect anything from you." I signed, deflated. "Just my mother's bills to be paid so let's keep things simple."

I expected him to agree. I expected him to be furious with me however his gaze softened, and for a moment fear gripped me. Had he seen through me?

"You loved me," he said, and my heart nearly came to a stop. "You loved him too, but it wasn't anywhere near what we had… what you felt for me. I know it."

All I could hear now was the thundering of my heart in my ears.

"I don't underst-" he paused. "Was it truly not enough? Was I truly not enough?"

I turned away and returned my gaze to the wall. However, although it was transparent, I could no longer see anything. I decided this was too much and so I turned around and headed over to the table to grab my purse from earlier. I had been so distracted I couldn't even remember ever putting it down. I reached out for it and just as my hand grabbed the strap, his hand closed around my wrist.

My gaze lifted towards his and he saw the tears in them. I could no longer hide them but I did do all I could to keep them from falling.

His expression remained unchanged.

"I didn't say you could leave."

I glared at him and tried to wrench my hand from his grip but he wouldn't budge.

I kept trying. "Xander!" I called on a sob and suddenly I flew backwards.

I landed smack on my ass, and he rose to his feet.

For a few seconds, the fall took the breath out of me but then shame came along and overwhelmed me even further. So I hurried to scramble to my feet. I once again grabbed my purse off the floor and was heading toward the door. Before I could get to the door, I felt his hand close around my arm.

"Let me go!" I nearly screamed, but he was spinning me around and pulling me to him. His strong arms held me tightly.

I tried to pull away from the intimate embrace but then he was kissing me… deep and hard.

I melted into him, his taste once again liquefying me down into nothing. Like a balm for my shattered heart. It reminded me of memories my head had long forgotten but my heart could never rid itself of. Of tender touches… of innocent, star lit skies, of hope, and of love in its purest form.

And it reminded me of lust… fiery and frenzied… and of intimacy that made me tremble.

I truly had never loved another the way I'd loved him, and so I could do nothing but submit as this kiss reminded me I probably never would.

XANDER

Somehow my kiss steadied her. The tears in her eyes did something to me… to my very soul.

Once again we lost ourselves in each other and by the time we pulled apart all of our defenses had melted away. She buried her face into my chest and threw her arms around my neck and I couldn't bring myself to do anything but hold on to her.

Just for tonight it could be different, I tried to convince myself.

Tomorrow's another day to be bitter, but just for tonight, pretend she is yours. *Allow* her to be yours. The proposition was too attractive to refuse, but just then, there was a knock on the door and it was more than enough for us to pull apart. She jerked away, but before she could go too far, I held onto her hand and refused to let go. Then I pulled the door open and addressed the waiter.

Most of our food had remained untouched unfortunately, but there was nothing I could do about it.

I gave out the instructions for the bill to be handled, and we were on our way.

"Where's your valet ticket?" I asked, and although she hesitated, she finally just handed her purse over to me, her gaze lowered and turned away.

With a smile, I searched through to find the card and in no time, her car was brought around.

I accepted the keys from the valet and we both got in.

From here, I knew my way straight to my home, and that was where we headed until midway through, she finally rose up from her stupor.

"Where are we going?"

"My house," I replied.

I thought she would object, but she didn't. Instead she leaned into the seat and stared straight ahead.

Soon we arrived at my downtown apartment, and she followed after me.

Unsurprisingly enough, and despite the current nature of our relationship I didn't have any qualms about bringing her to my own home.

It was rare I let strangers in if ever, and especially within the context of this kind of intimacies, but with her, it didn't feel strange. She stopped at the foyer, but as I watched her I couldn't help but notice she didn't even bother to look around. "Do you want anything to drink?" I asked, and for the first time since we arrived she lifted her gaze to mine.

"I need to go home."

I was far from surprised but this time I wasn't going to let her run away. A smile curved the corners of my lips because my entire body was brimming with so much arousal and annoyance it was quite difficult to contain.

"My bedroom's on the second floor," I told her, "at the end of the hallway."

Without a word, she nodded and went on her way. I watched her go, heading up the floating staircase, and she disappeared into the hall above. Afterwards and with a sigh, I turned around and headed to the kitchen. I'd drunk enough and so there was no need to have any more alcohol for the night, but I couldn't help but grab onto a bottle of whiskey, as I needed the added kick to be able to handle her the way I wanted.

I poured some of the golden liquid into a tumbler, and flushed the drink down my throat.

It burned, in the most perfect way, and I set the glass down to think. Tonight I truly wanted to take my time with her. To exhaust her completely until it no longer occurred to her she needed to return home.

Just for tonight it would be like the last four years didn't happen, like she didn't destroy me, and we were still madly in love. Show her what she gave up... what she carelessly threw away.

I turned towards the refrigerator, grabbed a bottle of water, and was soon on my way up to her.

OLIVIA

I n his bedroom, I didn't exactly know what to do. I stood in the middle of the expansive room, sober but yet still somewhat disoriented.

Tonight, I felt just a little bit more exposed… more vulnerable and it didn't make me feel good. But the source of it all was clear thanks to my emotional stint back at the club.

Taking a deep breath, I released my sigh and turned around to glance at the door.

The last thing I wanted was for him to come in here and meet me more unsure and unconfident about myself, so my gaze returned to the massive bed before me.

Truly, I felt exhausted enough to just collapse on top of it, but I also didn't want to make myself at home either. So instead I headed over to the lounge in the corner and sunk onto one of the chair arms. My purse remained in my grip, my legs crossed and that was how I shut my eyes and fell into a light sleep.

A short time later, or at least what felt like a short time, I was startled awake.

I wasn't sure why as there hadn't been a sudden sound or movement, but as my eyes came open to see the man seated on the chair opposite me, I understood why.

My heart jumped in my chest as I sat up to gaze at him.

"You're exhausted?" he asked, but I didn't exactly know how to respond. If I admitted it would be as though I was seeking out some sort of sympathy from him, but if I denied it would be as though I was unnecessarily feigning strength when we were both aware I had in fact been on my feet all day dealing with kids.

So instead, I straightened and chose not to acknowledge him. I didn't miss his near mocking smile.

Then he threw something towards me and I looked down to see what it was. It was a silk tie curled across my lap. My gaze lifted to his.

"What's this for?" my tone was groggy.

His instruction was simple. "Blindfold yourself.

I was sure I had heard him wrong, and so it took a little while for what he had just said to me to compute.

And the moment it did, my eyes widened open. He remained unfazed.

"What?"

"Put it on," he repeated in a no nonsense, non-negotiable tone as he rose to his feet. "Or do you want me to do it for you?"

The entire scenario played out in my head, especially as I watched him walk away from me and head towards the bed. He began to unbutton his shirt and shrug it off his shoulders, the muscles beneath shifting enticingly.

Things became clear to me then, but I had to question myself as to if I was interested in this.

The temporary impediment of my sight... the loss of control, the total submission.

I was never afraid he would physically hurt me but at this point of the night between us, I had already been more vulnerable and exposed than I could stand.

And so I rose up to my feet, willing to negotiate.

"Is this necessary?" he turned to glance at me, a scowl appearing on his face as his immediate answer. I watched as he began to undo the buttons of his slacks, and soon enough they were hanging open. He turned to me, and not till our gazes met a few seconds later did I realize I had been outright staring at his ripped torso.

"Do you want me to do it for you?" he asked, and the words sounded more like a threat than anything else.

And so I headed towards the side of the bed, away from him, and began to undo the buttons of my shirt.

"I didn't ask you to take your clothes off," he said. "The only instruction was that you blindfold yourself."

At this, I sighed, and fastened the silk tie over my eyes.

My heart rate had already begun to speed up.

"*Now* you can unbutton your blouse," he said, and a shiver went through me.

I couldn't help but wonder. *Was this some kind of power play or was he just trying to further humiliate me?*

Sure, he wanted to enjoy this, to savor every moment even at my expense, and this definitely made me feel upset. I needed to take back some of the power in the room.

I considered how I could possibly do this. He probably would suspect my taking off my clothing quickly as trying to just get it over with, but what if I take my time... draw it out... make him wait.

And so that was exactly what I did. I slowly finished unbuttoning my blouse, pausing to let it hang off my shoulders before slowing letting it roll down my arms to the floor.

"Perfect," I barely heard the whispered praise, and this immediately made me pause.

He laughed softly, but I didn't miss the underlying note of mockery. He was goading me... toying with me... and I was falling for it every step of the way.

He had once again become quiet and I had no doubt he was watching me.

I ran my hands down my torso and flipped the button of my jeans open. The room was so quiet now I could hear every snick of the zipper as it descended. My hands moved over to my hips and I slid my jeans down my legs till they reached my ankles and my hands followed the same path up as I kicked the jeans away.

My hands didn't stop until they reached the clasp of my bra. I turned my back to where I knew he was still standing and let the bra roll off my shoulders to join the growing pile of clothing surrounding me.

With my new confidence I needed to see the look in his eye. Was this doing anything for him or was I just making a fool of myself? Without turning around I reached up to remove the blindfold.

"Don't," his voice broke the quiet. "Finish what I asked of you."

I was prepared to ignore and refuse him, however I couldn't help but feel a wave of exhaustion come over me at this dance we'd both been involved in so far tonight. And so I decided to do what I truly wanted.

After all, I held no fear whatsoever towards him.

And so I took a few steps forward till my feet connected with the bed and I settled onto it. In no time, the covers were pulled down and I laid on the bed.

"Finish yourself," I said to him and quite the silence followed after that.

Eventually though, I felt the bed sink down under his weight and understood he was coming towards me.

And suddenly I was exposed. I could instantly feel the cool air of the dim space tighten my nipples. Goosebumps broke out all over, and I felt his hands on my ankles slowly working their way up my calves. When he reached my knees he pushed them wide and moved between them as his hands continued to explore further up my thighs. He stopped and drew lazy patterns around my panty line. I was astounded at how much I could *feel*... by how tense I had become. Waiting... uncertain.

I could feel the heat emanating from his body as he loomed over mine... and finally even noticed his scent. It was something sweet and smoky and... then he began to pull away.

He was currently toying with me and I became frustrated.

Xander... I felt his name rise to the tip of my tongue, however the call never sounded. He didn't leave the bed and so I waited and listened... fighting the urge to hold my breath.

I wanted his lips on my skin... kissing me and touching me... slowly... purposefully. Very vivid reminders came to mind of the last time we had been in bed together in this way, and how the orgasm he had drawn out of me had left me quivering.

I was so aroused now... painfully so. I couldn't help but squirm... in anticipation and with immense self-consciousness.

I was acutely aware of his presence, and ached to reach out to touch him but somehow, I managed to keep my hands to myself. I gripped the sheets by my side, especially as I felt the light brush of his lips on my stomach. My body jerked at the unexpected touch... heated and wet and then he pulled away. The anticipation haunted me as I wondered where he would kiss next.

I felt him move closer towards me, and it seemed as though he was looming over my face.

"*Xander,*" I called out, my hand lifting with the intent to take the tie off. "I'll do whatever you want, but I don't want this over my eyes."

His response however was once again stern. "Stay as you are," he said, but the frustration overwhelmed me.

"Just *fuck* me!" I cried out, and heard his answering chuckle.

He kissed me once again, on the same spot on my stomach and then he leaned forward and I felt his lips on mine.

His kiss was unhurried… as he took his time in coaxing my lips open with his and he went deep.

His tongue slid into my mouth, licking against mine and stroking… sucking until little whimpers began to escape me.

But then he was pulling away again, and I almost went after him.

With one hand however, he pushed me back onto the bed and I was forced to lie back down nearly panting. He got off the bed, and I reached toward him, needing his heat over me.

"Take the rest off." he said and I hesitated. But I soon came to accept the more I held back, the more torturous this would be for me, and the more he would enjoy it. And so I did what he asked. I was fully naked and exposed, and although I tried my best not to get too self-conscious about it, reminding myself this was Xander, it was quite difficult too.

Thankfully I felt him return to the bed and his hands closed around my thighs. My breathing slightly shuddered at the touch, and he was pulling them open. A few more seconds passed and his lips were between them.

I cried out… the heated weighty feel of his tongue connecting with my now swollen clit.

I was soaking wet, and he only added to this. My thighs tightened around him, keeping him in place but seeking some sort of relief from the excruciating sweetness that was now winding my body tight.

My hands searched and soon found his hair, and I slid my finger into the thick mass, grabbing tight.

"Let go," he said, and began to pull away when it became obvious my grip was more for revenge than anything else.

"Let go," he said again, "or else I'll shove my cock down your throat."

I stilled, but I couldn't help but admit, I was tempted.

I wanted him in my mouth too I realized, but first I wanted him ramming into me... hard.

"*Xander...*" I breathed, the frustration and anticipation now truly overwhelming me. I felt him lean forward once again and his breath was washing over my face.

"What do you want?" he asked.

And I cried out again. "I've already told you."

"I want details. I'll give you what you want but I also want to enjoy myself so you can't be too smart about it... and you cannot demand anything fast." he said, and I decided to comply.

I took a deep breath and tried to settle down... to accept my fate, and in a way it made this begin to seem as though we were making love more than anything else. I wanted to get over this and get out of bed, while he wanted to remain in it with me for as long as possible.

And so with this in mind I came up with my first request.

"Fuck my mouth," I told him. "I want your cock in my mouth."

For a moment everything went still around us... but I heard the soft huff of laughter from him. And then he complied.

Blow jobs were far from my favorite thing, but I'd only come to find this out after I'd broken up with Xander and began dating Josh.

I realized it was more than the act itself but the person you were performing it on, and how you felt about them. With Xander, every sigh and groan and strain of tone made me excited, and brimming with contentment at the effect that my suction had on him. And so I'd fist him even harder... even when my jaw began to ache, simply to be rewarded with the warm stream of his release filling my mouth and then sliding down.

I'd loved it, and had lapped every bit of him up, unwilling to let any of it go to waste. With Josh, I'd never been able to go that far.

And so now, as I felt Xander grab onto my thighs to pull me even further down the bed my heart began to race.

Soon his thighs were over my face, and I couldn't help but to reach to hold onto them, to somehow ground me.

I felt the strength of the muscled limbs, and couldn't help but moan. Soon enough, I also felt the thick, plush head of his cock brushing against my lips and I didn't need any more nudging to go ahead. One of my hands closed around the hard length and I was pulling him in.

"Mmn..." I moaned aloud as this brought many, many memories to mind.

I knew how to milk him, and as I began to take him even deeper, hollowing my cheeks, gripping him tightly and sucking hard, I felt my stomach continuously flip in utter joy.

"Ahhh…" I heard him cry out at the additional pumping of my hand, and as I sunk down even deeper and took him all the way to the back of my throat.

It occurred to me how probably ravenous I looked, but I didn't give a fuck. All I cared about was that I receive his release… the warm sweet rush that had once made me feel quite lucky to be his.

I didn't expect this kind of emotional satisfaction to arise this time around, but I was certain my satisfaction would be wholesome regardless.

And I was right… a few seconds later as I fondled his balls he lost control and was shooting down my throat, however his load this time around was heavier than I could remember it ever being.

I nearly choked on it, but this soon became inconsequential as the sounds of his exertions and the slight trembling of his body registered. He continued to fuck my mouth and I consented, milking him of every ounce of release left in him until his dick finally left my mouth with a pop. I licked my lips, savoring the wetness and sloppiness and wanted more than anything in that moment to see him. To see his head thrown backwards and his chest slightly heaving as he tried to contain his labored breathing.

But instead, I licked my lips and decided to wait, and soon enough he was back to normal.

"*Fuck*," he cursed and I couldn't help but bite down on my lip to conceal my delight.

"No one could ever blow me as well as you could Olivia," he said and the thought of anyone else even doing this to him caused a surge of jealousy to shoot through me.

It was all soon contained however when suddenly he was leaning down and his lips closed around the nipple of one breast.

I whimpered at the sharp jolt of arousal to my core, and just like that all contrary thoughts faded to pleasure as he began to fondle my other breast. He sucked hard on one peak, and then the other, proceeding afterwards to trace kisses down my torso and then his tongue was dipping into my belly button.

My back arched at the touch, but before I could even recover he was suddenly pulling my legs apart, and once again returning his lips to my sex.

His tongue slid inside of me, thrusting and licking, my hips writhing against his face searching for my own release. There was something about the way he touched me so intimately like this it nearly drove me out of my mind every time. Or perhaps it was the fact it was *him*... and how in love I had been with him... and still probably was.

He didn't let me come from his ministrations on my sex. Instead... he planted unhurried and unexpected kisses along the insides of my thighs, and then his cock was nudging me open and sliding in.

He was far from careful as he immediately thrusted deep, going all the way till he hit the end of me. I cried out at the delicious friction, the pleasure rolling and rolling and pummeling into every part of me.

I clenched and unclenched around him, taut and greedy, my hands going around his body to hold him close to me, as tight as was possible.

And he began to move... pumping his hips... every stroke intent...

All my reservations scattered into nothing and it wasn't long after, his did too.

He collapsed against me, trying to catch his breath, his frame dampened with sweat. And then slanting his head, he kissed me, and I felt myself begin to fall apart.

As his tongue slid against mine, slow and sensually, I felt his hand go behind my head to slowly hoist me up.

It barely registered to me what was happening.

But soon enough the silk fabric was slipping away from my eyes.

He pulled his lips away from mine... briefly, but even that seemed unbearable. However before I could complain too much, his lips were back on mine.

I held him even more tightly as he continued rocking into me, his hips grinding and his pace now particularly slow.

I loved it... every single moment of it... every single breath of his. My hand slid up his back needing to feel the exertion of his body... the exertion of his frame, the shift of his muscles beneath damp, heated skin.

And before I could stop myself... my lips lowered onto his shoulder to press a wet kiss onto the curve, needing to taste him. It was just as I remembered... sweet and warm, and the rush that ensued left me heady.

I collapsed back onto the bed, my eyes coming open with my need to see him. His were shut but I understood why he had taken off the blindfold. We'd now passed the point of teasing, and at this stage we needed to be one with each other even though neither of us would ever allow ourselves to admit it. I watched him, mesmerized, and wished he'd open his eyes so I could look into them. His expression however showed he was too far gone. Twisted and almost pained at the pleasure as he began to fuck harder and harder into me. I eventually decided I was more than content to just watch him. To watch how his lips parted breathlessly at the onslaught of these overwhelming sensations.

Soon though his eyes came open, and I was immediately tempted to shut mine. I was able to resist however even though I could barely keep them open anyway. He slammed into me, over and over again our bodies moving in one beautiful rhythm, but on one particularly good thrust I felt all the way to my soul, my eyes clenched shut to control it. I turned away, as it rocked my entire body, and I was coming with a long torturous moan. I felt my mind go blank, the only thing registering, the waves of pleasure crashing against me, my shivering frame and the weight of his body on top of mine.

My hands moved down to grab his ass, my legs circling around him as I couldn't help but twist and writhe.

This sent him over the edge also and he was shooting into me, thick and warm.

I loved the sound he made at his release, raw and unrestrained, and reverberating through the both of us. Afterwards he collapsed onto me and I buried my face in his neck, holding him tight.

I should have let him go, just as I had previously but I couldn't. And so I steeled myself for the embarrassment of when he would jerk my hands away and rise to his feet. When he would announce he was once again done with me and it was time for me to take my leave.

However… and to my surprise it didn't come. Seconds passed and then minutes and still his face was buried in my neck as he tried to catch his breath… as he tried to gather the fragments of his brain back together.

And so I shut my eyes, relishing the tender and shared aftermath for however long it would last.

But then I fell asleep.

XANDER

I knew the moment she fell asleep... and I didn't want to move. My entire mind however was aggrieved, insisting I shake her awake and remind her what this was between us, but I couldn't bring myself to do it. My body couldn't bring itself to because once again, it had found its perfect bliss... incomparable, soothing, warm and sweet bliss.

I couldn't understand it. I could only ever feel this way with her and as I slowly lifted my head to stare down at her face, I couldn't understand why. Perhaps we were truly meant to be, however my pride wouldn't yet allow me to accept this.

At this moment however, it had taken a back seat... with me still inside her.

I was well aware that my weight would soon be crushing her, so I stayed until I could no longer afford to hold as much of my weight off her as I had been doing.

Pulling out of her was near heart wrenching... especially at the wetness and loss of heat that followed and to this she winced.

I was certain I'd woken her, but she soon settled back down and I was allowed to roll onto my back by her side. She however followed, amusingly, and once again had her arm and leg draped over mine like no time had passed.

For a moment I wondered if she was faking this, if she was perhaps awake but was trying to weasel her way into staying but the longer I watched her, the more I understood this could not be true because I knew exactly how she was when she was asleep. Perhaps she had changed over the years... but I doubted her sleeping pattern would. I could even almost identify the rhythm and pace of her breathing when she was so deep in slumber in this way, and so I decided to temporarily suspend the skepticism towards every single thing she did.

I watched for a little longer but didn't allow myself to wrap an arm around her. I was scared that if I did I'd truly remember what having her as mine completely and thoroughly had felt like.

And if I did, then I would truly be in trouble... even though deep down I suspected I already was.

Otherwise, why else would she be in my bed and why else was I now shutting my eyes... content. I drew in a deep breath, released it and was soon fast asleep.

T he next morning, I woke up feeling disoriented.

And so it took me a while to even agree to open my eyes. I didn't want to face what was out there... waiting and gnawing.

He was not in bed with me just as I had expected, but still, I could feel the lingering warmth of his presence. Perhaps though it was simply from my imagination because recently, it was becoming difficult to separate what was real from what was not.

Like for instance, why the hell had he let me sleep over? He hated me, and on more than one occasion had made me very aware of this. But perhaps he didn't loathe me completely? I couldn't help but wonder. Perhaps deep inside and in some corner, hidden very, very far away was a tiny hope that perhaps our meeting again and coming together in this way wouldn't be futile. That yet another path could sprout from it... but then I doubted so. I looked around from the empty bed to the spacious room, and couldn't help but admit to myself that what I was currently nursing was a pipe dream.

And so I pushed the covers off me and sat up, refusing to remain here any longer.

It bothered me that I'd stayed this long, and made me wonder how I was going to face him.

Exhausted, my face fell into my hands for a few moments as I tried to recollect myself and all of the memories from the previous night.

Soon I had most of it, and was glad to see that I had no regrets. Since I didn't plan on suddenly racking up any, I finally pushed off the bed and rose to my feet.

I found my clothes still strewn all over the place, grabbed my underwear and bra and easily found my purse.

I didn't bother looking at myself in the mirror because I wasn't exactly certain as to what I would see there.

And so I went out of the room and began to head down his magnificent hallway.

His magnificent apartment or should I say home, because I was certain just his bedroom was comparable in size to my entire living area and kitchen.

He had truly done well. I couldn't help but realize it as I took a look around. It was one thing indeed to hear of his humongous success but then it was a completely different thing to be able to take it in this closely.

My only hope was that he continued to do well, even despite our antagonism towards each other.

Soon I was heading down the gorgeous floating concrete stairs, and the nerves began to set in. I was going to be facing him again and I didn't know how I was expected to act. It truly was a damn shame I had fallen asleep so quickly and easily because I had missed probably the only opportunity I would get to enjoy him in that way... unconscious and vulnerable, just like I had in the past.

With a sigh, I soon arrived at the ground floor and wondered how I was going to find him in this massive house.

The scent however of a meal being prepared drew me in and I headed over to meet him in the kitchen making breakfast.

My heart was touched as for a moment, I imagined he was doing this with me in mind. But it was too hard to believe. The signals were definitely now becoming too mixed and I had no clue as to what to do. *Go ahead and speak to him or to just take my leave?*

Unable to decide, I pulled my defenses up and went over. When I arrived at the counter however he didn't turn around but I doubted that he wasn't aware of my presence after all we were the only two present in the house. There was no way he wouldn't have heard my movements till now.

And so I forced my mouth to speak.

"Morning."

He didn't turn, but I was certain he was very aware of me. But still I didn't leave. I promised myself however that I would, and so I began to count down from ten. Three seconds later he turned away from the stove with a skillet pan in hand, and I saw the eggs, bacon and sausages that were in it. It brought to mind the countless times in the past when he had made breakfast before sending me on my way, and so for a few more seconds my gaze was lost on him. He found a plate, and then brought it over to the counter to transfer his meal onto.

I watched him, wondering when and if he ever planned on responding to me or even look at me. I wasn't truly complaining though and allowed myself the extra minutes to admire his frame because who knew if I would see him again. Who knew if because of the lines we had crossed this time around, if he would ever let me back into his arms?

He was bare chested, and the slight reddened marks down his back were visible and brought me a sense of satisfaction that made warmth coil within my stomach.

His lower half was encased in a pair of dark sweat pants, and all in all he looked sexy enough to eat all over again. I wanted to fuck him again... just one more time before I left but I doubted he would be open to this. With a sigh, I turned around and began to make my way out.

I was sure he would speak... that he would reach out to me but instead all I heard was the sound of pouring coffee. I turned around to see he had purposely decided to ignore my presence and it hurt. Hurt more than I would have expected.

He hadn't even offered me a glass of water.

Tears stung my eyes as I watched him pour the coffee into his cup, and just before he turned around I continued on my way.

I managed to hold it all together until I got outside, however I soon remembered I didn't have the keys to my car. Thankfully, he had brought it here instead of his, but it killed me that I would have to return to ask him for my keys. It made me almost furious even, especially when it occurred to me he had probably ignored me on purpose, knowing I would have to come back.

Perhaps he knew this… perhaps he had let me go knowing I'd realize this and return.

What kind of sick, deranged game was he now playing with me? Furious, I headed back into his apartment complex. I found my way up to his floor, and was soon pounding against the door. A few minutes later, he pulled it open, a frown on his face at the very sight of me.

"My keys," I demanded with gritted teeth, and his gaze perused me slowly from the top of my head to the base of my feet.

It felt so condescending, and never had I felt so ashamed. He stepped away then but turned around to continue on his way back into the house without so much as a hello or response. I watched him disappear around the corner as he returned to the kitchen, and I knew I wouldn't be able to take one step forward. So I looked around the foyer, swearing to myself that I would leave without the keys if I didn't find them there. I didn't and so furious, I turned around and exited the house.

It annoyed me even further that his door was so heavy, so even though I tried to slam it shut behind me, it just didn't work.

I cursed at him in my heart.

XANDER

Linda called me, and I was so surprised when receiving the call I almost didn't know what to do.

She laughed as soon as I answered and I could tell something had made her quite surprised.

"You still have the same number," she said. "I thought you would have changed it."

"I didn't," I replied, more than glad to hear from her. But then I immediately sensed the exhaustion in her tone.

It had been so many years since I had last seen her, but all my fond memories of her remained. Of how she laughed so easily and how she never held back in teasing her daughter along with me. She had cared for me and approved of me, and so I couldn't imagine now how I had for even a moment hesitated with handling her medical bills.

However she didn't know I was involved, and probably never would so I cautioned myself to take care when speaking to her.

"I just thought of you," she said, "and decided to give you a call. I have quite a lot of time to kill these days."

Kill was definitely the wrong word to use, but I didn't bother pressing her about this because then I would have to reveal that I was aware of her present condition. I hoped she wouldn't say or listen to any words as ominous as that because it was sure to sap her of her ability to fight.

"Where are you?" I asked. "Can I come pay a visit?"

This was a bit dangerous I admitted, but her esteemed daughter couldn't possibly be around her all the time, and I did truly want to head over myself to check on her. However, her response surprised me.

"I'm at the hospital having testing done today, but I would love some company," she continued, "can you come around 4 PM?"

"Um…" I started to respond, but then she intercepted me.

"I won't take no for an answer. We haven't seen each other in years, and I'm sure we have a lot to catch up on."

I couldn't argue with that and agreed. "I'll be there," I promised her and the conversation came to an end.

And so later that evening, I found myself strolling down the hallway of the hospital.

I wasn't surprised at all when she mentioned the hospital, and neither did I bother to feign as though I was, which I was certain was a surprise to her. But if there was one thing that I'd loved about her from the onset, it was the fact she never pried too deeply. She listened and then gave and accepted information as it was delivered to her.

Soon I arrived at her door and knocked on it and her voice sounded over for me to come in.

She smiled the moment she saw me, but it was so tired my heart ached.

"Xander," she called and I went in. She held out her IV tethered hand.

I took it gently, and couldn't help but notice how frail it now looked, how frail in general she now seemed. She had never been overweight, but she had never been as skinny as this either. She was still so beautiful though, and as I stared into her familiar smiling hazel eyes, I could see the unmistakable similarities with her daughter.

I looked around, and soon found a chair by the corner. So I brought it over to sit right by her bedside.

"How have you been Linda?" I asked and she shrugged. "I'm hanging in there. We're here for some detailed tests and then afterwards we will be informed as to how best to proceed."

I nodded, stroking her hand in mine, softly... gently.

"You'll be fine. You'll get through this."

She studied me and then smiled again.

"You're aware of the details aren't you?" she asked and I paused briefly to consider if I was in the mood to feign ignorance. Before I could respond anyway she spoke. "I suspected as much."

This surprised me. "You did?"

"Yeah," she said. "A week ago we couldn't afford anything but then suddenly, I'm in a private room and treatment is rapidly underway. My daughter has done well for herself but she doesn't make as much money as you do, and we don't have any rich relatives. I also know that we've maxed out our credits in dealing with this cancer. So... I had to consider you."

I didn't have a response to this.

"She contacted you?" she asked.

I nodded.

"I thought the two of you parted on bad terms."

"We did," I replied.

"She told me she messed up," she said and I lifted my gaze to hers. To this I didn't give a response.

Her mother looked away thoughtfully. "She messed up but still went to you... I wonder how that made her feel."

"We're fine," I tried to reassure her. "We're fine. And if it makes you feel any better, I'm doing this because of you, not her. I've known you since I was a teen and you were once a very important part of my life. And it'll always be that way."

She turns to me, a smile on her face. "And what about Olivia?" she asked. "She too used to be someone extremely important to you."

I grew thoughtful as I considered this statement, and she waited patiently for my response.

I lifted my gaze to hers.

"If you don't want to respond you don't have to," she said to me. "This is between you two and I am her mother. I'll understand."

I smiled again at this, and chose to speak. "Olivia…" I began, thinking about how I could word this properly. "My attachment and dependence on Olivia was very different from the one I had with you. Obviously…" I smiled, but then at the devastation I had gone through, the smile soon wiped off my face. "I expected more from her than anyone else or perhaps it's better to say I just expected the most important things from her."

The seconds ticked away, and although I thought I would be able to say more, I soon found out that I couldn't.

"I understand," she says. "I guess you will be unhappy then if I reject your help?"

I smiled at her. "I will. But Olivia will be devastated."

At this, we gazed at each other for the longest time, and then she nodded her head, and looked away with a smile. "That daughter of mine is quite stubborn isn't she?"

I smiled again at the understatement of the century.

"She would be extremely upset if she found out I'm aware of her using your funds to handle the expenses, right?"

"You know her," I said. "But I don't think she knows you very well. She expects you to reject this."

Her mother smiled. "I should. I would… because yes I do hate charity, but if it means that I get to stay around a while longer to be with her, and to guide her then I will take as much charity as is offered. In the face of love and death I have found that pride means very little."

"Mmn," I replied. "But still I think its best that we keep things just between us both for now."

She turned to me again and smiled. "Most definitely. You're a great man Xander. I'm very happy my daughter met you."

To this I nodded, and couldn't help but wonder if my father's sentiment towards my meeting Olivia would be the same. Pushing the sour thought aside, I took Linda's hand in mine once again, delicately... and just then the door to the room slid open.

Whoever had come in seemed to go immediately quiet, and I didn't need to turn to see who it was.

Her mom's gaze moved between mine and her daughter's behind me. I considered rising to my feet so I could take my leave, but decided to first of all see how Olivia would react to my presence, especially given what had happened between us at my home earlier that morning.

It hadn't been intentional at all, as her keys had been with me in the kitchen. I'd expected her to come after me, but she'd been impatient and short-tempered, and thus things had turned out the way they had. I had no doubt it had completely sealed off whatever light had been about to break through in our relationship with each other, especially given the somewhat affectionate night we had shared together. Perhaps a simple apology and explanation would repair it, but I didn't possess any capacity whatsoever to be courteous to her.

"Mom," she called, and I turned then for a glance at her. She met my gaze briefly, brows furrowed with immense displeasure at the sight of me, but the scowl immediately disappeared when her mother turned to her.

I was amused, but regardless, decided it was indeed time for me to take my leave. Her mother however reached for my hand the moment I rose to my feet.

Then she stared into my eyes. "Thank you for coming to see me. I'll be able to see you again right?"

"Of course," I replied. "I'll pay you another visit soon."

She let me go then, and without bothering to pay any attention to her daughter I turned around and walked out of the room.

OLIVIA

All of this was quite bizarre.

First of all, I'd been so shocked to see him that my soul had nearly left my body, and then we had acted like complete strangers. It was the way it should be, especially given the hostility from earlier that morning, but then it was equally as strange because this was the same man that had been inside me just the previous evening… the same man I had fallen asleep with.

It made me feel as though we were both deceiving ourselves and playing a game neither of us knew the rules to or stakes of. Or perhaps he did and I was the one that was clueless.

I watched him as he made his way out of the room, dressed very similarly to how he had the previous weekend when he'd come over to my apartment.

Blue jeans, a crisp white dress shirt, with the sleeves folded up to his elbows.

He looked welcoming, but yet striking and for a moment I couldn't help but imagine him without the clothes on which wasn't in the least difficult since I had been privy to this over and over again.

In response, my body instantly began to overheat, and so the words were out of my mouth before I could even stop myself. "Mom, I'll be right back."

I dropped my purse on the lounge chair and hurried towards the door

I found him in the hallway, strolling away and wondered if he would even turn if I called out to him. The plan had been to do what I could to catch up with him so I could inquire on what I wanted to, but at the reminder that I was on less than friendly terms with him, I decided against it.

"Xander," I called out, and to my surprise, he stopped in his tracks. He then turned around to face me.

"Let's talk," I said, and he didn't seem to object to this. When however, a few seconds passed and I realized we were both waiting for the other to make the first move, it became clear to me at least in this moment what the current game we were playing was. Who was subservient enough to succumb to the other's wiles?

My insides were instantly set ablaze.

I hated him so much in that instant that I wanted to strangle him. This complete disregard for me was truly dehumanizing and too unnecessary. But then again he had come to see my mother... and I couldn't understand why. Or perhaps I did. Perhaps it was extremely clear I was the one he truly loathed... and no one else.

I decided we would have absolutely nothing more to do with each other, and now that he had come to see my mother, I knew he was bluffing earlier about cutting off our access to the needed funds.

I should have known better... he was far from heartless and she at least meant something to him.

For a moment, I had forgotten about the heart of the man that I had fallen in love with.

It turned out he hadn't truly changed. He was still extremely and passionately furious at me, and I deserved it but I didn't need anything from him so this didn't need to plague me.

And so I turned around and walked away. There was no need for me to go after him, or to even speak to him, and so with my heart aching I headed back to my mother's room. And as for my car, he knew where I lived. So if he ever wanted to return it then he knew where to find me.

"Livvy."

"No," was her immediate response, and I couldn't help my smile. She turned the page of her notebook, without even bothering to look up and then picked up her fork to dig into her macaroni and cheese lunch.

"Wow," Danny exclaimed. "Not even a hello?"

We pulled out the two chairs before her as we arrived at her lunch table, and even then she didn't bother sparing either of us a look.

"We have a guest," Danny said, as we set our trays down and took our seats, however she seemed to have completely tuned him out.

"Hi Olivia," I said, and she kept writing. But then her pen suddenly stopped, and it seemed as though she had frozen in place.

I wasn't too surprised by this reaction, especially when I recalled the almost dazed way with which she had reacted to me from the first time we had met in front of the boys' locker room.

Her gaze slowly lifted then, and I felt my heart begin to pound in my chest.

She had caught my interest… almost a year prior but I hadn't thought to do anything about it until I had heard her curse at her best friend while previously acting mute with me. From that moment on, I hadn't been able to get her out of my mind and so of course I had to plead with him to bring me along to lunch with them.

He'd been taken aback, and somewhat reluctant, warning me that Olivia didn't necessarily do well with strangers and it'd made me laugh thanks to my first-hand experience with this.

I couldn't help but wonder though if she was generally that reserved, and unwilling to communicate with strangers in general or if it was just me. A part of me hoped that perhaps I had caught her eye too, and thus she'd simply just been too nervous to speak to me.

She was indeed a loner from what I had noticed so far, and seemed to enjoy and even prefer it when most of our other school mates exhibiting the same demeanor seemed uncomfortable instead. I guessed this was what had made watching her so enjoyable.

Our gaze finally connected and I didn't know what to say.

Neither did she. Thankfully though Danny was present to rescue the both of us.

"See, I told you we had a guest."

She looked away then, and when she shut her notebook, I could tell very clearly that she was readying herself to escape.

I panicked. "Do you hate me or something?" I asked, a smile still on my face so she wouldn't feel too alarmed by the question.

Her eyes slightly widened.

"What?"

"You never speak to me, or seem to want to be around me for even a second. I just came now for instance and you're already looking for a way to escape."

I watched as a frown came across her face. "And… and your conclusion is that I hate you?"

I could see she was about to give the unspoken verdict of if she considered me an idiot or not.

I shrugged, and lowered my gaze down to my plate to stab at a piece of lettuce. "You never know," I replied. "I mean… there might be other reasons but this one seems to be the most plausible?"

"Why would I hate you?"

Laughter ensued from Danny, but my gaze returned to hers.

"Don't take it to heart Xander," Danny said. "She's like this with everyone, even me and we've known each other since we were five."

I studied her, features soft, eyes kind… but then couldn't help but be amused as it all darkened into a scowl as she turned to Danny.

"She likes to escape everyone?" I asked and he laughed, eyes sparkling.

"Nope… just you," he said underneath his breath but we all heard him loud and clear. She grabbed the bottle of water by her side and began to twist it open, and although it was beyond clear how she intended to attack him with it, she remained fairly calm about it. I was mesmerized, and couldn't look away as she began to pour a little bit of the liquid into the cap.

"Don't you dare," Danny warned her. "It's going to hit Xander too."

This made her pause just enough to glance at me, but then she didn't quite meet my gaze. She gave things a moment of thought… and then she kept going, and I think that was the moment I fell in love. I watched, beyond amused as she aimed the water at her friend. He leaned towards me in an attempt to avoid the hit, so her gaze moved between the both of us… conflicted… and then she gave up.

I knew she felt frustrated and somewhat ambushed, and needed her space to herself. I also didn't want to take any more of her time than we already had, so I said what I wanted to.

"Why don't you ever come to our basketball games?"

"Livvy doesn't like basketball," Danny revealed, and for a moment, I was upset both by the fact he had responded for her and that she didn't like basketball.

"You wouldn't want to come to our game on Saturday?" I asked, and both of them seemed to pause.

And then she met my gaze.

"She'd love to," Danny replied on her behalf once again, and she seemed struck.

"*Danny*," she gritted her teeth.

"I've been trying to get her to come watch me play for years, but maybe this time around she'll actually accept?"

His eyes were full of hope, and I couldn't help but send her an equally expectant gaze.

To both of our surprise, she sighed. "Alright," she replied with a small voice, and I felt my heart do a little dance in my chest.

By that Saturday, I was brimming with more excitement and anticipation than I'd ever felt on the court. However I was also growing increasingly nervous because the seats were already filling up, and she was nowhere to be found.

Suddenly, an arm came around my shoulder and I turned to see it was Danny.

"She's late to things," he explained to me, and something about the fact he knew this about her hit me with a twinge of jealousy.

"She'll be here," he assured me before walking off to meet up with our other teammates.

The game soon began, and not till we had our second intermission did I finally notice her.

She was seated midway in the bleachers, and she had her gaze on me. I was struck, however the moment our eyes met she instantly tried to look away. I waved to her but she didn't respond.

"Xander!" I heard some catcalls, and looked over to the group of girls at the forefront. I smiled politely at them but returned my focus back to our team.

We resumed once again and through it all I couldn't stop myself from looking up at the bleachers, and to my surprise as time went on, she didn't take her gaze away from mine. I would look at her and smile, and the first time she returned it I stopped dead in my tracks. This earned me a ram into the shoulder and then I was staggering backwards.

"King!" I heard the shout just as I landed on my ass. The whole court seemed to gasp but I didn't care. All I did was look for her, and when I saw that she had risen to her feet in concern, I was so filled with delight that I completely collapsed and laid on the floor, not feigning pain but needing to rest for a few moments, to catch my breath and calm my racing heart. We took another break then and I had a few abuses rein down on me from our coach for being so distracted. But I didn't care.

Just before we returned back to the game, I glanced up at her once again and at the concern in her gaze, I couldn't help but mouth over to her. "I'm fine."

And to my surprise, she nodded.

It suddenly became even harder to breathe.

OLIVIA

I wasn't exactly sure what was happening but I couldn't say I hated it. I also couldn't say I didn't notice all of the looks the other girls all around the court were turning their heads to give to me, all because Xander King was only looking at and responding to me. If only they knew I was just as confused as they were.

First of all, he had invited me to this game which Danny had informed me officially indicated his interest in me, but that had been quite difficult to believe. Now however... as he waved to me once again before heading back into the game, my heart nearly stopped in my chest. I couldn't wave back since too many people would see and speculations would spread, and this saddened me.

He was already going too far by even giving me this much attention, because sure he was popular and sure he was desired by almost every girl at Emerson High, but he had never singled anyone out, or paid attention to anyone in particular... until now.

We weren't even in the same grade.

He was a senior and I was just a sophomore… so how and when had he even noticed me enough for all of this to begin happening?

"Olivia!"

At the sudden chorus, I looked up to see a few girls that I definitely recognized as being sophomores hurry over to take the empty seats by my side. I was immediately over-whelmed at their widely interested eyes and badly concealed envy.

"What's happening? Why is Xander paying so much attention to you?"

"Who's Xander?" I asked, and truly had no idea why I had said that.

They all looked confused.

"Um…" they looked then towards the court to see him talking with one of his teammates, but then he turned towards the bleachers and I didn't miss the frown that came to his face as he sighted the girls that had surrounded me.

In that moment I realized, and for the first time ever I might add, I'd been avoided by my peers in the past solely because I'd been too unpopular to be given any attention whatsoever.

Now however with Xander King's gaze on me it was no longer the case.

To be the center of this much attention was not all bad, I couldn't help but admit, however all of these attentional eyes on me made me want to leave, but I couldn't help but think it would make him unhappy. After all, he had been the one to invite me.

"You really don't know who Xander is?" one of the girls eyed me suspiciously, and I sighed.

"The one who's been waving to you," she added.

"That's Danny's friend," I replied.

"Xander," one of the girls corrected and I nearly rolled my eyes.

"Sure... whatever."

It was clear to them then we weren't a couple, and I was far from deserving of this new found attention.

Thankfully, the message hit home, and so all four of them got up and went on their way.

I pulled out my iPods then, blocked my tears and brought out a book.

From time to time I watched the game and the score, but never Xander which hurt, but there were too many eyes and the last thing I wanted was my name circulating across the school when I'd never even had a proper conversation with the guy.

Soon, the game came to an end and I immediately gathered my things, ready to leave, but then Danny was hurrying over to me from the court.

"We won!" he said dripping in sweat.

"Great," I replied.

"Wasn't it fun to watch?"

"It sure was," I replied and he pushed my shoulder lightly as if to say 'I told you so'.

"I'll change quickly," he said. "Let's grab a burger so we can celebrate before heading home."

I had nothing else on my agenda for the night, so I nodded and waited for him.

I looked around too but could no longer see Xander. I was disappointed and hoped my not watching him hadn't discouraged him from whatever this... was between us. Soon Danny called me and I headed out to meet him. What I met however was an old Chevrolet truck waiting outside, with Danny at the front seat.

"Livvy get in," he called out to me.

I was reluctant, especially when I saw the breathtakingly handsome boy that was in the driver's seat and watching me with the kindest of smiles on his face.

"Where's your car?" I asked Danny.

"I didn't drive it," he replied. "My dad needed it for the day so Xander offered to give me a ride home."

And so I joined them, sitting in the middle because what other choice did I have.

Ronnie's Diner had the best burgers I'd ever had, as Danny and I had long ago discovered, so I almost couldn't help my excitement as we all settled down to eat.

I wasted no time in enjoying that first bite, and as my head fell slightly backwards and my eyes fluttered shut, I couldn't stop the soft moans that escaped my lips.

At the sound of Danny's laughter however, I came back to my senses, remembering we had very important company present, at least to me.

I could feel the intensity of the gaze he had on me, and couldn't bear to meet his eyes. I brushed my hair over my shoulders without a word, and continued on with my meal. They talked about their game and tried to pull me into the conversation, but when it became apparent I had little to no interest or knowledge about any of it, they gave up.

I was content to just listen to them both, amused at some of Danny's grievances and excitement until eventually he rose to his feet and went to the bathroom, leaving Xander and me alone.

I could see through the periphery of my vision that he was boldly watching me now, but once again I looked at him.

"If you're not a fan of basketball then what sports do you like?" he asked.

I cleared my throat and responded. "I'm not a fan of sports."

"So what do you do for extracurricular activities?" he asked.

"I have a part-time job," I replied, and his brows shot up. "You do?" his eyes sparkled with interest and I almost couldn't look away. Especially as his hand ran through his hair and then he leaned back into the booth.

"Yeah," I coughed wondering where my voice had gone. "At the animal shelter."

"Oh…" he smiled. "You love animals?"

His smile was messing with my lungs. "Yeah."

"You want to work with animals when you're older?"

At this I couldn't help my smile. "No, I thought I wanted to, which was why I looked for work at the shelter to get a feel of it."

"You don't enjoy it as much as you thought you would?"

"I do," I replied, now engaged since I hadn't really spoken about this with anyone in the past. "But I didn't realize how emotionally draining it would be. Animals are a lot of work."

He laughed. "Of course they are."

"We don't have any pets at home so I thought it was going to be all sunshine and rainbows getting to spend so much time with them but…" I shook my head as I brought my soda to my lips. "I don't think it's for me."

He laughed again and the hearty sound gripped me. I loved how relaxed he seemed to be in my presence, and wondered if the time would come where I would ever become that way in his.

That was if we even became friends or anything after this. I still wasn't even sure what he was doing hanging out with me and Danny once again or… my eyes widened suddenly. *Was I the third wheel?*

Was there something going on between him and Danny, and I was brought along to deflect attention. Danny was bi. No one knew this except me perhaps, but maybe Xander was also aware?

"What is it?" he asked as he noticed by expression.

"Nothing," I replied and lowered my head to pick up my half eaten burger.

"So what do you want to focus your attention on in the future?" he asked, and I truly wondered about his questions as they were quite specific and peculiar. I mean, why wasn't he asking me about more trivial things like movies or whatever else people our age talked about. I had no clue, and it made me wonder what Danny and I talked about when we were together?

This made me realize we didn't necessarily hang out together a lot, but when we did and since we knew each other's families, attended the same classes, and were all in all familiar with each other's history, we never quite had a shortage of topics to talk about when we did meet up. There was also the fact he was always trying to steal my homework, so a lot of our time together was filled with us arguing and fighting over his lackluster approach towards his education.

I studied Xander as I chewed, and decided to actually think on his question and give an honest answer... "I'm thinking that I might go into social services... or become a teacher. One of the two."

"A teacher?"

"Yeah," I replied.

"You seem really soft hearted," he said. "You either want to work with animals or kids."

"They're the two most easily abused," I said without a thought, but it was straight from the heart. "And if they're not abused then they're neglected. I want to do what I can to take care of them."

At this, he went completely silent, but I couldn't help but notice the smile on his face had faded some. I wondered why but before I could work up the courage to ask, Danny returned.

"Hey," he said and took his seat. "What did I miss?"

Neither of us responded to him for some unknown, unspoken reason.

"How am I going to get home?" I asked Danny, as we walked out of the diner.

"Xander will take you," he replied casually and I looked into the diner to watch him by the counter as he spoke to the cashier.

"What?"

"You both will drop me off first since my house is first along the way, and then he'll take you home."

I smacked him loud and hard across his arm.

"Ow!" he exclaimed. "What the hell was that for?"

"What do you mean by he'll take me home? What's all this about? Why is he suddenly hanging around us?"

At the true befuddlement in my eyes, Danny burst out laughing.

"You're using me as some sort of shield aren't you?" I asked. "Like a decoy? Why the hell are you dragging me into your personal affairs?"

He just kept laughing, shaking his head and before I could ask any more Xander returned.

"What's funny?" he asked, but Danny simply threw an arm over my shoulder.

"Xander, I present to you the smartest but yet most obtuse human on the planet. Are you sure you want anything to do with her?"

My eyes widened then up at Danny. Xander shook his head, a smile on his face and then he turned around to head towards his truck. With the back of my elbow I shoved Danny mercilessly in the side.

XANDER

She didn't say a single word.

At this point, I was well aware that she wasn't as quiet as she had initially projected, but she was quite uncomfortable around people she wasn't familiar with, or didn't particularly feel the need to get closer to.

And with this, I had my first question for her as I drove her home. "Why do you keep your circle small?"

She glanced at me, and I felt the tightening of awareness in my chest.

"Do they need to be large?" she asked, and in that moment I was certain I fell just a bit more in love with her.

I smiled. "Perhaps not."

"Do you have a large circle?" she asked.

"Hmm," I thought about it. "I don't think so."

"Do you even have a circle?" she asked. "I don't actually see you around with anyone. You know a lot of people and are generally welcomed everywhere, but you stick to no one. So isn't my circle with just Danny larger than yours?"

My smile widened even further. "I guess you have a point?"

I heard her smile as she looked away.

We kept driving in silence as she stared out of the window, and as I looked ahead I couldn't help but notice the stars were out.

There were so many across the sky, and I could understand her current fixation on them.

"They're beautiful, aren't they?" I asked, and a few seconds later she replied.

"Yeah."

We continued the rest of the drive in silence, with both of us stealing glances at each other from time to time. At one point, our gazes actually met and I couldn't help my smile. She smiled too in response and my heart jolted in my chest. Soon we arrived at her house, and I didn't miss her slight hesitation in disembarking.

"Thank you for the ride," she said, and I couldn't hold myself back anymore. So I held onto her arm and stopped her from leaving.

"Olivia," I called, and she settled back down, something akin to alarm in her eyes. I was instantly remorseful at touching her so suddenly, the last thing I wanted was to startle her.

"Yeah," she replied, her voice small.

I stared into her eyes, all the hair on my body standing up. I couldn't believe how nervous I was in doing this but then again, I knew I had to.

I could already tell she wasn't the type to handle ambiguity well, and so it was only a matter of time before she would begin to find every which way possible to avoid me.

"I…"

She waited.

"Would you go out on a date with me?" The words finally found their way out of my mouth. "A proper date?"

Her eyes widened to the size of saucers.

At least for a whole minute afterwards, she remained mute, and through it all I didn't know whether to be worried or amused.

Eventually, I couldn't take the silence but was slightly consoled because at least she hadn't gotten out of the car and ran for the hills.

"I couldn't get rid of Danny today," I tried my best to lay all of my cards down. "Plus I doubted you would have agreed to even come out with me otherwise."

My laugh was nervous and despite the cold evening, I could also feel the sweat that was beginning to bead across my forehead.

She cleared her throat. "I thought…" she began, but then she stopped and shook her head.

"You thought what?" I was near losing my mind with curiosity.

"Nothing," she said, and began to push the door open. My hand instantly shot out with panic but before I could alarm her again, I held back. My heart deflated as I watched her leave and hurry away towards her house. I continued to watch her as she went into her house and then shut the door behind her. It took at least another five minutes before I could work up the strength of heart and mind to drive away. My hope however had been crushed and left on the floor.

OLIVIA

PRESENT DAY

"Who's back?"

Elise had just joined me in the break room, and since I could no longer keep thinking myself into the ground, the words had spilled out.

"Xander."

Her eyes widened as she turned to me. "What? But wait… he's been in LA so by back you mean…"

I brought the protein bar to my lips and took the last bite, and at this my message seemed to compute.

"Oh," she said just as I rose to my feet, and headed over to toss the wrapper into the trash. Then I headed towards the coffee pot and groaned when I found it nearly empty. I considered it a blessing anyway because it meant I could focus my attention on making myself a fresh pot as she spoke with me. It would be less uncomfortable I imagined, than having her watching me closely as we conversed about this. I was already jittery enough of everyone and everything thanks to Xander freaking King.

"Oh," she said again, and I sighed.

A minute passed.

"Does he… want to get back together?"

"Absolutely not," I replied, as I watched the coffee begin to drip. "I mean I don't think so. What I think he wants is pay back."

"Pay back? But you didn't actually cheat on him, right?"

My heart instantly went sore at the mention once again of the matter that had torn us apart.

"Yeah, but he doesn't know that. He thinks I did and so he will forever hate me for it."

"What sort of pay back exactly do you think he's seeking after all this time?" she asked, but I didn't particularly have any response that I wanted to share.

I'd only known Elise two short years since we started working here together, and although we knew quite solid details of each other's lives there were some things I'd kept to myself. Like my rendezvous with Xander for instance, and the recent deterioration of my mother's health.

I couldn't help but wonder if it was time to share so I could get a second opinion on how to dig myself out of the over-thinking hole that I was being constantly plagued by.

"Olivia?" she asked and I turned to gaze at her.

"He's already gotten what he wanted," I finally said, unable to hold back, and her eyes slightly widened.

I shrugged.

"And he hasn't walked away?"

I thought of the fact I hadn't yet seen or heard from him in a week. So perhaps he had, but he also hadn't returned my car. Or perhaps he completely forgot about it. I'd never ever felt so confused in my entire life.

"Do you want him to walk away?" she asked, and I looked up at her.

"What I did was unforgivable."

"You didn't actually cheat on him," she reminded me.

"But I made him think I did. I broke his heart."

She sighed. "So you don't want to try? To fix things and explain."

"No," I smiled.

"Why?"

"He's extremely rich. How do you think that looks? *Oh now that I'm successful you want me to be in your life?*"

"But you did that so he could become successful."

"I did that because I didn't know how to trust anybody... and I was scared. Perhaps I should have had more faith. Or perhaps he should have had more faith. Truly, I thought he'd know me enough and reject what I said. At least argued that I couldn't have betrayed him so easily. But he just accepted it as though he had been expecting it... as though it was an out he had been searching for. He accepted it and just walked away."

A long silence followed as I lifted the coffee pot to pour myself a cup.

Suddenly there was a knock on the door, and we both looked up. We'd been expecting to see one of the other teachers sneaking away too for a little break but instead, who we saw nearly made my heart drop into my stomach.

"Hi," he said as he walked in, and Elise turned on her thousand watt smile at the handsome stranger. He returned it, and then fixated his gaze on me as he walked over. I was lit up with joy from the inside as I set my mug down, and in little time, I was being encased in a hug.

I couldn't help it then. The dam that had been holding back my frustration and unhappiness broke and the tears came sliding down my face.

"Livvy," he breathed and all I could do was try to catch mine.

Later that evening, Danny and I were seated on my couch with my legs resting across his. His foot massages were legendary, and so as I basked in their incomparable stress relieving magic, I informed him of why I currently didn't have a car in Los Angeles.

"You left it at Xander's?"

"Yeah," I replied and he was so confused.

"I thought you two hated each other?"

"We're adults," I said. "We don't have to like each other to get what we need from each other."

"Wow," he laughed. "Fifteen year old you would hate you so much."

"I would hate her too. What a snob. But nineteen years old Olivia is the one that I hate the most for being so audacious and for ruining my life."

"I'll get the car back for you." he offered, and I murmured my thanks.

"Are you sure you want me to though? I think it could be a good way for him to keep you in mind? Maybe if he sees it long enough then he'll start to long for ways for you both to get back together?"

"No," I shook my head. "It's time for us both to move on."

"He hates me though," Danny said, "and for the life of me I still can't figure out why. So I really don't know how I'm going to get him to listen to me when I demand your car back."

"I think you're the perfect person for the job," I said, my tone small and heavy with guilt. "If you go get it, he'll be disgusted enough to let it go."

"And why is that?" Danny asked.

I lifted penitent eyes to his. "I smeared your name before him?"

His gaze narrowed. "How?"

"You'd never forgive me," I replied.

"Spit it out," he said, and I did.

He went silent afterwards, and not till I nudged him with my foot did his attention return back to me.

"I'm sorry?" I apologized, but he shook his head to refuse it.

"Why are you sorry? You did what you thought was best for the both of you, and plus by that point I wasn't even close to Xander. We were somewhat acquaintances until he got you and then I was tossed away. From the onset I've always been the means to an end for you two."

"You're making it sound so bad."

"It's not," he replied. "But I'm glad I know now. Back then I'd always wanted to know so badly why you ended things with him."

"Why didn't you pry?"

"Like you would have told me if I had. I've known you for too long, enough to know that you only share what you want to when you're ready. And moreover, so many changes were happening in my own life at that time too so I figured it was time for us all to move on? I was in New York living with Craig, and as long as it brought you the peace that I could see you needed, I wasn't too concerned."

"Yeah," I said thoughtfully, because as I looked back now, I wondered if that *peace* that I'd obtained from breaking up with Xander was worth it.

A long silence passed between us, and then he resumed his heavenly ministrations on my foot.

"So, how's the restaurant?" I asked. "And Craig?"

The smile that came across his face made warmth curl up in the pit of my stomach.

XANDER

For the first few seconds, I was certain that I was hallucinating and the person before my door wasn't actually there.

"Long time no see," he spoke, and it took all of the self-control I'd built up over the years for me to respond solely with my words.

"What the hell are you doing here?" I asked as calmly as I could manage.

At this, the light in his eyes which had seemed genuinely happy to see me dimmed.

He sighed. "I'm here for Livvy's car," he said and with the affectionate moniker, I felt the familiar burn of jealousy when it came to him and his relations to her in a corner of my heart.

I'd never truly been jealous of anyone in my life but him, and the way in which Olivia held him so dearly to her and for so long, with the exception of everyone else. And nothing seemed to have changed because once again, he stood shameless before my door on her behalf.

"You truly have the audacity to come here?" I asked, and he watched me, his gaze almost kind.

I wanted to punch him in the fucking mouth. Thankfully though, I was able to rein in my temper and ponder on what to do like a rational adult.

"Tell her to come pick it up herself."

I started to shut the door in his face, but at his surprise, I couldn't help but slightly pause.

"Wow," he said and I stopped. "She was sure that when you saw me you'd be disgusted enough to let the car go."

It took me quite a while to process this statement, and when I did I finally understood his amazement. He'd expected I would hate the both of them enough to instantly hand the car over, but instead I was insisting she come by herself to pick it up. And it truly made me wonder what this revealed about my emotions towards her.

"You're still in love with her aren't you?" he asked, and something slammed so heavy into me that it took my breath along with it.

One week after Danny had left LA and returned to New York, I still didn't have my car.

It was tough to constantly try to convince my mom during my visits to her house over the weekend as to why it was still being serviced, especially because it was the second week in a row. In two days it would be the weekend again, and I was certain that having it serviced was an excuse that she would no longer buy.

I called Xander. It took me the entire day to work up the courage to do so, and not until I opened my mouth and the words came out did I even believe I would be able to speak. After what I had done with sending Danny over to pick it up, I was certain we were done since it would appear I had once again provoked him and touched a sore spot. However, and just as I expected it hadn't affected any access to my mother's health care, and it made me feel so guilty.

As usual, he didn't speak the moment he answered, but I was undaunted, grateful he had even picked up at all.

And so despite my heart pounding so loudly in my chest that I could barely hear my own voice, I managed to speak. "I need my car."

Another bout of silence ensued and as a result I could no longer sit still. So I got to my feet and began to pace the now emptied classroom.

"Where are you?" he asked, and at the sound of his voice, calm and composed I couldn't help but release a deep sigh of relief.

"Um... I'm still at work. But I'll take an Uber and pick it up."'

"Are you done with work for the day?" he asked, and I couldn't help but be confused. Why was he asking?

"Yeah," I replied.

"I'll pick you up," he said, and before I could say another word the line disconnected.

I held onto the phone, and it was only when a knock suddenly sounded on the door that I was startled enough to realize it was still against my ear. Pulling it away, I turned around and saw that it was Elise.

At first, as I stared at her I felt relief but then as the seconds went past a sense of panic began to rise within me.

"Olivia?" she called and it was only then that I came to my senses.

"Yeah," I replied.

"I'm leaving. Do you need a ride?"

"No," I replied. "I'll call an Uber," I said and she smiled.

"Say hi to your mom for me," she said and waved her good-bye. And just like that the door was shut behind her and I was left alone. To wait.

Thirty minutes later and with no word whatsoever from him, I realized I hadn't even asked when he would be arriving.

I wanted to call him again, but I truly didn't want to be subjected to another bout of heart palpitations and to give him yet another chance to intimidate me so I just sent a message.

"When will you be here? I'm about to leave."

I wasn't expecting an immediate response but still I waited for at least a full minute after I'd sent it to see if there would be one. There wasn't, I sighed and left the classroom to head towards the bathroom. Texting him reminded me of our past and how I had always gotten a response as quick as lightning whenever I'd contacted him in our earliest years together.

Starting from the very first time.

After he had nearly shocked my soul out of my body by asking me on a date after he'd dropped me off at home. I'd returned in a daze and leaned against the shut front door until my mother had appeared.

"I was just about to call you. You're late. Wher-"

She'd stopped when she finally noticed my state.

"What's happening? Are you okay?"

"Yeah," I breathed, my face burning.

Her gaze had narrowed at me but I hadn't given her the chance to further inquire as to what had left me in such shock.

I ran up to my room, half excited and half terrified. It had been almost midnight before I'd finally gotten my senses together and then it'd dawned on me I'd run away from him. He'd asked me out and I'd run away.

The one boy I hadn't been able to keep out of my mind for a few years even though I was convinced there was no way he could ever even be aware I existed, not to talk to much less thinking he would ask me out on a date.

Perhaps it was a bet?

"Ah," I said aloud. That explained things. They'd probably made some sort of prank amongst themselves in the locker room or something to see how quickly it would take me to fall for him?

This sounded absolutely plausible to me, and the longer I thought about it the more annoyed I got until I couldn't help but call Danny.

"Was this a bet?" I asked, knowing he wouldn't keep this from me or even allow it if he was aware. He would never have even allowed Xander to approach me. However he seemed confused by my question and groggy.

"Are you already asleep?" I'd asked and his patience had worn thin.

"What do you want?" he'd groaned and I had found my first smile since Xander had shocked me.

"He asked me out," I said, my voice smaller than I had ever heard it. "Is this some sort of prank?"

At his silence I went on. "It is, isn't it?"

Danny's response had been a sigh, and at the sound of shuffling movement I was aware he had sit upright in his bed.

"I thought you liked him," he said.

"I do," I replied. "But…"

"Livvy," he said. "Sometimes I'm truly astounded at you. A guy you like asks you out and your first thought is that it's probably some sort of bet or prank?"

"Isn't it?" I'd muttered, otherwise wasn't this too ludicrous to believe?

"He likes you," Danny had said, causing my heart to slam against my chest.

"Truly likes you. Why is that so hard to believe? And why would you think that if I had even gotten a whiff of this being some sort of bet that I would have allowed him anywhere close to you?"

He was right, I realized.

"Yeah."

"So…" he said

"'So… what should I say?"

"What do you want to say?" he'd asked.

And so a few minutes later, I'd typed out my first message ever to Xander King.

I reviewed it over and over again, and then with my eyes tightened shut, pressed send. The message had been received and it had marked the beginning to a path in my life that I truly wondered now if it would ever be possible to get off from. He had replied instantly and the first words he'd texted back to me were. "Hey."

"Hey," I'd replied back and he sent a smiling emoji.

"The last two hours have felt like two years to me," he'd said and my heart had grown wings, attempting to fly out of my chest.

"I'm sorry," I apologized. "I wasn't sure... that I'd heard you right."

"Neither am I... right now I mean," he'd texted back. "You said yes?"

"Yeah," I replied. "Yes. I'll go on a date with you."

In the present, I stood before the sink in the bathroom, and wondered about the paths that we had both taken since then. It had been painful but yet we had ended up here once again.

'He's still in love with you,' Danny's words to me from a week earlier came to mind, and at the time I hadn't given it more than a moment's thought because I was certain he absolutely had to be joking. However now, and as I thought of the fact he was once again heading over to meet me, I couldn't help but allow myself for a moment... just a moment to consider the fact maybe there was a sliver of hope for us? Hope for us to clear the misunderstandings and perhaps start all over again?

With a sigh, I washed my hands and exited the bathroom after drying them. If I were to tell him now... to tell him everything... and how I'd always wanted the best for him though my methods had been extremely poorly executed, I had no clue what his reaction would be. Perhaps indifference? Perhaps mockery? Perhaps fury?

Either way, every part of my being told me this would be a bad idea, and I would remember and be drenched in shame every time the memory came up in the future. Extreme shame because he was sure to reject me.

Which was why when I returned to my classroom and met him standing in the midst of it, I wasn't as swayed as I should have been.

I was, however, happy to see him because for a moment, I allowed myself to remember I'd shared this dream with him... of how I'd spend my days in the classroom. And then he'd shared his with me, of how he'd be in technology, unsure yet as to which products he would be putting out to the market but excited about the unique smartphone design he was tinkering with.

He turned towards me as he sensed my presence, and my airways shrunk to the width of straws. He was more formally dressed than I'd ever seen him thus far, because although he had on a usual suit, pin-striped, he also had on a vest underneath that fitted his torso remarkably.

My throat instantly felt parched.

I went past him, keeping as far of a distance away as was possible, and then returned to my desk to take a seat.

It was where I was the most comfortable, so I couldn't help but hope the moment I lowered onto my chair I would regain some much needed semblance of calm. I was right and soon, I was able to breathe… fully and deeply.

"Do you have my keys?" I asked, as I began to fumble with the scattered files and stationery I had on my desk, feigning the appearance that I was putting everything in order so I could take my leave since school had ended for the day.

His response however made me stop. "You sent *him* to come pick it up?"

Somehow I wasn't surprised this was the first question he was asking me. What I realized now that I *was* surprised about was the fact it had taken him this long to do so, and a little part of me couldn't help but acknowledge I had taken the risk of letting Danny go on my behalf just so it could bring us to a place where Danny's name could be mentioned.

And so I steeled my spine, and slightly cleared my throat.

"He offered," was what I said in return.

He cocked his strikingly handsome face at me.

He smirked, and although it was dark it also came across as him being quite amused. And then he glanced briefly away.

"Is it that you truly don't give a damn whatsoever about me or that you truly have no regard for me?"

I reviewed the question, and although my brain was fuzzy, I was soon able to point out to him that it was the same thing.

"I just wanted my car back." I replied, a quite innocent smile on my face because truly, my intention wasn't to aggravate him any further. And I did need my car back. And as to what I wanted out of this conversation with him I wasn't quite sure but I did know I wanted to push him just a bit, so we could unravel this matter between us rather than gloss over it, or just completely abandon it like we had in the past.

However, when he straightened and slipped his hands into his pocket, I lost a bit of my courage because there was something in his gaze that informed me I was going too far and suddenly, all I wanted was to move on with my life, starting with getting my car back.

"He was in town," I said to him. "'And the last time I tried to get the car back you weren't exactly cooperative."

He watched me without saying a word further, and although I tried not to be affected, I couldn't help but squirm under his gaze.

"Xander," I called. "Let's stop making each other miserable, and let's stop meeting up. If you leave the keys at your front desk, I'll ensure that someone comes to pick the car up, and then we can be done for good."

He scoffed. "Done for good?"

"Yeah," I nodded.

"But what if I'm not done with you?"

My heart ground to a halt.

XANDER

We were now at a stalemate, however I was now very aware of where I wanted this to go.

I saw the confusion flash in her eyes and then the uncertainty and then finally the concern. "'What?"

I smiled. "You heard me. And your keys have been at the front desk since you left. You can pick your car up whenever you want or never. All up to you."

I turned around then and began to walk away, however I heard her scuffle out of her chair and just before I could pull down the handle to her classroom door and walk away, I heard her hurried footsteps behind me.

"What do you mean?" she asked, her hands closing around my wrist to stop me the moment she caught up to me.

I felt the burn of her touch, so I jerked my hand out of her hold.

As a result, her balance almost went out of kilter but she was soon able to regain it.

"What do you mean... you're not done with me?" she asked.

"Exactly as it sounds," I replied, and she looked struck, almost even to the verge of tears.

She then paused, straightened, took a deep breath and released it.

Then she boldly fixed her gaze on mine, and I could see the tension slowly slip out of her shoulders.

It made me feel somewhat relieved.

"Until your mom's out of harm's way, and her expenses have been fully taken care of," I said. "You'll do what I want, when I want it."

"I'm picking up my car today," she said, "and then I'm going to get my mother off the support that you have provided for her. I'll pay for her medical expenses myself."

I was stunned at her response, but not completely, so I was able to hold onto her wrist and stop her from walking away just in time.

It however escalated into a scuffle due to her resistance, as she tried with all of her might to be released from my hold. I didn't budge, and instead brought her with me till her back was against the wall and my frame caging her in.

"Let me go," she gritted her teeth, her chest heaving.

I stared into her brown eyes, and for a second couldn't help but feel remorse and pity for what we had come to in comparison to how we had begun. Where had everything unraveled and frayed, and more importantly was it even possible to weave it back into place or was I just wasting my time? Did I even want to or was I just particularly enjoying tormenting her?

"You can't do this here," she breathed her gaze glancing at the door and then returning to mine.

I stared at her, still unable to let go.

"Did you really mean that?" I asked. "That you no longer want my support for your mother's medical expenses. Are you really going to let your ego impede her healthcare?"

"If she knew this was what I had to go through to ensure her health was restored then she would rather I did nothing," she spat, and I couldn't help the twinge of remorse that pulled at my heart. However, I ensured not to let even a bit of it show and instead smiled.

"And what exactly are you going through?" I asked.

She went mute, but her scowl deepened as I leaned forward into her, my hips nailing hers to the wall.

"You can't respond?" I asked, as I began to grind my hardness against her crotch.

Her lips once again parted in a harsh inhale. She tried to pull away from me, but ended up supplying even more pressure against where my hardness was pressing against her softness.

"Stop treating me like a whore," she cried.

"Isn't that what you are?" The words came out of my mouth before I could stop them, and at this she went completely still. As the shock of my words rang between us, my hold on her hand automatically loosened. And then she was swinging it into the air.

It struck the side of my face, and although her strength wasn't exactly blinding, the fury behind it was enough to turn my head away.

I accepted it... for my utterance, and allowed the tension between us to reach its boiling point so it could begin to simmer back down. However when I returned my gaze to hers they were damp with tears.

"How dare you?" she breathed, and once again the question I had been dying to ask her for too long slipped out of my mouth.

"How could you?" I asked. "You knew how I felt about you. You owned my heart. You knew it would destroy me. So how could you?"

"You think you deserve an explanation now? After what you just called me?"

"You've hit me," I replied. "Let's call it even. I deserved it and you... "

She goaded me on. "Go ahead," she said. "I deserved that name?"

At the hurt in her eyes, I could no longer hold back. I slanted my head and kissed her.

She resisted me, which I had expected and so my hands had already closed around her arms to keep her in place. She moved her face away but pretty soon her resolve dissolved and she gave in. The kiss was brief but deep and it was just what we both needed... to rest, and to truly albeit brief, revel in each other.

The question left my lips again. "How could you?" I asked. "You loved me... I know you did. So... what happened? Did he force you? Did something happen?"

She watched me and I could feel the slight trembling of her frame.

"Why are you only asking me this now? Why didn't you ask back then if you had doubts that I would ever do something like that?"

"Not only that," I replied. "I couldn't process why you would actually do or say something like that to me. Save for the fact you had, that meant it was final, and I didn't know how I was going to look at you again. I didn't know how we were going to come back from that. I still don't know if it's even possible."

At this, she stared at me and then moved her frame once again to displace my hold. I let go then, immediately, and took a step backwards.

I watched her, and something in her eyes made a different question come to mind.

"Did you lie to me? Back then?"

My heart slammed into my chest and at the slight widening of her eyes I couldn't help but sense that I had hit a nerve.

OLIVIA

He was getting too close... much too close to the truth, and so I panicked.

I pushed him away, and he staggered backwards a few more steps.

I couldn't say a word... I couldn't trust myself to open my mouth and so I moved, my legs shaky but still managed to make it over to my desk. Without looking at him, I then began to pack my things up.

"Olivia," he called but I didn't respond, however I could feel his presence just as heavily as I felt my own.

I didn't expect him to wait forever, but I also couldn't help my disappointment when once again and without another word, he turned around and walked away.

I collapsed back into my chair unable to move, and not till a knock sounded on the door startling me did I realize that tears were streaming down my face. I instantly turned my face away to hide, scared out of my mind he was the one that had returned.

I heard the footsteps of whoever was walking over to my table, but I couldn't look at them and so I kept my face lowered and hidden in my lap.

"Olivia?" I heard Elise's voice and was shocked. But then a big wave of relief hit me at the same time and the tears seemed to come even harder.

"Olivia?" she called again and began to come around the table. I could no longer hold on to my whimpering then. She heard it all and it shocked her.

"Olivia," she gasped and then she lowered to wrap her arms around me.

It took longer than I was happy about for me to retain my calm, and through it all I tried to hide the pain that had soaked my face.

Eventually though, this became obviously impossible as she sat on my desk, and refused to leave. Not till I explained all that was happening and why she had caught me in such a state.

It took a little more coaxing, but I finally gave in, unwillingly to keep it all inside of me. Perhaps this was the entire crux of the problem. That I kept things inside of me so much and so unnecessarily it made me make mistakes and see and judge things from my perspective alone.

And so I revealed the truth to her, and for the first few minutes after she was completely silent. I leaned back against the chair, my gaze on nothing but the amateur art on the wall by the kids I had hung up.

Eventually however, she spoke.

"Olivia," she called. "Do you want him back?"

The billion dollar question.

"Be honest with me," she said. "Be honest with yourself, because I feel as though you still haven't made up your mind and once again are looking for an easy way out, just like you did the last time."

At her words I looked up, and couldn't help saying the truth as I was currently aware of it.

"I don't know," I replied.

"Alright," she responded. "Fair enough, but I have a second question for you."

"What is it?" I asked almost knowing then what was coming,

"Are you still in love with him?"

The next morning, I stepped out of my apartment to find my Uber waiting to take me to my mother's home. However what I also saw was my car, parked in the spot that was designated as mine. For the longest time I could only stare at it, but in the end I decided to just ignore it. And so I entered the Uber and headed over to my mom's, and it was only when I was midway through I realized I truly would have to explain to her once again where my car was and this time around, more likely than not I would have to tell the truth.

This wasn't my major concern however I found, because what now was, was the fact he had finally returned the car and I had absolutely no idea what it meant.

Thankfully though, all of these concerns were soon flushed out of my mind when I arrived.

She was just cleaning up from baking a batch of muffins, and the scent was like a warm hug. Immediately I went over, my arms wrapping around her waist from behind. It was almost as though she had known it was just what I needed.

Amused, she turned around to look at me.

"Hey."

"I love your muffins," I said and she smiled even harder.

I couldn't look away from the exhausted lines around her eyes.

"I know," she said. "I thought you might want some. Plus I woke up this morning and was suddenly craving them."

"You could have told me to bake them for you," I said, as I moved away and headed into her fridge in order to take note of what she needed replenished for the week.

"Well, you're going to be cleaning out my closet with me today so I have to fill you up with energy don't I?"

I'd just tossed some grapes into my mouth at the announcement, so I turned to her in shock. "What?" I mumbled.

"Don't touch the blueberries. We'll need those for the next batch."

"Mom," I complained and headed back to her. "Your closet is enormous."

"Exactly and most of the clothes in there I haven't worn in years. I want to begin decluttering."

At her words, I couldn't help but turn somber. "Why are you decluttering?"

"Doesn't it feel better?" she asked, as she brought over two glasses of milk for the both of us. "You've told me to do it for years but I never have. Why hoard so much when others don't have any? I'll only keep what I need and what still fits, and give the rest away."

"You'll gain the weight back," I told her. "You'll need those clothes."

"God, I hope not," she exclaimed. "I've tried to lose all of this weight for the last twenty- five years. Who knew that cancer was the answer?" she laughed, however it only just brought tears to my eyes.

"That's not funny," I said, and she understood that the joke had crossed a line.

"I know baby," she said, and gave me a hug.

Things became much too quiet and broody between us after that, but it wasn't long before I found just the quiet comment to lighten up the air between us.

"I'll help you on one condition," I said.

"What?" she looked up from peeling the wrapper off her muffin.

"I get to keep whatever pieces I like."

At this, her face contorted in surprise. "You'd want to wear any of my clothes?"

"There are some vintage items in there that are priceless. Those I am definitely bringing home with me."

Three hours later, we were buried in clothes and labeled boxes, and I had to find a way to console myself.

"We're making progress, right?" I asked. "That better be the case."

And to this she laughed. "Sure, we are. You might even have to spend the night here if we're not done early enough."

"Ma," I complained.

"Why?" she asked. "Is there a problem? Do you suddenly have a date?"

At this I laughed. "Yes mom, I do."

She shook her head at me, amused and then returned to sorting and folding.

A few more seconds passed between us and then she spoke up. "Speaking of dating, how are things between you and Xander?"

"We're not dating Mom," I explained to her.

"I know," she smiled. "But there was a lot of tension between you two at the hospital, and I'm curious. Has it been resolved?"

At her words I couldn't help but completely push him out of my mind, my gaze on the button down blouse that I had found and was slowly taking a liking to.

I didn't want to lie to her, and so responded directly. "Things haven't yet been resolved, but hopefully they will be soon enough."

"Does this have to do with why you broke up with him?" she asked, and I truly didn't know what to say as her inference was an understatement.

"Yeah," I replied. "Without clarifying that and somehow resolving it, neither of us will be able to move forward... together, even if we wanted to."

My mother stopped then and turned to place her full attention on me.

"So what's holding you two back? Why haven't you resolved things?"

"It's not something that's so easy to fix Mom. If the matter was so simple we wouldn't have broken up because of it years ago."

"So what was it?" she groaned, and I couldn't help my smile at her frustration.

I also couldn't help wondering if perhaps the issue was pretty simple, but felt so complicated to me because beneath all of it, I believed it was my fault.

Sure, one could argue, especially me, that I'd had my valid reasons but still... and at his attitude so far... at his reaction to all of this, I couldn't help but consider now that perhaps I had been too careless... with his heart and with what we had.

"We were drifting apart," I told her. "Back then. We weren't keeping in touch as much as we once did and it was understandable because of how we'd both gotten. I thought I was doing him a favor and doing what was best for us at the time, however I didn't realize it was really because I was just scared."

I continued folding and waited.

"Olivia," she called and I tried my very best to keep my emotions in check.

"I called him, and told him it was best we broke up because our paths were too different. I didn't want to hold him back because he'd always feel guilty that he couldn't spend as much time with me as he wanted to. And plus he had a trip at the time with his friends to New York but was considering not leaving. They were going everywhere in search of investors to start their company."

My head lowered even further. "I just wanted him to be free. And plus I couldn't trust him. I didn't know how to trust anyone. Not after Dad. And not after Mathew," I added, and as my stepfather's name came into mind, I couldn't help but note the deep frown that came across her face.

"What'd you do?" she asked.

"He wouldn't break up with me. He said we were just going through a rough patch and it was to be expected. We were young… we were trying to find our own way, and so we were more focused on our own goals."

"Olivia, what did you do?" she asked.

I muttered my response underneath my breath. "I told him that I cheated on him." My tone was low, but it seemed as though the words echoed all over the small space.

"You cheated on him?" she asked, her tone equally as low.

"I didn't," I corrected. "I just let him believe that I had."

"With whom?"

"Danny."

OLIVIA

Fifteen minutes later, I was seated back at our counter with a cup of warm chamomile tea in hand.

My mom was nursing one too as she leaned against the island counter on the opposite end, deep in thought just as I was.

Since my admission, she hadn't asked anymore questions and had instead thought to console me.

However I couldn't stand the silence any longer.

"Talk to me," I pleaded with her, unable to meet her eyes.

"You shouldn't have done that," she said and I rolled my eyes.

"Jeesh, thanks Mom."

"I'm right," she said. "And I need you to acknowledge this outright because if you don't, then you won't be determined enough to handle things now."

My gaze lifted to meet hers.

"What do you mean?"

"You're still in love with him, aren't you?" she asked. "You want him back."

I went quiet. "Why does everyone automatically assume this?"

"Because everyone can see how much you're hurting from this… how distracted you are."

Another stretch of silence.

"Olivia," she called.

"Hmm?"

"Do you want him back?"

"It's impossible," I replied. "If he wasn't so wealthy then perhaps I'd have the audacity to try but now that he is, will anyone believe it's because I suddenly realized how much I loved him when I was the one to break his heart when he didn't have a penny."

"You don't owe an explanation to anyone. Except him. Have you given him one?"

I sighed again. "Why does no one seem to be allergic to humiliation except me? Haven't you met Xander, Mom? Does he seem like someone who is that lenient to you? That understanding and forgiving?"

"He is," she replied, and at this my head snapped up to meet hers.

"What?"

"To those he loves, he is all of these things. I feel as though he wants you back," she said. "With all of his heart, but he doesn't know how to make this happen without it seeming as though he has no backbone and you have him wrapped around your finger."

I scoffed. "Sure… I do."

"I think you do," she said and that surprised me even further.

"Mom," I called and she met my gaze

"I mean it," she said. "I mean if it wasn't the case then why would he accept to-"

She suddenly stopped, and with the guilt that came over her face something cold slid through me.

"To what?" I asked. "Mom…"

"He agreed to cover all of my medical expenses, didn't he?" she said, and my heart dropped into my stomach.

For the longest time, I couldn't speak as a hot rush of anger surged through me.

"He told you?"

"Of course not," she said. "But I'm not dumb Olivia. Where else would you have gotten the funds to handle all of this when we're both aware of how much debt you incurred from the first time."

"So he did admit to it?"

"What would have been the point in denying it? Did you expect him to argue with me to protect your pride or something?"

I didn't think that I'd ever been so confused before. In that moment, so many things ran through my mind but more importantly her reaction.

"And you're okay with this?"

She smiled as she gazed fondly at me. "He told me that you were quite worried about me finding out because you knew I hated charity. So he too was surprised I wasn't ready to sound the alarm the moment I found out."

"Why aren't you?" my voice trembled.

"Olivia," I called. "You had to go to Xander to save my life. To make sure I can remain here a bit longer for you. Without me, you have no one. If I have to beg on the streets to ensure I can be here then I'd do anything."

"It just hurts that you had to go to him when I know that you would have chosen not to. And after all of that, you thought I would so easily throw it back in your face because I was too proud to accept charity?"

Tears filled my eyes.

She set her cup down and headed over to me.

"Olivia."

"Mom," I shook, and lowered my head but in no time she had me in her arms. I couldn't breathe and so I sobbed into her neck.

"I'm so sorry."

"No," she whispered. "I'm the one who's sorry. I wasn't financially equipped from the beginning to fully deal with this. I put you under so much stress and concern."

I held on tightly to her, and would never know how long passed before my hold on her loosened. She pulled away then to look into my eyes and although I tried to hide, she managed to hold my face in her hands so she could stare at me.

"It's been so hard on you hasn't it?"

I smiled. "I don't know if I have the right to say that."

"You do," she assured me. "It has been hard on you… and it was hard for you and so you had to make decisions that weren't necessarily the best. But at the time it seemed to be. If he truly loves you then he should at least consider showing you mercy. And if he doesn't then it's his loss. But at least you'll know that you tried."

"So you're all for me telling him?" I asked.

"I am. Don't make the same mistake again by taking this decision out of his hands. It's not yours to make. Plus, he might not believe you now or be willing to be lenient, but Xander knows you. Deep in his heart. I believe so. And I also believe it is because of this and because of the fact that he wouldn't have expected you to ever do something like that he still has such a sore spot for you. Otherwise why is he still unable to let go of you?"

"He's hostile to me, Mom. You're the only one that he's kind to."

At this, she smiled. "Well that is understandable. I didn't break his heart into a million pieces."

"Mom," I complained and she held me even more tightly.

"Talk to him," she says. "Clearly… directly. Share your heart with him and expect nothing. At the very best he'll believe you but at the very least, you'll both be able to wipe the slate clean and move on. And also, life is long… so who knows what will happen down the line. My point is, get rid of the regret, correct your mistakes the best way you can, and let life deal with the rest but do not be sloppy about your own responsibility."

At her words, I inhaled deeply and then exhaled.

Tears filled my eyes again and she pulled me back into her arms.

OLIVIA

Later that evening, I was shooed home by my mom to set things right, and I was terrified to my very bones. And so the moment I returned home, I did nothing but pace back and forth in my living room for at least half an hour, before realizing I didn't even have my phone in hand. I went to search for it and then got ready to place the call but then as I placed it against my ear, I realized I had absolutely no clue as to what to say.

Still it started to ring, and I couldn't end it because he would know I was the one who called.

Shit I cursed under my breath, unable to find any ounce of calm until I reminded myself what this call was for. You're not trying to get back together with him or obtain anything from him. You're not expecting anything from him. You just want to set things right so that we can both move on. Whatever he decides to do afterwards is none of your concern.

Easier said than believed and accepted, but nevertheless, I tried my very best to keep this at the forefront of my mind.

The call rang and just when I was certain he wouldn't pick up, my heart deflating, he did.

"What?" he asked, and I was even more on guard.

And so I cleared my throat and began.

"Um… I wanted to speak to you about something," I informed him.

"What?" he repeated, and I sighed. Things could go a bit easier on me if he didn't sound so hostile, but then perhaps expecting any part of this whatsoever to go easy on either of us was the delusion.

"Are you home?" I asked.

"Why? You want to come over here?"

"No," I replied. "I just…"

"You just what?"

I wanted him to be focused so he would listen… so he would hear me properly but again, this wasn't something I could control.

"Nothing. I want nothing," I told him. "I just wanted to say my peace."

He went quiet and I knew then he was paying rapt attention.

"I wanted to explain what happened, four years ago."

Finally… the words had come out of my mouth, and although they had been low, I was certain he had been able to hear me loud and clear.

He didn't say a word in response and so I took it as my cue to continue on "Back then, I-"

"If you have something to say to me," he suddenly interrupted me. "Then do it in person."

And just like that the call was brought to an end.

For the longest time, the phone remained against my ear. It happened so fast my mind needed time to process, and when I eventually did, it registered then my heart was pounding so hard in my chest I could barely breathe. I collapsed onto my couch, beyond spent and it was then I realized just how much strength and courage I had to work up to be able to place the call. But yet he had refused to listen to it and I wanted to scream. Things would have been over now. I would have been able to breathe and perhaps move on but-

I stopped myself.

He hadn't ended the call because he didn't want to hear what I had to say, but because he wanted me to have the courage to say it to his face. Perhaps he wanted us to speak about it, or even fight about it afterwards but what it seemed he didn't want was that I would just say what I wanted and then that would be that. That would be the final page and the conclusion between us. Or perhaps was I just being hopeful?

I shook my head to clear it, because the last thing I needed to nurse now was any sort of hope whatsoever because it would lead to my shattered heart all over again.

This was simply to wipe the slate clean. This was simply so we could both address the demons and move on. I rose to my feet on albeit shaky legs.

I grabbed the keys I had found deposited in my mailbox, grabbed my purse and was soon on my way to his house. I would need to contact him again so he could give the instruction at the front desk to let me up, and this was the part of the trip I was dreading because I couldn't help but expect he would refuse to see me. That he perhaps had absolutely no interest whatsoever in paying any attention to me and whatever I had to say.

Still I drove onwards until I arrived at his building and then I called him. His phone rang to disconnection several times, and then he eventually picked up.

My heart and soul was wrenched with so much anxiety and frustration that I was near tears.

"I'm here," I said to him. "Are you home? Can you let me up?"

He was silent for a long while and then once again the call abruptly ended. I couldn't wait to get this over with… to get all of this behind me so that at least whenever I thought of him I would stop feeling so sick to my stomach.

Thankfully, the front desk let me up upon my arrival. With a deep sigh of relief, I headed towards the elevator with the granted access card and was on my way.

My steps began to slow as I arrived at his door.

I stood before it for a few minutes, trying to work up the courage to knock or to at least press the bell. When I realized however he was probably watching me thanks to the cameras he had everywhere, the fire was lit under my ass.

I rang the bell and it took a while.

At least five minutes passed with me standing outside before the door was pulled open. By then though, I was already halfway done with him. Most of my nerves had dissipated and I was ready to say what I wanted and then take my leave. It was truly a miracle I even waited this long, but I knew due to his contribution to my mother's expenses, if I left now my heart would soften again at him for being kind, and I would return to try to get myself heard.

I wanted absolutely no recurrence of the present and I immediately got ready to speak to him at the door if it was even possible.

"I'm not going to take much of your time but-"

My words instantly halted midway, because he wasn't the one that opened the door. Instead, it was a woman, and she was strikingly blonde and gorgeous and with the prettiest set of green eyes I'd ever come across. I couldn't stop staring at her.

"Yeah?" she smiled.

And for a few seconds after, I still remained stumped.

"I uh…" I tried to see into the apartment. I was ready to turn around right now and be on my way.

"I-is Xander home?"

"Yeah he is," she said. "Is he expecting you?"

I looked up into her kind eyes. "Um yeah, he is."

"Oh alright come on in then," she said and I was ushered in. There was soft ambient piano music flowing throughout the house, and it was relaxing to say the least.

However I felt anything but relaxed. I was ushered into the house like the stranger I was and my gaze automatically went to the kitchen. There was no one there, but she did stop and asked me what I wanted to drink as though she owned the place. I couldn't help but be curious then. *Was this a woman that Xander was in a relationship with?* That queasy feeling that threatened to push all the contents of my stomach up my throat returned.

"No, I'm fine. Xander?" I asked.

"He's out by the pool," she replied and I watched as she began to stroll over, barefoot and dressed scantily in a black dress that barely reached the middle of her thighs.

She went out through the wide patio doors, and I paused for a moment to ask myself one more time if it would be that bad of an idea to cancel this. I mean was I going to say all that I wanted to in front of her?

With a sigh, thoroughly confused and cursing Xander in a corner of my heart, I walked out onto the patio and indeed met him seated in the lounge area. Before them was wine and a platter of little bites- cheese, crackers, ham, grapes, the works- and then there was Xander seated with one leg crossed across his knee and his phone to his ear as he took a call. I watched him for a bit even though he didn't spare me any look whatsoever, and then headed over with as much confidence as I could muster.

I took my seat as we arrived, while she proceeded to plop down beside him, draping herself against him like a second skin. Her legs were tucked in underneath her, as she picked up her phone and a piece of cracker. She also leaned forward, all of her cleavage exposed to me as she picked up a piece of cheese, bit into it and then turned around to offer some to him. He shook his head, and then in that moment, our gazes met.

I was seated across from them, and he watched me as he listened to what whomever was on the other end of the line was saying.

He nodded and responded curtly and appropriately, his gaze on mine.

Suddenly the woman leaned over, a blueberry in her mouth and then she slanted her lips over his.

The pain I felt in that moment was like a shard of glass stabbed through my heart. My entire body went numb and for a moment my breathing ceased. Still however I didn't dare react.

I watched outright just as he did, and then he pulled his lips away from hers. He turned to watch her as though suddenly aware she was present. She blushed at him, placed one last kiss against his lips before turning towards me.

"He hates it when I do that," she said, and I had no clue as to what she was talking about. I prayed with every moment that passed, his call would come to an end so I could escape this misery, but he took his sweet time. The woman sent her attention over to her phone while I stared ahead at nothing, wishing I truly could kill myself. Eventually the call was completed and he leaned forward to toss the phone onto the coffee table. He then picked up his glass of wine, and as he took a long drink, his eyes remained on mine. He drained it, set the glass down, and finally spoke.

"Go on, say your peace."

XANDER

I didn't know how to react to her.

Here she was, willing to speak and I didn't even know if I was willing to hear what she had to say. And so I allowed Jessie to remain, unsure of whether this would be enough to stop Olivia from speaking. From her demeanor and tone I sensed resignation. I could very clearly see she had absolutely no hope or intention for a reconciliation, but was instead willing to speak and reveal all to set herself free. Selfishly… all over again. It made me wonder what she would say… it was a mistake and although she could never forgive herself that it was now best for the both of us to move on?

She hadn't even tried… not once since my return had I even seen the hope in her eyes that perhaps just maybe she would attempt to rebuild what was broken between us. But instead she had been careless and crass, even sending *him* to my home to pick up her car.

I didn't know how to feel about her.

In this moment, my affection for her felt more like a curse than anything else, especially because I wanted it to remain just as much as I wanted to escape from its clutches.

I watched as she lowered her gaze in thought, and then returned it to mine, steel determination in them. She was driven to get whatever this was off her chest and be on her way... leaving me hurt all over again and perhaps even broken.

I suddenly couldn't stand to be touched, by anyone or anything but I also didn't want Jessie to be gone.

Having her in Olivia's presence as she prepared to have such an intimate talk with me was incredibly condescending, but I didn't want to be overly considerate of her just as she never was with me. And so I waited until she began.

"I told you I wanted to talk to you about what happened four years ago."

"About how you cheated on me?" I asked, and a heavy silence fell upon the room.

Even Jessie seemed to lean away from me then as she realized exactly who this was and what was happening. She straightened, sitting properly and then eventually she turned to me. The instant our gazes met, she knew what she had to do. She got up and walked away much to Olivia's surprise, and thus we were left alone together.

Olivia briefly watched her leave, but I knew it was simply a way for her to calm the nerves she was probably feeling inside before she had to speak to me.

Afterwards, she returned her gaze to me and I watched her, grief filling me up as my heart couldn't help but register this was the one person that even now, occupied a special place in my heart that hoped for something magical. No one before or after her could ever compare, and I couldn't help but glare at her knowing full well she was resigning herself to a goodbye.

"I uh…" she couldn't hold my gaze, but I could see she was determined and nothing would stop her.

"I'm not here to explain because I expect you to forgive me… I mean… I hope you do, but I also know I don't deserve it. I'm just here because… I thought I would be okay with it but I can't stand the fact that… our story ended with me cheating on you."

At these words, alarm slammed into me. However I remained calm and didn't speak.

"At the time… I was insecure and I uh…" her smile was bitter. "You might not believe me but I really loved you and my idea of love then was sacrifice and compromise and wanting the best for the other person even at your own expens-"

"Get to the point," I growled as my emotions began to boil. When it came to her it was too easy for me to simmer out of control whether physically or emotionally, and for the first time I wondered if she knew that. If she was truly aware of how much of an effect she had on me, because if she really did then I still couldn't wrap my head around how it would have been possible for our relationship to have degraded the way it had.

She held my gaze then, eyes softening as she looked at me the way that she used to so many years prior. I used to get lost in her eyes… the love I found there and the adoration… and the reminder currently made it too heartbreaking to bear so I looked away.

"Danny's gay," she said to me, and for a few moments her words couldn't register in my brain. But when it finally did, my attention returned to hers.

"What?"

"He's gay. In high school he identified as bi because he didn't want all the backlash, and just thought it would be generally more acceptable but he's gay... and so..."

She couldn't have slept with him.

My frown dug into my forehead.

"What?"

She lowered her head then, and could no longer look at me. "I'm sorry," she apologized.

"So many girls had their eyes on you then... I kept hearing the stories... and saw how conflicted you were about spending so much time away from me. You were travelling all the time to try to get funding along with Mark and... I could see it made you unhappy to be away from me for so long. We weren't even speaking as often because you were working all the-"

"You told me it was fine-" I couldn't help but cut her off. "You told me we were fine."

"We were, and I never held it against you. I loved that you were going so hard after your dream and I was doing the same for mine too but... you always felt so guilty all the time and I felt as though... I was holding you back. I loved you too much to do that. So I... let you go."

I glared at her, unwilling to believe I was actually hearing what I was from her.

"Are you joking?" I asked bitterly amused. "Is this some sort of game you're playing?"

"You know it's not," she replied. "I was insecure and you know my family's history. My dad and then my step-dad and what they did to my mom... the way you were... the distance... I... didn't expect-"

"You didn't expect me to be loyal to you! To cheat on you eventually like they did to your mom?"

She inhaled deeply and exhaled. "This is why I said that I'm not here to ask for forgiveness. At the time I was terrified, and I did what I thought was best. And... although it hurt us so much... it brought us here today... it brought you here today. After we broke up, you moved immediately and focused solely on your company and look at how things turned out for you. It will always hurt that I lied to you in that way, and that I broke your heart but... I've come to terms with it. It broke me too... and..."

"... and?" I asked, still unable to believe what I was hearing, but then in a way, and if I agreed to put my anger aside then I would be able to understand her. But I didn't want to... not so easily when she could just have easily told me all of this back then and we would have worked through it.

"I have no regrets" she said, and the rage that burned inside me nearly left me blind.

"You have no regrets!" I spat. "You have no idea what you did to me, do you? I've hated relationships since then... haven't been able to commit myself to anyone since then. And you have no regrets? You've dated around since then haven't you? Carried on with your life? Been happy?"

She lifted her gaze to mine, and I hated that she still refused to cower.

"You're asking because you want to hear that I've been miserable right? That I haven't been able to date anyone else either, that I'm just as broken?"

I went silent.

She sighed. "Even if I admitted to these, at the end of the day you would never believe me."

"Admit to it," I insisted, but then as the words fully registered to my brain and what they implied I corrected them. "Admit to it if it was true, and admit to it if it wasn't. Since you've finally decided to come clean then do it completely."

At this she sighed, watched me and then she spoke.

"I had been miserable for a while."

"You were miserable when we were together?"

"I was miserable because I had decided to end things with you... and... this is a surprise to you isn't it?"

"Because you put up a front?"

"No, because you were too busy to pay attention like you used to."

"You encouraged me."

"Yes I did and I love that I did. The most important thing to me was that you fulfilled your dream because I knew just how happy it would make you. Xander, you're too ambitious to be held down or held back… and if I had hindered you in any way, eventually down the line the resulting contempt would cloud the way you felt about me."

"What if I didn't want to be free?" I asked, and she became quiet. "What if I wanted you to remain by my side? To keep my feet on the ground?"

"You didn't want that."

"How do you know? Did you ever ask me? Sure, I'm worth a lot now, but what gave you the impression I would have complained if having you in my life had only allowed me to have a lot less? All I wanted was for the software and our phones to hit the market, and do well, and what I wanted even more was for you to be by my side while I tried to figure it all out."

I could see then, the realization coming to her gaze and the slight fear that perhaps, just maybe she had been too hasty.

She rose to her feet, and I couldn't help my smile. "You're leaving?" I said darkly.

"You never stopped to ask me either," she said. "You chose not to fight for us… to just walk away."

"Because I was in fucking pain," I said, my tone increasing.

"And so was I," she said unfazed. "But after you didn't question… after you heard what I said and then just turned around and walked away, I couldn't help but convince myself I had done the right thing. You can't see it this way now because currently things have gone incredibly smoothly for you but back then… none of us could have predicted any of this. None of us could have seen the future."

I could see now and accept that neither of us was going to obtain the satisfaction we had both been hopeful to gain from this. And as she turned around to walk away, I couldn't help but feel as though I was once again receiving the short end of the stick.

OLIVIA

I walked out of the apartment with a lump in my throat. My stomach knotted and I hurried to the elevator. I pushed the button for the parking garage and slumped against the wall. Tears clouded my eyes and as my stomach rolled and I threw my hand over my mouth, willing myself not to get sick as the elevator came to a sudden stop.

The doors opened and I ran to the trash can next to them to retch as the tears slid down my face.

I didn't have high hopes for the conversation but I was hopeful he would at least understand me. Understand, I only wanted what was best for him at the time. Maybe I should have spoken to him more about it then... but he would have never understood at the time. I was his distraction and I couldn't do that to him.

I stood back up and wiped my mouth with the back of my hand and slowly made my way to my car. Opening the door, I just sat in the driver's seat, staring at the cement barrier in front of me. When it became too blurry to make out I rested my head on the steering wheel.

My phone rang and I thought to ignore it, but it could be mom. I couldn't make out the Caller ID so I hit accept. "Hello." I tried not to croak.

"Livvy?" Danny questioned.

"Oh God, Danny, I…" The words stuck in my throat.

"Livvy? What happened? Is your mom okay?" Danny's voice pitched high as my sniffling echoed through the connection.

"He knows… I told him." I choked. I didn't even know what else to say.

"I take it that it didn't go well?" his voice was concerned.

"It doesn't matter… I'm too late anyway." I stated dejectedly.

"It's never too late, Livvy. It probably just seems bad now, but I'm-"

"He wasn't alone." I interjected.

"What?"

"He said I could come over to explain knowing he had a blond bombshell to greet me at the door. He even kissed her in front of me. Trust me… I'm too late." my tears started to dry.

I'm too late. The words echoed in my mind like a skipping record.

Danny's sigh was audible through the line. "Livvy, it's been four years. What did you really expect? He would remain celibate? He hasn't carried around the guilt you have."

"I didn't expect... I... I think I still love him." The confession felt like acid in the throat.

"Of course you do. Did you ever really stop?"

Sometimes I wondered if Danny knew me better than I knew myself.

"I don't know," I mumbled, feeling raw from my emotions.

"You do. You just need to accept it. Really put yourself out there. Did you make it clear you wanted to try again?"

"I don't know... no... not really. If he rejects me I don't know that I will recover. I lost him once and it almost killed me. I can't go through that again." the truth echoing in my words.

"If you want him, you need to fight for him." Danny said like the true optimist he was.

"You are forgetting he already has someone." I said bitterly.

"That Barbie has nothing on you Livvy." he said. I laughed without humor. I couldn't handle any more baggage today.

"I'll have to take your word for it."

There really wasn't any more to say so the call came to an end and I left the garage to head home.

The next few days went by in a blur of sadness, self-doubt and anger. I couldn't settle on an emotion long enough to process what to do from here. Xander hadn't called after my confession. Not that I expected him to, but the hope still lingered.

I was no closer to figuring out what to do or say or if I should do anything at all. Maybe I needed to give him more time to decide what he wanted if anything between us.

Perhaps I should make another move to talk to him. And so my thoughts continued to whirl in my mind like they were running on a hamster wheel.

And what was with the woman at his apartment. How long had he been seeing her? Had he been with us at the same time? Did I really mean so little to him? Was he really so cold he could just use us both? Did I really want to be with him if he could? Ugh! I needed to get a grip. I just didn't know how without talking to Xander again and I just didn't think I could do it yet without losing control and either bawling or screaming at him.

I knew I needed to talk things through with someone but wasn't quite ready to accept any advice. With that in mind I decided to wait and talk it through with my mom when I went for our weekly visit this Saturday.

XANDER

The sleepless nights came back.

The longing and the yearning left me feeling more haunted than I had ever been. It had been fairly easy to not think of her before… earlier on when I had her in my grasp and at my beck and call but now…

Now she was truly gone, and there was probably no reason to get her to return without revealing the hold she still had over me. It was as though I had shoved myself into a dark hole and shut it closed.

And in that dark hole all I could think of was her.

In the past, work had been there to push me through and at the time, it was the most effective distraction because everything had been new. The challenges were new, the goals we were working towards were new, the experiences and the people too. Everything was different and far away from all I had known from her and the hurt she caused me, but now it was no longer the case.

Nothing was new and it was near impossible to drown myself in work as my mind weighed heavily on why I was unable to forget about her. On why I was unable to uproot her out of my life. So on a bright Friday afternoon, I found myself canceling my meetings and wandering out of the office. I knew where I was headed, and despite the fact I was well aware it was a bad idea, I couldn't stop myself.

But I needed to feel some sort of connection to her, without directly coming in contact with her. And so I visited her mother instead.

Her home had remained the same since high school, and since it was where I had spent almost all of my time with Olivia, it wasn't hard to recall.

She was surprised to see me just as I had known she would be, while I on the other hand was glad to see her. I walked in preparing my heart to recognize the mementoes and I saw it all. The dark red couch that Olivia and I had spent more afternoons on than I could care to count, their small kitchen which had the uncanny ability to get overwhelmingly dirty no matter how little a meal had been cooked between us. And of course all the photos on their mantle... of Olivia in all her stages of growth.

My eyes floated over to the one in particular of her as a baby, and all over again... my heart softened. Why was I so heartsore for her, I couldn't help but wonder. She had hurt me deeply but then as I thought back to all her reasons behind it, one thing I couldn't get off my mind... I couldn't help but be immensely glad for the fact she hadn't actually cheated on me. Like she'd said she had... like she'd made me believe for so long. That singular fact was what had plagued me... made me hate her... made me unable to ever consider a relationship with her because I couldn't get over the fact that by doing that, she had deemed me worthless. Worthless enough to be hurt in such a way.

But now... I didn't know what to think.

And so as her mom came over and pulled me into her embrace. I held onto her for longer than should have been normal, because I didn't exactly know what to say either.

And then I let go, my frame straightening and my expression neutral.

She gazed at me with a smile. "You came to see me?"

I simply nodded and we headed straight to the kitchen like we had in the past. I sat down on one of the stools and she headed straight to the freezer. "Do you still like corn dogs?" she asked. "Or do you want me to make you a sandwich?"

"That's strenuous," I said and got up. "You take a seat and I'll get the corn dogs ready."

"No," she refused, and all but swatted me away as I approached her. "You're my guest. One I haven't had in four years, so I'm going to heat up some corn dogs for you."

And so she did, and while I watched, countless memories from being in this kitchen began to return to me.

After she popped them into the microwave, she turned around to study me.

"You're not supposed to be at work?"

"I am," I replied. "But... slow day."

She nodded with a smile as she watched me, and it made me wonder again just what I was doing here.

"What's the update on your treatment?" I asked, just as the microwave dinged and she turned around to retrieve them. "You don't know?" she asked. "You're not speaking with Olivia?"

At my silence, she brought the corn dogs over to the counter and dished them onto a plate.

She didn't need to ask me how I liked them, and so I watched as she spread some sour cream over them and then retrieved some pickled jalapeños from the fridge.

"I'm so happy we have these," she said. "I got into an argument with Olivia about two weeks ago at the store when I insisted on picking them up. She didn't see the need."

At this I smiled, my attention on her motions so I wouldn't think too much about her daughter.

"There are no cumin seeds though," she said. "Sesame, okay?"

I nodded, and in no time she was pushing a plate towards me. There was one before her and as she began to eat, I had to inquire aloud as to why she wasn't seated.

"It's good for me to move around," she said. "And if I don't face you then how else can I cajole you into speaking? Otherwise you might just forget I'm here even though you're in my house.

At this, I glanced at her and then returned my attention to my meal.

A long silence stretched out between us until she spoke again.

"You've finally ended things with Olivia, haven't you?" she asked.

"Things between us ended four years ago," was my response.

I looked up just in time to see her smile.

"Things ended a lot between you two when you were still in high school. Have you forgotten how we bonded?"

"You'd come over even though you both weren't talking, and you'd have dinner right here. And even when she came down, you both wouldn't talk and then you'd leave. Just like that. I enjoyed watching you both, but it was also one of the reasons why I approved that you were with her. I loved how you couldn't stay away. Especially when she wasn't even around. When she'd go on trips with her cousin, you'd still just come over to have dinner with me but I knew it was because you wanted to be near her somehow."

At her words I stopped eating, and set the corn dog down.

I realized why I was here, and so I rose to my feet. However she stopped me, her hand reaching out across the counter to rest on mine.

"Don't go," she said to me. "Stay a bit longer. We don't have to talk about her."

I somehow couldn't reject this offer, so I returned back to the stool.

"I know as her mother it might be uncomfortable to hear things like this from me, but trust me I didn't go off speaking to her either. She won't listen to me."

"She doesn't listen to anybody," I couldn't help but say, and at this she laughed softly. "Good, it's nice to know that we're talking about the same person."

I lifted my gaze and at the curve of her lips, couldn't help but feel just a little less burdened.

A long silence followed between us, and then I asked. "She said she was affected... by ..." I looked into her mother's eyes. "By her experience of your relationship with her father?"

At this her mother smiled just as she finished off her corn dog.

"I regret that," she said. "I wished I had called things off earlier than I did, but I'd thought I could fight it and win. That I could stay and show her that with just the right amount of endurance and attention even the most broken of relationships could survive. I was dead wrong. I should have let go when it was time, and perhaps she would have been less scarred. I used to worry about that but then she found you. She trusted you so wholeheartedly... at least she seemed to and I was so relieved. I had no clue about what happened between you two until just a few days ago."

I stared long and hard at her, and the only words that could come out of my mouth... that I finally wanted to come out of my mouth were, "she didn't cheat on me."

"I know," her mother said.

"I hated her for so long, because I thought she had, and it broke my heart more than I knew was possible."

My gaze back down to the corn dog. I picked it up but then set it back down.

And then the truth spilled out of me.

"I don't want her back," I said, "but yet, I don't think it's possible for me to picture my life without her. I never could, even before she came to me about your medical expenses. I thought of her from time to time, and always knew someday something would happen and it'd make our paths cross again."

It didn't even make sense to me at the time as to why I'd desire this, because given what I'd thought she'd done, I was sure we could never return back to each other. But now... I guess it sort of makes sense as to why I'd never been able to completely get her out of my mind.

I want her back, I wanted to tell her mother, so I could get it off my chest, and express it to someone else who cared, but I found I couldn't.

And so I simply rose to my feet.

"Thank you so much for your reception," I said, and she came over to give me another hug.

And with that, I turned and left the house.

"W hat?"

I stopped in my tracks just as my mother pulled the refrigerator open to retrieve some milk.

When I asked, however, she took her time in responding. "Mom!"

"A couple of days ago," she replied, and I felt my eyes sting with tears.

"He came over and you didn't tell me?"

"He didn't seem like he particularly wanted you to know," was her response.

"You're my mom!" I accused, and she turned around to face me, noting the slight tremble in my tone.

"You do care about him." she said, and I turned away with a scowl. "You can't exactly blame me now can you?" she said. "I could talk about you with him, but I can't exactly talk about him with you, can I? You never want to bring him up."

"For good reason," I shot back.

"What good reason?" she asked. "What good reason exactly?"

I grabbed the handle of the cart then and proceeded to push it ahead, away from her.

"You see what I mean?" she said. "You're walking away again. Maybe this is why things are dragging out for so long. Why he's unable to find his way back to you, even though he wants to... even though you both want to."

"You're wrong. I still love him, Mom, but... but he's moved on. He has someone else. My heart is breaking all over again for him and... I just can't do this here!" My steps hastened away before she could see the tears had fully broken through and were now running down my face.

Back in the car, I drove us quietly home, with neither of us saying a word to each other. Today however, I couldn't go in with her and thankfully her groceries for the week were not much so I wasn't worried she couldn't carry them in on her own.

"You're headed home?" she asked.

"Of course," my gaze snapped to hers. "Where else would I go?"

"Olivia," she called, but I couldn't meet her gaze. "You're hurting and so is he. I'm not saying it's going to be easy for either of you to figure this out, but you're both going to have to start somewhere."

"Mom," I complained. "I told you... he has someone. What do you expect me to do?"

"Just… text him or something. Tell him he left his wallet at our home or something."

At this, I turned towards her, a frown on my face.

"Did he?"

"He didn't but… be creative. C'mon. Tell him you want to talk to him about dropping in to see your mother when you two are no longer together and he's supposedly seeing someone else."

"And then what?" I asked. She gave me a naughty look that somewhat horrified me, and then she turned around and headed into the house.

I almost couldn't take my eyes off her until she disappeared out of sight.

XANDER

"When are you leaving?" I asked Jessie as I gauged the portion of pasta that I would be making.

"A bit more for me," she said. "I'm starving."

I turned to stare at her, and she smiled brightly. I couldn't help but shake my head.

"I just asked you a question," I pointed out.

"You have a massive house Xander," she said, "and I know you can accommodate me for a few more days. That shouldn't be too much of an inconvenience for you, should it? Unless… you're reluctant to because of her? You're worried because of her right? Because I overstepped my bounds and kissed you in front of her? Once again I'm sorry about that. I shouldn't have."

I didn't bother responding, but at the reminder, I also couldn't shake off the slight prickling of guilt that I'd been unable to shake off since then.

I had so far managed it by convincing myself that I didn't owe Olivia anything. Not my loyalty, or anything else but I also didn't want to sink to the state of acting in the manner that had brought us here in the first place regardless of whether it was merely an appearance or not.

"Drop it," I said to Jessie and hoped she would understand by my tone it was not to happen again. I did however wonder at the repercussions though because thus far I was yet to hear from Olivia again and I wondered if I ever would. I forced myself as I had been doing thus far not to think about it, and to continue on with the task at hand.

And so the rest of the dinner went on peacefully. A few minutes later however, a text message arrived on my phone so I set down the jar of carbonara that I had just twisted open.

I was expecting a report from our financial adviser Craig, so I expected the notification would be on that, but when I see a message from the one person that was constantly plaguing my mind, I was a bit perplexed.

"I need to see you," was what she wrote.

OLIVIA

He didn't respond, and I couldn't exactly say I was surprised.

I was still seated in my car... waiting... contemplating... hoping?

I had absolutely no idea what I was doing, but I couldn't get out of the car either.

"You're both going to have to start somewhere," my mother's words sounded over and over in my head, and more than ever I wanted to calm myself down enough to listen.

To her... and perhaps to myself.

I recalled the last time I had been in his apartment and how I had departed with the conviction I wouldn't be contacting him anymore. Why then over the past few weeks we had been apart had tears come to my eyes every time I'd thought about him? I wasn't unfamiliar with the pain and wretchedness that came with losing him, and in the past, I'd eventually learned how to survive it, healed and even moved on. But now it all seems to hurt even more… twice as much because I only now realized the wounds had never healed. I'd just found a way to seal them tightly enough to stop it from both bleeding out and festering.

But now, I had ripped those bandages off and I didn't know how I was ever going to be able to seal the wounds again.

I didn't want to go on with my life in this way… wounded… and yearning for a person I knew no one else would ever compare to. I didn't want to go on feeling as though I'd lost something, and as a result I would always be somewhat incomplete.

I couldn't forget about him and I didn't have the courage to insist on getting him back.

My gaze returned to my phone once again, and the state was the same. There was no response, however I was certain he had probably seen it.

I shouldn't have had the guts to do this but if he was as unaffected as I wanted to believe, then why had he gone to my mother's house?

My forehead lowered onto the steering wheel and I didn't even care how hard the contact was. It was going to bruise for sure but that was the least of my problems. I wished I could leave the car… to walk into the house and continue on with my evening, but everything in my being conspired to make me wait.

Tears filled my eyes once again, as I wondered truly on the path to take. Was laying my cards completely before him rather than pretending, the way to go? Why couldn't I put aside my ego and my fear that he would reject me?

But as I thought about it further, I didn't think this was the case. I supposed I was fighting so hard to hold on to my dignity because of how successful he was. Because a part of me believed he would always believe his being so wealthy, was the true reason why I was pushing so hard to bring us back together.

I lifted my head up from the wheel and pushed my hair out of my eyes.

Then I picked up my phone and although every fiber of my being cautioned me I was making a mistake, I couldn't help but type out exactly what I wanted to say.

"If you weren't as successful as you were, I would probably be doing all that I could to earn you back," I wrote.

I reread the message, and was sure I had lost my mind. However before I could come back to my senses, I squeezed my eyes shut and pressed send. After all, what more did I have to lose, and at this point however Xander chose to respond to this was okay by me. As long as he responded to me. I sighed and couldn't help but blame my mom and her words to me earlier for this stint of lunacy. When I woke up the next morning and things were a bit clearer, I truly wondered how I would feel. Would I bash my head against the wall or would I be indifferent?

I sighed again and then pushed the door open so I could get out of the car. Now that I had done this, my body seemed to be cooperating with me once again. However, just as I picked up my phone the notification arrived.

My heart slammed into my chest, and for a few seconds, I couldn't bear to look at it.

It might not be him, my mind told me. *It might be your mom or Elise.* But then why would either of them be texting me right at this moment. So I gathered my courage, and looked, and my breathing turned haggard. His words were simple.

Come over.

Was all he responded with, and I made up my mind now to completely dispose of reason. So far I had used my head, and all it'd seemed to do was lead me into mistake after mistake.

So for this night, and this night only, I was going to follow my heart. And when I calmed down enough to listen, I could hear that its instruction was very quiet and simple.

Go, was all it said.

XANDER

"She's coming over?" Jessie asked. "Really?"

I didn't know how to respond, because I wasn't certain. Olivia hadn't responded, but more importantly I was still trying to find the reason why I had invited her over the moment I had read her message. Not long ago I had been certain I wanted nothing to do with her, at least for the evening, but now…"

I looked up and stared ahead at nothing.

"Xander," Jessie called.

I heard her but wasn't ready to respond just yet.

"Xander," she called again, and with a sigh I turned back towards her.

"I think your pasta's ready," she said, and I returned my attention to the boiling pot.

Grateful for the distraction, I busied myself with taking the pasta off the stove and over to the sink. I ran the water for too long over it as I once again got lost in my thoughts, and it was only when Jessie once again called out to me that I came to.

"Wow, Xander," I heard her say. "I didn't know you were this much in love with her."

At her words, I turned around once again to scowl at her, and in response she laughed. The sound mocked me.

"You should know by now you can't intimidate me. We've known each other too long. She too doesn't seem to be intimidated by you, so I'm at least happy about that. It would've sucked to lose you to someone who didn't have balls."

At her words, I couldn't help but smile.

"She has something alright," I said, as I shut the tap off to allow the water to drain through the sieve.

"She invited herself over?" Jessie asked, and although I was well aware she was fishing for information, I didn't particularly feel comfortable discussing Olivia with her. I even considered perhaps it wasn't appropriate for her to be here when Olivia arrived. However I couldn't send Jessie away just because of Olivia. Given her words though, I could tell we were going to have something of a serious conversation and I didn't know if Jessie's presence would hamper this.

"Do you want me to leave?" Jessie suddenly asked, and I startled. I then turned around to gaze at her.

"I can see the wheels of your mind spinning," she said, as she picked up her glass of wine. "Don't worry," she said. "I'll make myself scarce the moment she arrives."

"No," I immediately refused, and was a bit taken aback by my objection.

"No?" she asked as she heard my words, but noted the contradicting expression on my face.

"Stay," I said. "Please."

"Are you sure?" she asked. "It didn't seem like she was too happy about seeing me here the last time and I don't care to be a third wheel."

"Doesn't matter," I responded, and then I knew why I wanted Olivia here at this time.

"Can you hold on a bit?" I asked Jessie, "with having dinner?"

At her silence, I turned around to see the cock of her brows.

"Have it with us," I said, and a smile slowly spread across her face.

"Isn't that asking too much of me?" she asked. "I still have feelings for you, you know."

I was aware of this, and for a moment worried perhaps I had taken her proven ability and assurance to push her feelings aside so we could remain friends too much at face value. Perhaps it was a facade and she was more affected than I had imagined?

"Those wheels are spinning again," she said and laughed softly. "Stop over-analyzing everything Xander. I'm not fine but I'll stay. Plus I've long come to accept things as they are. We're friends now and I meant it when I said that. Who knows, I might even be able to knock down some walls between you two."

At this, an alarm blared through me so I turned around to face her.

"Do not interfere," I warned. "Olivia... she attaches meaning to everything. One wrong word and everything could unravel, even though I have absolutely no idea what is intact right now but... things could be worse."

"I'll try," she said, but I didn't trust this lukewarm assurance.

"I swear," she promised at my scowl.

I continued on with dinner, and about thirty minutes later, the call from the front desk came. By then, Jessie and I were enjoying yet another glass of wine, the meal long ready but neither of us eating with the hope that perhaps Olivia would join us. I couldn't believe how much effort I was putting into receiving her.

I instructed them to let her in, and soon enough the doorbell sounded. I considered letting Jessie greet her, but since I had been the one to invite Olivia over, I didn't want to be a complete asshole. So I headed over to the door, and took a deep breath. I could see her through the peephole and although I didn't want to look, I eventually succumbed to the desire to see if she was just as nervous as I was.

When I looked however, I saw she had a baseball hat on, and with her head slightly lowered and her frame still, I couldn't see or read much from her demeanor. With another sigh, I pulled the door open and to my surprise she stumbled forward. I realized she had been slightly leaning against the door. Perhaps like before, she hadn't expected me to open the door on time.

My hand reached out automatically to catch her, and then she was in my arms.

She soon recovered from her slight misstep, and she lifted her gaze to stare into mine. My heart skipped several beats as I stared at her, and then as she parted her lips to speak my gaze lowered to them. I wanted to kiss her, I realized so badly I could barely suppress the near overwhelming desire. However Jessie saved me.

"Is that Olivia?" she called out, and as her voice sounded across the room, and seemed even to be coming towards us, we both came to our senses. She jumped away from my hold while I let her go, and then Jessie appeared.

"Olivia," she greeted, and I couldn't help but note the shock in Olivia's eyes. She looked between Jessie and me, and I saw the accompanying hurt. Without a word, she turned around but before she could leave, I caught her arm and pulled her into the apartment.

OLIVIA

I wasn't expecting much from Xander by way of courtesy, but this... by all standards was going too far. And so even when he held onto me and tried to pull me into the house, I refused to budge.

"Let me go," I said, on the verge of tears. I had never felt more stupid and foolish in my entire life, and to think I had sent him that text message, hopeful and drove all the way here. I wanted to bash my head against a wall or preferably into his head, and hopefully he would come away with the most damage although at this point I was certain we both deserved it.

He however pulled me effortlessly into the apartment and never had I felt more embarrassed. I couldn't imagine she was watching all of this and so I immediately tried to salvage the situation. "I'll come back," I said, just loud enough for her to hear me. I even managed to add a smile. "I don't want to intrude."

However, with the way Xander held me, I was able to turn around to see she was no longer in our presence. I turned a confused gaze to his, and met his entrancing, ice blue gaze.

"I'll come back," I told him, but then to my shock, he leaned forward, and latched his lips onto mine. The kiss was soft, and before the shock could even register, his tongue was sliding into my mouth.

The kiss continued on for a few seconds, with my strength and resistance waning along with it, and then he pulled away. I was dazed and so confused that my eyes immediately opened to meet his. That same hostility and coldness was still there, but I could almost understand why he had kissed me.

It was a truce, and a kiss I was all too familiar with from our times in the past. Whenever this kiss was given, no matter the fight, we had always momentarily managed to lay down our defense before the other. He let me go, but I held on a bit longer so that the strength could return to my legs. The moment it did, I moved away from him and then he shut the door. Without a word, and without the worry I'd pull it open by myself and exit the apartment, he turned around and headed towards his kitchen.

I gave myself a little while to get myself together, and to consider for the last time whether I should continue to participate in whatever game he was playing here. Whether to hold on to my dignity or find my way out. However as I looked towards the kitchen then back at the door, and then inwards at just how much that truce kiss had affected me, I couldn't help but succumb. And so with a sigh, I shook my head and reminded myself no matter what happened, I had already long decided that for the night I would be foregoing reason. And so I turned and continued towards the kitchen.

My steps were slow… as I was unsure of what sight I would see, or in what state I would meet them.

I was relieved to find that things seemed to be platonic and casual. She was seated on one of the breakfast bar stools with Xander across the counter as he dished out the creamy pasta from the saucepan.

"Olivia," she called then, and I turned to see the genuine smile on her face. It wasn't condescending in any way, but felt somewhat sad. I suddenly couldn't help but take a closer look at her, and it made me for some reason realize she wasn't the threat I had perceived her to be.

"Come take a seat," she said, and tapped the stool next to her, however there was no way I was going to take it. So with a nod, I headed to the stool by its side instead.

"Xander made carbonara pasta," she said. "We made it a while ago but we've been waiting for you to arrive so we could have dinner with you. Have you eaten?"

"Um…" it took a while for me to process all she had just said, and as I did so, I set my phone on the counter, took my hat off and settled on my seat.

I pushed my hair out of my face wishing I had brought a hair tie along so it could be out of the way,

When I however still felt her gaze on the side of my face, waiting for my answer, I realized it was a great thing my hair could cover my face.

"I'm not hungry," I said, and felt Xander's gaze lift up to mine. I couldn't help but hold it, momentarily struck.

He looked so handsome and domestic, that my heart began to melt all over again as so many memories of him in this exact state came rushing back to mind. He wasn't the best of cooks, but I had been, and I'd like to think a lot of the skills I had shown him, since most of the time he had insisted on being in the kitchen with me, had rubbed off.

His hair was pulled away from his face with a band, and I couldn't help but appreciate how the rest of the mass fell beautifully down in layers to his shoulders.

He was dressed more casually this time around in a simple white t-shirt, and dark sweatpants. This however triggered a recognition within me, and so I couldn't help but turn towards the girl by my side to see she was in a similar t-shirt and a pair of jean shorts. Granted, nothing indicated the t-shirt was his, but all over again, that dark queasy feeling returned twisting my gut, making me suspicious, and making me wonder why I was putting myself through torture in this way especially as I thought back to the kiss she had given him the last time I'd been here. They were living together, so what was I doing here?

"You have to at least have a bite," she said to me. "Xander's a great cook but I'm sure you already know that."

"He's not," I said without thinking, and as the words escaped my lips, I felt both of their gazes lift towards mine. Xander's was the one I focused on but it was brief, and then he looked away. He turned around after he was done dishing the pasta onto two plates, but I didn't miss the slight curve of his lips in a smile as he looked away.

She laughed out, and at the beautiful sound, I couldn't help but turn towards her. Once again I was reminded of how gorgeous she was, and couldn't help but notice she looked this good even without any makeup besides some eye liner and a peach lipstick.

"I'm sure he isn't and that you're better," she said. "I have absolutely no skills whatsoever in the kitchen so I guess whatever he makes for me is instantly elevated to gourmet status."

I returned my attention to Xander then, and watched as he picked up the plates to bring to us. All the nerves in my body instantly tensed up as I wondered what he would do. He came over, took the seat by my side which put me between him and the girl, and then handed one of the spoons over to her along with a fork. He set the other down before us, not quite directly before him and to my surprise handed me a fork.

I was so surprised that for the longest time, I stared at him, but then the girl's laugh soon drew my attention away.

"You two are too cute," she said and I was confused all over again as to what was happening.

"Eat some," he said, and I didn't know how to refuse so I accepted the fork from him.

It looked amazing, and my mouth couldn't help but water as I took in the creamy bowl garnished with parsley.

"This looks amazing Xander," she said and instantly dug in.

"Do you want some wine Olivia?" she asked, and picked up the bottle before her to pass it over. "It's white, and dry but we could get something else for you if you preferred?"

We? The word rang in my ears, but before the bottle could reach me Xander took it and set it aside.

"She can't drink," he said. "She has to drive back home."

"Oh," she said, and I was tempted to say the same.

It was clear then whatever this was, would eventually be coming to an end tonight. I had no complaints. It was already too strange for me to fathom.

But then as he dipped his fork into his bowl, and it was acceptable I shared the bowl with him I couldn't help but feel warm. Too warm. So warm it seemed as though there were no hostilities between us and the last four years hadn't happened.

He lowered to pull a forkful into his mouth, and at the added proximity to my face, my heart began to beat so loudly that I wondered if he could hear it. He glanced at me then, as his tongue slipped out to lick the cream off the corners of his lips and the punch to my gut was excruciating. Because I could recall the countless times in the past when I had been the one to kiss those slight spills off his lips.

I lowered my head then, needing to keep my mouth busy before I did something silly like lean over to force a kiss on him.

The one he had delivered to me at the entrance door lingered in my heart and mind, and as I ate, I didn't know if it was the reason why my knees continued to weaken, or if this was simply the effect of Xander being cordial and eating beside me.

"Olivia," she suddenly called, so we both turned to glance at her. "Xander tells me you're a teacher?"

I almost turned to him, as I needed every valid excuse to look at him, however I stopped myself because he was too close. I could hear everything and feel everything and there was no doubt it was the same about me to him.

"Yeah," I replied as I swallowed, and realized I at least needed some sort of drink.

Xander didn't necessarily like to drink water as he ate, and preferred to do so after so I understood why we didn't have any before us. I turned to him then, and just as I expected he did the same and whatever I had been about to say was wiped out of my brain. He was too close, and so I couldn't help but try to lean away.

However, this almost sent me falling over. His sharp reflex and ironclad grip shot out to grab my arm, and thus I was saved from abject embarrassment, the kind I doubted I would be able to recover from.

The girl gasped while Xander dropped his fork, and searched my startled gaze.

"Are you alright?" he asked, and I wished so much we were in the past because I would have told him exactly how his very presence was responsible for almost pushing me over.

"I'm fine," I said, my face slightly burning at the almost disaster. It made me lose my appetite, and wonder once again what I was doing here.

"You needed something to drink?" he asked, and I almost turned to glance at him again.

I caught myself in time and nodded, and in the next moment he was rising to his feet. I was surprised and startled all at once as I watched him head over to his massive steel refrigerator. He pulled the door open and then retrieved what I instantly recognized as cranberry juice- my favorite. And he was well aware of this.

In our earliest days together, we could barely afford it so it would be a treat he would bring my way from time to time, and I would nearly kiss his face off in gratitude. So as he brought out the huge jar of it, and then retrieved a glass to begin to pour, I couldn't take my eyes off him. I expected he would bring the whole jar over so I wouldn't have to ask for a refill later on, but instead he took his time in returning it to the refrigerator and then brought the glass over to me.

We were all quiet as we watched, and it was as uncomfortable as it was endearing.

"Thank you," I said and began to truly wish the girl wasn't here because I could no longer tell if I was holding back from speaking my mind to him like I usually did because of her presence, or if it was because of that damn truce kiss he had assaulted me with in the foyer.

With a sigh, I lifted the glass to my lips, wondering at the turn the night had taken, from not even expecting him to respond to me in the first place to now having dinner with him, and even sharing from the same bowl.

I twirled another forkful, and unexpectedly we both lowered our heads at the same time. We both stopped then, our gazes fixated on the other, and then he sent his fork into his mouth. I did the same, and couldn't help but feign clearing my throat in order to regain some semblance of calm. It was a cool evening, and the house was equally as chilled, however I couldn't help but feel the heat burn up my spine and fill my chest.

"Um," the girl finally spoke, and we both turned to glance at her.

"Alright, I thought this could be an easy, tension free dinner but I don't think I'm qualified to share a room with you two, so I'm going to finish my dinner somewhere else."

I didn't miss Xander's slight frown at her words, but before he could stop her she had grabbed her plate, glass of wine and was already stepping down from her stool.

We both watched her leave, neither of us particularly happy that she was, but we weren't exactly trying to hold her back either. I suddenly grew even more nervous, as I realized that although I had wanted her to leave from the onset, it was quite possible that Xander and I were unable to remain in the same vicinity with the other without going at each other's throats or lips for that matter because of her presence.

And so I watched helplessly as she headed up the stairs, and soon disappeared before I was forced to return my gaze to our meal.

OLIVIA

I still couldn't understand why we were sharing the same bowl I realized, and so I stopped, straightening my thoughts until it came to me. It was because I had initially refused to join them for dinner when they had waited for me before beginning.

This courtesy however, I was certain was done on behalf of the girl so I didn't expect the same needed to be continued after her departure after all I had once walked into this kitchen and he had ignored my very existence. Or perhaps… and as my mind once again went back to that kiss, this was a new era?

I had no clue.

I eventually set my fork down, however he didn't speak. He just kept quietly eating, and I was forced to watch him since I didn't want to continue and neither did I want to interrupt him either. It seemed as though he was deep in thought, and so I just stared ahead, my entire body aware of every bit of his presence but unable to react.

I was prepared to wait until he was done before speaking, but then he surprised me even further when he reached for my glass of juice and brought it to his lips. I turned then to watch as he tilted the glass backwards, and sent the drink to his mouth. I watched the bob of his Adam's apple, and then returned my gaze to his just as his eyes turned to me. I knew what was going to happen without a shadow of a doubt, and so after he set the drink down on the counter, we both paused for a few moments, and then he was leaning his head towards me. My eyes fluttered shut, and once again we were engaged in a kiss that felt too right.

What were we doing? What was happening?

My mind screamed at me to pull away, but I refused. I couldn't. Instead, I deepened the stroke of my tongue against his, licking into his mouth though slowly, but with a fervency that told of my desperation to have all of him. His hand lifted, and then curved around the back of my neck to keep me in place, and my lungs nearly gave out.

I could barely catch my breath.

But then I remembered the last time I'd been here, he'd kissed the girl.

Sure, it wasn't in the same way he was kissing me now, but was more than enough to remind me this was going too far, despite the earlier permission I had given myself to not reach for reason tonight.

And so I started to pull away from him, but he held me in place.

"Xander," I breathed into his mouth, and he realized I was trying to pull away, so he broke the kiss off with a slight gasp.

I felt the ground beneath me dissolve, my hand grabbing on the sides of his shirt to keep myself stable. Our foreheads were leaning against each other, and I didn't think I could face him yet without recollecting myself. So I pulled away, and turned my face away so I could catch my breath, and was certain he did the same. However from the moment we broke away from each other, that almost gnawing need to kiss him once again returned. However I couldn't let myself.

"Who is she?" I asked with the one ounce of reason that had returned to me. I wasn't certain he would respond and so I went on to clarify my reason for asking.

"I just... I don't want to be unfair to her if... but I was hoping..." I couldn't bring myself to complete the statement.

He didn't respond, and as the time ticked away, it began to almost feel as though I had hallucinated the last few seconds of complete and unrestrained vulnerability between the two of us.

I was about to rise to my feet when he spoke up.

"Isn't it amusing, how you seem to consider everyone else apart from me?"

At the bitterness in his words, I turned to watch as he pulled the bottle of wine over to him. He grabbed my glass of cranberry juice, drank it all, and then began to pour himself a drink.

"What do you mean?" I asked, and he turned to me.

"You don't know what I mean? What did you mean then by *'you don't want to be unfair to her?'* So it's alright to be unfair to me?"

I sighed, and could do nothing but watch as he once again lifted the glass to his lips, and in a few seconds had completely drained it.

I gazed at the bottle, and wished that I too could have a sip because I didn't know how I was going to continue discussing this with him without some sort of kick or buzz.

"If I take an Uber home," I said. "Can you send my car over tomorrow?"

I sensed him turn to me, and immediately did the same and explained so he wouldn't misunderstand.

"I want a drink," I said. "Actually I need a drink."

He pushed the glass towards me, and then he refilled it. I accepted it, still not certain how things would go if I did. If I set it down and got up to leave then nothing would happen between us and coming over would have been an absolute waste of time. However if I did drink, then I was almost trapping myself with him with no idea of how the rest of the night would unfold. I instantly knew the option that I preferred.

I lifted the glass to my lips, and took a long drink. I heard him scoff and couldn't help but wonder if he was aware of my internal battle. Perhaps he was because he was in a similar state? I turned and gazed at his striking side view.

"I asked you a question earlier?" I said to him, "who is she?"

"An ex-girlfriend," he replied.

A stretch of silence passed between us before I spoke again. "If you're not going to say anything else. *You* told me to come."

"I indeed told you to come," he said. "But you asked to see me."

"Oh," I said under my breath and heard his slight huff of laughter by my side.

I shut my eyes briefly, and hoped he wouldn't subsequently point out the truth to the complaint he had just made about the way I treated him. However I wasn't so lucky.

"See what I mean?" he said. "You're always so eager to dismiss me?"

I held his gaze, my heart slightly softening at his tone. "Do you really think I'm dismissing you?"

"When it comes to you, I don't know what to think anymore."

I watched him, and then unable to stop myself I leaned forward once again and kissed him, softly... but before I could pull away, his hand was once again curving around my neck. I loved the weight and the heat of his touch against my skin, and the way it caused goosebumps to break out all over my body.

It seemed like forever, but at the same time as though no time had passed at all before his hand moved away, forcing me to respond in kind. I stared into his eyes.

"I guess I'm quick to dismiss people that impair my ability to think straight," I said and a soft laugh escaped him. He turned away then, truly amused.

"That's not true," he said. "Nothing impairs your ability to think clearly. Or at least what you deem is clear."

"Really?"

He returned his gaze to mine. "Yeah."

"So what am I doing here? Kissing you in the same house that your ex-girlfriend is in."

To this he didn't give a response, and more than ever I wanted to inquire about the full nature of their relationship before we moved any further.

And I did want to move further, that much was clear to the both of us, but I had no clue how to proceed.

His hand returned to the back of my neck, stroking as he lost himself in his thoughts.

The gentle caress gave my heart wings.

"What... what are you thinking about?" I asked.

It took a few seconds but he soon responded. "The text you sent to me earlier," he said and my heart clenched tight.

He turned to me. *"If I wasn't as successful, you would be doing all that you could to earn me back?"*

I watched him, unsure how to say everything I wanted to say.

"I know..." I tried my best to gather my courage. "I know that I've made some-" I stopped myself. "At the time I didn't believe it to be a mistake and even now, I'm reluctant to call it that. I just... I think... I know doing what I did is grave enough to keep us apart indefinitely... especially because you're as successful as you are right now. If you weren't then perhaps I wouldn't be so scared that my attempt to reconnect with you will be construed as opportunistic."

"Your attempt to get back together with me?" he said. "What attempt?"

I couldn't help the slight tilt of my lips in amusement. "I'm here aren't I?"

He straightened. "Say what you want," he said. "Exactly. I won't ask for or give you anything more."

My heart began to race as I watched him, and considered if I would truly have the guts to ask for what I wanted.

A few more moments passed as I tried to form the words in my mouth, and although they were quite simple I couldn't get them to leave my tongue. I gave up and instead chose something much more plausible and perhaps soothing.

With a sigh, I gathered my wits and responded.

"You," I said, and just so I was certain he hadn't missed what I had said, I expatiated.

"I want you," I replied. "Tonight. Inside me."

"Is that all?" he asked, and once again something dark and hurt in his eyes stopped me from responding the way that I wanted to.

And so I leaned forward and kissed him again, but just then I recalled there was something I needed to clarify first.

"Her." I said turning behind to glance at the stairs. "Make it clear."

"We're friends," he replied. "She used to be one of the earliest interns at the company but she eventually left for Chicago. We've remained in touch since then, platonically."

"Oh," I replied, however I still wasn't satisfied because knowing Xander, he didn't easily allow people into his personal space and it made me wonder just how serious their relationship had been.

"When is she leaving?" I asked.

"Does it matter?" he replied, and I felt that all too familiar sting of hurt in my heart.

"What you asked for was tonight," he said.

And that's all I was going to get- I couldn't help but complete in my mind.

I thought about it, and thought about it again and then I remembered my admonition to myself for the night, to discard reason. So I grabbed the glass of the remaining wine he had before him and drained it.

"What if I want more?" I pushed out. Then I got to my feet and with one look at him began to walk away.

XANDER

With bated breath, I watched as she walked away and waited to see what she would do.

She reached the foyer, and turned, and I swore to myself I wouldn't get up to stop her if she did indeed head towards the front door. My temper was already rising at the very possibility she would once again be so nonchalant, but then she stopped and inhaled sharply.

"Aren't you coming?" she asked, and I didn't need any further invitation or confirmation. I rose to my feet and followed her.

She knew the way to my room, however when she arrived at the top of the stairs she stopped and turned around to wait for me.

"What is it?" I asked. "You know the way, don't you?"

She held my gaze, boldly. "I don't know if it's occupied," she said and I couldn't help my smile because I knew exactly what she was fishing to confirm.

Shaking my head I didn't justify the comment with a statement and headed onwards on my own.

Truly, I was beginning to see now it was either she didn't understand who she was to me or she was well aware but couldn't believe it because otherwise, how could she even fathom I would let someone else in my bed after she had been in it. In all the years we had separated and beyond Jessie, I had never been able to bring anyone home with me. Jessie remained the exception because at some point, I had been moved by her as we had truly connected, and imagined perhaps I could move forward with her and leave Olivia in my past.

It hadn't worked, and so here we were once again. I pushed the door open, and turned around to grab onto the front of her shirt.

It was somewhat rough but that was the intention, and so when her gaze slightly widened in alarm, I felt a rush of pleasure jolt through me.

With my hand over her head, I slammed the door shut and then pushed her against it.

I heard her gasp just as I lowered, and slanted my lips against hers. She threw her arms around my shoulders and just like that, we were once again completely and irrevocably lost in each other.

I didn't know what had come over her tonight… why against all odds she had decided to come here but in a corner of my heart, hung the suspicion maybe we could move forward.

And so as my hands curved around the sides of her neck to keep her in place, I was determined to kiss her harder and more deeply than I ever had. Perhaps... just perhaps through this, she could feel the things I had tried to tell her over and over again but it seemed too hard for her to believe enough to be willing to fight for me.

She had set up so many hurdles in her mind about what we could be, and how far we could go and I realized now there was very little I could do to remove them. She had to do it on her own, and till then all I would do was respond. Because the one thing that terrified me the most was I would once again pour my heart into trying to convince her and for her to erect yet another hurdle and break me all over again. The pain that suddenly gripped me at the reminder of the devastation I'd gone through the first time around, I couldn't help but kiss her just a bit harder.

"*Xander,*" she breathed as if it bruised her. She broke away then, her gaze ablaze with desire and suspicion, and at my slight smile she realized now it had been intentional.

I didn't expect her to move away, but I did expect her to be hostile and so when her hands flattened against my chest to push me away, I couldn't help my smile. She headed into the room then, pulled her blouse over her head and flung it aside. I saw as it landed on the floor, and turned to watch her as she began unbuttoning her jeans as she approached the bed. I was entranced, and could do nothing but watch as she tugged the tight fabric down, revealing the taut ass underneath and the skimpy lacy underwear that passed through the ridge between. I was so hard I could pound nails, and not till the jeans completely peeled off her legs and flung away, did I remember to breathe. She turned around to face me and I could see she was emboldened. With her gaze on mine, she unclasped her bra, her beautiful breast spilling forward and then the scrap of material was thrown aside too.

I expected her to also take off her underwear, but then she stopped and I couldn't help but be amused. And so leaning my weight on one leg, I folded my arms across my chest and taunted her.

"Why stop there?" I asked.

"I need to give you something to do don't I?" she replied. "Why don't you try taking it off with your teeth?"

She then began to climb onto the bed, and then settled on the slightly rumpled sheets.

It registered that I needed to move so I could join her, but I couldn't help but just watch her.

"She hasn't been in here has she?" she asked as I eventually began to approach.

"And what if she has?" I asked and she glowered at me. I reached her then and stopped before the bed to stare down at her.

"Then I'd rather fuck you on the floor," she said.

"We fucked on the floor too," I shot back, and her gaze darkened even more.

She didn't speak, and for a moment I was certain I had gone into the territory of hurting her.

I didn't miss the slight tremble of her lips and then she rose to her feet.

I knew then that her intention was to leave but I wasn't having it, and so I caught her, my arms going around her midriff.

I crushed her body to mine, but she grabbed onto my arm and tried to pull my hold away.

"I'm not doing this," she said while I buried my face in her neck to breathe in her scent.

"You're mad?" I asked

"Let me go Xander," she said.

"Where?" I shook her. "You drank, remember? You can't drive."

"I'll take a cab. Send my car over."

"If you leave your car here for the second time you're never going to get it back again," I said to her, and at this she turned around to catch my gaze.

There was nothing polite or soft about the look she gave me, and it aroused me near to the point of pain. I loved her eyes, how lethal they could get when dealing with me but yet how soft and passionate they became when dealing with kids. She was perfect in every way and the words that I hadn't spoken to her in years nearly slipped out. Thankfully I caught myself just in time as her hand went around the back of my neck to jerk my head down to hers. She crushed her lips to mine, and I couldn't help but laugh at how brutal she intended it to be.

She was feisty, always giving as much as she got or even a bit more, and I loved that about her. I loved everything about her, even her stubbornness and over-thinking… and her taste, how it never failed to leave me dizzy even after all of these years. And so I kissed her even more deeply until she was turning me around. I let her and in no time was shoved onto the bed.

With her gaze on mine she lowered to her knees, jerked my legs apart and then hooked her hands into the waistband of my sweatpants. She tried pulling them down my ass but I made no effort to cooperate until once again, and with a hand to my chest she shoved me backwards. Amused, I landed flat on my back.

She managed to pull the pants down my thighs, and then they came off my feet. She crawled towards me then, her naked body astride mine as she gripped the bottom of my shirt and pulled it over my head.

I was so charged and heated, that my lungs struggled to keep up. She kissed me on the lips and then on the tip of my nose, my cheek and then I felt her gaze on mine. I didn't want to open my eyes but I couldn't help it, and as I did, I found she was watching me intently and… tenderly.

She leaned forward and at the softest of kisses she placed on my eyelids, I felt my core begin to melt in response.

I sighed and took the time to recover as she began to trace the kisses down my neck and onto my torso. Her lips covered a nipple, sucking hard on it and grazing it with her teeth. I couldn't help but slightly jerk at the sting, amused because I didn't expect anything less than her mischievously teasing me. I loved how she kissed them and every inch of my body, soft, but yet fervently, as though she wanted nothing but to savor my taste and as though I was worth more to her than anything else in the entire world. She continued to trace the kisses down my torso, and then she arrived at my groin. She kissed through the light smattering across my crotch and then her tongue was sliding down the length of my cock.

I could feel it swelling even harder, as she gripped onto the base and then her wet heated mouth covered the broad lush head. She sucked, hard, and my back nearly arched off the bed. The strike of arousal to my core was so painful it was numbing, and yet was so sweet I couldn't help the moan that escaped my lips.

Being with her in comparison to other women had long been able to inform me that sex to me at least had a certain cap to its excitement.

However, with her my craving and yearning never seemed capable of being sated.

After our first few times, it had become less and less about finishing and more about how long I could spend intimately connected to her.

I loved the scent of her skin... the taste... the heat...

Then there was the feel of her frame on top of time, like the present and sometimes underneath... fragile but yet more than capable of dominating.

My hand reached out to hold onto her head, small and delicate, but incredibly fervent as it bobbed up and down on my length.

I loved the sounds she made, and how slurpy they could get and several other times in the past when she had pulled away just in time so I could release onto her face came to mind.

It almost sent me over the edge as another bout of arousal slammed into my weakening frame. She licked up and down the painfully hard length with the flat of her tongue, and then she was lowering even further to pull my balls into her mouth.

I let my groan ring out across the room, uncaring even if Jessie could hear us. For a moment I couldn't help but feel somewhat penitent about this, but I had long requested for Jessie to take her leave but she had insisted on staying and I understood her underlying strategy behind this. It was part of the reasons why we'd remained friends when I had been unable to maintain such lingering attachments with the other women I had relations with.

Jessie knew her boundaries or at least she acted like she did.

She knew when to push for my attention, and when to retreat and never took offense. She knew from even before we'd started dating where and with who my heart still was, despite broken, and how I had been unwilling to pick up the pieces. Instead, I had ignored it for the longest time because I had been too scared. Too scared that if I had indeed cleaned up the damage, then perhaps I would have been able to truly forget Olivia and move on. And at the time, nothing had terrified me more.

It wasn't even that I had hoped to eventually reconcile with her, or perhaps I had… somewhere deep inside, but I had never allowed myself to admit it. And so all I had done was accept the carnage of my heart the way it was… as the way it was meant to be.

It hit me now that I was willing to stay broken for Olivia, and I could barely catch my breath.

What was this hold she had over me, and by putting up a front now and turning a cold shoulder to her advances, wasn't I hurting myself more than I was hurting her?

Her mouth sank even further down my cock then, taking me all the way to the back of her throat and suddenly I needed her lips on mine. And so the moment she came back up and before she could suck on me any further, I leaned forward, grabbed onto her shoulders and pulled her up against me.

It was a bit of a struggle with a slight complaint escaping her at the sudden shift, however I soon crushed my lips to hers, and she melted into me.

"Mmn," she moaned, and the sound reverberated through me like a charm.

"*Xander,*" she breathed and I had to pause briefly to catch my breath. I felt overwhelmed by emotions that swarmed me… to an extent I had never really imagined could be possible. And so I crushed her frame to mine, burying my face in the crook of her neck and inhaling her scent deeply.

Soon enough, she caught onto my emotional state, and her arms went around me.

Afterwards, she began to nibble along the outline of my jaw, moaning so softly and sweetly that I began to fall even more in love with her.

Then she kissed me… over and over again until I was near losing my mind. And so I turned suddenly and sharply till she was underneath me.

"Xander," she complained, eyes coming open to meet mine as I stared down at her.

The moment seemed to freeze in time as we stared at each other, and she began to brush the hair out of the sides of my face. I saw her gaze soften and tears begin to fill them.

I waited… needing to see them fall from her eyes, however when this began to happen, she tried to turn away.

"Look at me" I said, however she didn't listen.

"Olivia," I called, and she clenched her eyes shut as the moisture seeped out from the corners and rolled down her face.

I was satisfied with this display, because although not nearly adequate, it strangely gave me the hope that against all odds, we were on the same page or at least heading towards the path of being so.

And so I kissed her… delicately… softly, my tongue stroking passionately against hers.

She held onto me, harder than I could remember, breasts pressing onto the hardness of my chest as my cock stroked against the folds of her sex.

Eventually, she was gasping into my mouth and my desire to taste every bit of her surged. So I began to trace my kisses down her body. I sucked a hickey onto the side of her breast, determined for her to bear the very vivid and inescapable reminder of our night together for as long as was possible.

As though in retaliation her nails dug into my back and then seemed to drag along. It stung, but I had absolutely no complaints whatsoever. Thrilled even further, I continued tracing kisses down her chest and then with one hand cupping her left breast brought the sweetness of her hardened nipple to my lips. I sucked hard on it, loving the tiny whimpers that escaped her as a result. I licked across the pale pink, engorged bud, relished her slight quiver as my teeth grazed across it.

And then her arms were curving around my head, cradling it to keep me in place. Amused, I managed to break free so I could move on to the next breast, to lavish it with just as much attention. It was successful and by the time I was almost done with both, she was writhing so desperately underneath me I was certain she was going to come before I could even get to her sex.

"Babe," she called out to me as I licked a stripe of wetness down her torso, until the tip of my tongue dipped into her navel.

She shuddered, hands digging into my hair to grab at the roots.

I relished the slight sting, and even as I began to move lower, and a slight hesitation followed causing her to grab my hair even harder perhaps to stop me, I welcomed the pain.

It amused me she still reacted in this way because no matter how much I had eaten her out, she always hesitated when I approached, even though I had informed her countless of times the pleasure I derived from it was a very close tie to fucking her.

It had to do mostly with how good it made me feel to unravel her so completely, and in a way that I could pay more attention to than if I was an equal participant and thrusting into her. And so as I began to trace soft, intent kisses down her mons, I loved the slight jolts that came to her frame. I bit onto the tiny straps of lace that bound the delicate scrap of material to her hips and began to pull it down her thighs and legs.

Eventually her legs kicked it aside, and I was free to take in her pussy. The room was dim, only lit by the bedside lamp, and it was the perfect, warm ambience for us to completely lose ourselves in.

I kissed the heated smoothness, and then my nose was sinking in to relish her scent.

Both of her hands returned to my head to exert some sort of control, though she was unaware of this as she was now near the point of incoherence. I ignored it all, and in no time was devouring her in the way I truly relished.

I lapped her up, sucking and licking as her entire frame writhed and shuddered against me. So I grabbed onto her hips, and held her down hard against the bed.

"*Xander*," she whimpered, barely able to move in order to soothe all of the sensations that were barraging her. In little time she was coming hard, and I couldn't help but loosen my hold so she could move the way she needed to.

She palmed herself and then a hand was in her hair, grabbing it at the roots.

"*Xander*," she called over and over again... her frame trembling from the sweet assault.

Amused, I flipped her over and then moved over her to press a kiss onto the pulse beneath her neck.

I could have sworn I felt the pulse jump in excitement, and couldn't help but press one more kiss to it before moving downwards.

Trailing heated kisses along the curve of her spine, the dip in her back and then arriving at her ass. I kissed both cheeks, and included reasonably hard smacks that left slightly reddened bruises on her pale skin. She gasped in surprise, her frame slightly lifting from the bed but as I grabbed the soft round cheeks, pulling them aside so that I could eat at her from behind, her knees once again crumbled.

"Ahh," she cried out as my mouth once again latched onto her wetness and my tongue dug in.

"*Fuck... Xander!*" she cursed, her tone now severely heightened. She was fighting to pull away. I latched onto her thighs, trailed even more kisses down it and then flipped her over once again. Her legs automatically spread wide open for me, as well as her arms in a silent, but desperate plea for me to come to her. At her wiggling fingers, I laughed and obliged and soon our lips were once again connected... deeply... intimately.

"*Fuck me,*" she gasped into my mouth. "Please... *Xander please.*"

I was aching almost as desperately to fill her up, so I grabbed my cock and was soon sliding between the soaked folds of her sex.

Her arms curved around my shoulders, holding me tightly to her as she moaned into my ear. The sensations, wet and intimate as my cock slid to and fro between her legs, stroking and taunting made my vision spin, and not until I was finally pushing into her was I able to find my focus.

I slid in slowly at first, and then with my elbows beside her head on the bed, and her legs wrapped around my waist, I railed into her and found bliss. She cradled my head in her hands even as hers fell backwards at being so thoroughly impaled while I hid my face in the crook of her neck.

My heart was racing in my chest and what a delight it was to find that with her, I was always so smitten and excited and overwhelmed and near out of my mind.

I tried my best to last but as I began to move, my pace quickened involuntarily. On a particular sweet thrusts, just when I hit the core of her that made her nearly scream out, I would slow and take my time rocking into her.

The both of us soon became too starved for that precious release, and so any idea of making this last long was thrown out as we nearly fucked ourselves into oblivion.

Our breathing was haggard, hips in overdrive, lips kissing and biting, blood boiling.

I savored every single bit of it and soon she was coming with a scream that resounded across the room. I kept fucking her, unable to stop until suddenly, I too reached the edge and was flung over. I froze, an almost painful numbness striking my body... and then the pleasure crashed into me in sweet waves. It coursed feverishly through my system, leaving me shaken and completely without strength.

I collapsed onto her, my arms wrapped around her body as we both trembled against the other. I just needed to hold her, to remain somewhat grounded, and didn't even realize it when I eventually drifted into sleep.

It was what seemed like a short time later, that I felt her pushing me onto my back, and then pulling the covers over us as she laid against me. My eyes fluttered open, and before I could think of anything else, I reached out and kissed her. Afterwards I held her even more tightly to me and then happily drifted back into sleep.

OLIVIA

For once I couldn't find the rest that I craved.

He however seemed to slip right into it and I couldn't understand why. All along he'd seemed more troubled than I was, more haunted but now it seemed as though our positions had been reversed.

Still, I could do nothing but revel in his hold as the night passed by. We remained sprawled on the side of the bed since I didn't have any strength whatsoever to reposition him properly without waking him up. So although I didn't understand the current bliss he was in, I also didn't want to put a stop to it. So I kept pondering on what to do and what possible path we could both take from here.

There was no way I was going to be able to get Xander King out of my mind and forget him, regardless of what I thought about his success and how it made me hesitate in sharing my heart and intentions with him.

So I made the decision to bare it all to him, truly and wholeheartedly- my heart for him… my doubts… my remorse…

and my love. I also began to run through what would be the best way to present these to him.

In bed, as we were still so intimate, or perhaps in a more neutral setting so neither of us would be too mentally or emotionally muddled or clouded.

I couldn't help but admit the former was my preference, but given he could always walk out on me and thus make it quite difficult or even downright excruciating for us to find our way back together, I decided to go the more clear headed route. With this settled, I soon fell asleep and by the following morning, I was once again left alone. It made me begin to wonder why he never lingered around to watch me like he used to do in the past. He was always the first to get up while I would come awake later on to realize a pair of eyes were on me. He would never look away or move away, and when he eventually did, he would bring me with him as we headed into the kitchen to prepare a meal to start the day.

Now however, and as I got up to stare around the room, I saw it was empty. With a sigh, and unsure of what time of the morning it could possibly be due to the completely dark and drawn curtains around the room, I rose to my feet and began to search for my clothes. It had been an almost perfect night, or at least as perfect as I could possibly hope for between us, and I didn't want any worries or regrets or rejections to ruin it.

Just then however, I realized that his clothes were also strewn across the floor along with mine, and this was quite unusual of him as he would have picked up after himself even if he ignored mine. This made me wonder if he had truly left, so I began to head to the bathroom door. The closer I got, the more I heard the sound of running water, and it made me breathe easy to find he was still here, even though technically, it was *his* bedroom and apartment and he was meant to be here.

Pulling the door open, I got into the bathroom, and met it heated and filled with steam. I considered waiting for him back in the bedroom so that we could speak, but instead decided to for once, use my vulnerability to present my body and my heart to him.

So I let go of the pair of pants that I hadn't even known had been in my grip as I headed over to the stall. I knocked once but there was no response.

It seemed it was too noisy for him to hear me, so I simply pushed the door open and went in.

I met him with his back to mine, head lowered as the cascade fell and rinsed the soap off his hair.

He seemed to feel the sudden chill, and turned around to meet my gaze.

For a few moments he didn't say a word. He seemed frozen in place, and then he ran his hand through his hair.

"Hey," he said, and I smiled shyly in response, unsure of what exactly to do. He watched me a bit longer, and then scoffed in amusement. It was however not one of derision, but of endearment, and it made me feel good that I knew him enough to be able to so easily detect which was which. He moved forward to grab the bottle of shampoo from a corner shelf.

"I woke up and you were gone." I whispered, my heart in my throat unsure if this was the right time to let all my emotions out.

I had to lower my head to hide my blush. I then went underneath the water, and couldn't help my moan of appreciation as the warm cascade drenched me completely from head to toe. My eyes were shut but I could hear him moving behind me.

I most definitely couldn't shake off my nervousness, but I found I could still relish his presence with me in the stall. Soon enough he returned even closer, and then pulled me slightly away from underneath the cascade. I started to turn towards him but then his hands were in my hair, and working shampoo onto my scalp.

All intents of conversation or even nervousness began to drain out of me as I melted into his touch, unable to stop myself from remembering the multitude of times he had washed my hair in the past. I didn't say a word, so as not to break the spell but instead, lessened the rush of water out of the shower head. Our silence continued as he massaged my scalp, ran his hands down the long strands of my hair, and then brushed the entire mass over my shoulder so that he could get to the underside of my head. I couldn't help but begin to step backward then... slowly... purposefully until I was leaning fully against his naked body. I immediately felt his hardness as it poked against my back, and couldn't help my smile. I wanted to kiss him once again, but admonished myself to take things slowly, and to solely bask in this most precious time between us.

Soon however, he spoke.

"I missed this."

My eyes remained closed, as I responded.

"Me too."

The silence continued to stretch on as he expertly worked his fingers into my scalp, and then he stepped away from me. I watched him as he headed back towards the faucet, and turned it on to full blast. He began to rinse himself off without a word and my heart sank, knowing something had come over him. Afterwards and without a word, he stepped out and shut the door behind him.

I watched what I could of his figure retreating, before the heat fogged up the glass and once again he was gone from sight.

I grabbed a towel on my way out and headed straight to the bedroom. There, I sat on the bed needing the moment to examine why I needed to be away from her. I'd felt overwhelmed for a moment with a grief that was all too familiar, and at the reminder once again that she was the source of it, I could no longer remain and act as though all was right with the world.

With a sigh, I rose to my feet and headed over to my closet.

In no time I was dressed, casually as it was a Sunday, and there was nowhere I particularly had to be. It was probably the same for her but I didn't expect she would offer to, or be willing to stay any further with me.

But maybe I could do something about that? If it wasn't too late? If my sudden hostility hadn't once again closed her up?

What I truly wanted was for us to sit down and have a heart-felt conversation with each other, but just as I had concluded the previous night, I wasn't going to push for anything between us. I was going to move according to what she had the guts to demand from me, because never was I going to delude myself again into thinking my yearning and passion for her was enough for two.

I headed down to the kitchen, hoping I had enough cashews to do what I wanted. They were her favorite in comparison to other nuts, so I'd long developed the slightly heightened preference for them. Pecans were the preferred nuts of choice for the French toast recipe, but I'd always mixed cashews in there for her which she had loved.

Something within me hesitated though, trying to warn me off the idea, insinuating I was trying too hard and extending too much of an effort into getting her to stay, but I couldn't help it. I arrived quietly at the kitchen, and was glad to see that Jessie was still not up. It was pretty early, barely 8am, and she was a late riser so I was assured that Olivia and I still had at least a few hours without any interruption. Not that we would need it if a repeat of the last time occurred and she chose instead to leave.

Though perhaps my cold reception of her was also to blame, I didn't know how I could willingly bring myself to correct it either.

I couldn't figure it out, and so I concentrated solely on finding the nuts, blueberries, and a still unopened bottle of maple syrup. She loved to drizzle it across her toast since I never really liked a lot of sugar, so it was always the perfect compromise for the both of us.

Soon enough, the kitchen was filled with the scent of cinnamon and butter and it was soothing to say the least.

By the time I was ready however, she still hadn't come down. Regardless, I placed her slices on a plate, solely made up of cashews and blueberries, while mine were with pecans and no syrup.

I had two scoops of ice cream on mine and as I began to eat, I couldn't help but smile as I wondered about the last time I'd had such a sweet breakfast. I couldn't recall it, and realized then that my sugar intake when I was with her had quite the significant difference to when I wasn't with her.

I began to eat, slowly... taking my time so I wouldn't be done before she arrived. It wasn't hard as I had my phone with me and could catch up on work emails. Thankfully though, it wasn't too long before I heard her footsteps descending down the stairs. I was certain that it was her because Jessie would have been a bit noisier. Olivia's instead were light and careful.

I couldn't help but smile as I shook my head. I was seated on one of the stools with my back to her, and wondered if perhaps it would be best to stand up and head to the refriger-ator so that she would be drawn to head over. Eventually, I decided against this idea and remained seated, listening with bated breath at when and if she would come over.

She didn't, and with every second that passed my chest tight-ened further and further.

I abandoned what was left of my toast, and simply lifted the mug of coffee to my lips, nearly draining it all before setting it down once again.

She had left, and I couldn't believe it, or perhaps she was standing in some corner and just watching me. I decided then to turn around for a glance, unable to stop myself, and when I looked behind me, found she wasn't in sight.

There was no doubt in my mind that she had already arrived on the ground floor but had taken the easy route out and headed straight to the foyer. To escape. My hand curled into a fist as I considered heading over, however I kept myself glued to the seat, unable to vow this was the last I would ever want to hear from her.

I tried to return back to work, but the words refused to compute to my brain, so I gave up, letting the phone drop to the counter. I was about to rise to my feet when I suddenly felt her presence. There were barely any sounds to announce it, but an unmistakable awareness of her suddenly came over me, so I turned around, and indeed found her watching me.

My heart jumped in my chest, but I could feel nothing but relief. And then I felt myself slightly tremble at the realization she hadn't left. She watched me, eyes soft but nervous, almost contrite.

Her gaze moved to the untouched plate beside mine, and then to mine which was now only half finished and abandoned.

Then she looked at me.

She glanced at the plate once again and then back to me, slightly puzzled.

"Is that for me?" she asked, her tone small and almost inaudible, but I could read her lips very clearly.

It took everything inside of me to control my smile. "What makes you think it's yours?" I asked, and she bit down on her lip.

My gaze perused her body, the slight dampness of her hair, and the simple t-shirt tucked into high-waisted jeans that she'd worn over just last night.

All of it was now rumpled from being pulled at and flung onto the floor, and needless to say it brought back memories that now made it quite easy for me to turn away and let her be, assured that she wouldn't be going anywhere.

Still though, she didn't move so I waited, ready to grab her arm and yell her ears off if she took this as my lack of agreement and my response for her to walk away.

Thankfully however, she stepped forward, grabbed the handle of the stool, and then pulled it out to take her seat.

I could see she was trying to control her smile as she lowered her eyes from mine, and picked up the toast.

"Thank you," she said. "This looks amazing."

I didn't respond, but as she bit into it, I could see I didn't need to. She made a small sound of approval and it instantly shot a jolt of pleasure through me.

I could feel my limbs tingling in response to my body's awareness of her, and truly wondered when I would begin to get used to her presence now like I had in the past.

I didn't have too many complaints about feeling this way though because in the past, it was only after we had broken up I'd realized how important it was to feel excited about being around a partner.

And so I listened to her eat, as I tried to return my attention to my email. I succeeded, as I stumbled upon a particularly troubling one that took all my focus. What brought me back however was when I suddenly felt her warmth, and realized she was trying to reach for my plate. She stopped when she realized she'd been caught, her mouth stuffed as she chewed and her gaze sheepish. I looked down at my plate so I could figure out what she'd been reaching for, and saw that a small piece of my toast had gone uneaten and her fork had been about to go for it.

I turned to look at her once again, almost in disbelief she had clung to this naughty habit of stealing off my plate especially when I saw she wasn't even done with hers.

She tried to explain.

"It has chocolate cream drizzled across," she said, but I was still too stunned to speak so she added. "I was just going to taste it."

"You don't know what French toast tastes like with ice cream on it?" I asked and she scowled. I most definitely couldn't control my smile then, but luckily she straightened just in time to miss it, her nose wrinkling at my sarcasm.

She continued eating hers in silence, but I couldn't stand her sulking so I picked the piece up and placed it on her plate. She turned to me, eyes soft but yet lethal at the same time. I smiled then, briefly and her entire body seemed to pause.

She appeared somewhat struck as she watched me, and I didn't need to ask why. Instead I took advantage of her slight surprise and leaned forward to kiss the slight stain of syrup on the corner of her lips.

My heart jolted into my throat at the contact and the sweetness and her accompanying warmth and scent. She smelled like me I realized, like the shampoo and lotion I used and it caused joy to surge through me.

I didn't take it too far, didn't intend to so I started to pull away but before I could, her arms were coming around my body to keep me in place. She deepened the kiss, her lips coaxing mine open so she could slide her tongue in.

I let her, but didn't reach out to hold her. However it cranked up the heat simmering in my blood, warming me all over and bringing similarly sweet but innocent kisses to mind from the past.

One I could never escape was our first time together. That night had started with absolutely no intention whatsoever of us becoming intimate with each other, but had ended with the two of us connecting with each other in a way that had truly left me dazed.

Afterwards, I remembered leaving her bedroom and then heading down to her mother's kitchen to whip up some pancakes for her, and it had all been beyond heavenly. Soon she'd come to join me, dressed in my T-shirt which was oversized and ill-fitting on her petite frame, and I had never been happier.

I sighed at the memory, my hands lifting to cradle her face as I slid my tongue even further into her mouth to taste more of her.

Suddenly as my hands connected with her skin I found there was a wetness. Alarmed, I immediately moved away.

She however tightened her hold and tried to stop me, but I refused.

"Olivia," I called, grabbing onto her wrists and that was when I heard the sniff that she had been doing everything she could to hold back.

I pulled away completely, my eyes coming open to meet that indeed I had been right.

Tears were sliding down her face

"Olivia," I called again, and she turned her face away from mine.

I watched her and then let go as she struggled to return to the stool. I waited, and the moment she started to rise to her feet, I grabbed onto her hand and pulled her back down without a word.

She knew I wasn't going to let her go anywhere until she shared her heart with me.

"What are we doing?" I could hear the vulnerability in my voice and held my breath for her response.

OLIVIA

What are we doing? Isn't that the question? What *are* we doing? I couldn't believe how emotionally I was acting from just a kiss and a few words, but it hadn't been just any ordinary kiss because this moment in particular reminded me of a time I know would forever be ingrained in my memory.

It had been during my final year in high school and Xander was already a freshman in college. That weekend however, he'd ensured to be home to help me with a dreaded chemistry test I had been complaining to him about. He had shown up uninvited, so it had been the biggest surprise to find him waiting at the door.

I had been so moved and delighted, I had jumped into his embrace and my legs lifted off the floor.

Afterwards, my mother had left home for something she had to do overnight. I couldn't even remember what it was exactly now but it had been work related. She had hesitated leaving us alone, but then she had made Xander swear we would behave and for some reason she had always believed his assurances to her. I didn't blame her, he was dependable and trustworthy and up till that moment, he had been exactly that and more.

Until I had provoked him.

All through our lesson, her admonition had kept ringing in my mind, and coupled with the proximity we maintained with each other, it had almost been inevitable. I had initiated it and back then, I'd known just how to coax what I wanted out of him.

It had taken a few tries and multiple rejections, but soon enough he had melted into the kiss and showed me just exactly what he'd felt in his heart for me. It'd amazed me afterwards just how gentle he'd been with me that first time, and I had come to appreciate just how much better his caution had made the whole experience for me. Afterwards, we had been lying naked together huddled in my small single bed, and I had blurted out I wanted pancakes.

He'd laughed in response, and at the time was certain I was joking as it was way past midnight. When he'd realized however I wasn't, and after much cajoling he'd relented. We'd ended up in the kitchen, to find out disappointingly that there was no flour.

But he'd been resourceful, found some nuts and thus the tradition of having French toast instead had been established. It had been perfect.

Just like now, the sweetness had stained my lips and he'd kissed it off me, then I'd looked into his eyes and told him I loved him for the very first time. As the words had come out of my mouth and I'd realized just how intensely I meant it, it had moved me to tears.

And so here I was, years later and still so struck by the same realization I didn't know what to do with myself. I had thought with time, the susceptibility to him would fade, and for a moment I had been certain it had… but being with him once again was bringing me to a conclusion I couldn't ignore.

Sure, I could live without him and be alright, but having him in my life brought a spectrum of colors and excitement I couldn't help now but acknowledge and yearn for.

Was I once again willing to let it go?

Was it so easy to let go?

I turned towards him, but still couldn't find the courage to meet his gaze. Not yet. Not till I could work up the courage I needed to answer his question.

I accepted he would most likely reject me, however as I allowed myself to acknowledge the hold he had on my arm which prevented me from walking away, I couldn't help but consider perhaps I was wrong and perhaps there was a slight hope he wanted me in the same way I wanted him.

With my free hand, I wiped the moisture off my face and cleared my throat. Then met his gaze with a smile.

He didn't have one in return for me, so I was forced to discard the facade of nonchalance I was hoping to hide behind.

"Well?" he asked, and I tried to pull my arm away from his grip.

However he refused, and at this my throat clogged up again.

"Please let go," I muttered, my hand on his, and only silence ensued. Then I heard his voice.

"Is that what you want... what you really want?" he asked, his tone heavy, and I understood he wasn't in any way speaking about the current moment.

He gave me the time I needed to find the words I was looking for and eventually, the words were able to make it to the surface, his grip more steading now than to keep me seated.

"I..." I began. "I was wrong."

He went silent, and although I wanted to continue on without him, it didn't seem I would be able to.

"What?" he asked, his voice lower than I had ever heard it.

"I was wrong and I'm sorry. I... took things for granted. I took us for granted."

My voice became shaky, so I paused so that I could regain my control.

"I... I don't know how... we can... I don't even know if it's possible. But I guess I have to lay my cards down. I want you... I want you back in life. Is... this possible?"

"And what about your text?" he asked. "Or didn't you mean that?"

I turned to him, a bit puzzled as I wasn't exactly certain as to the message he was referring to. He met my gaze and upon pondering further, I finally realized he was referring to what

I had sent to him the previous night before I had even made my way here.

'If you weren't as successful as you were, I would probably be doing all that I could to earn you back.'

I thought about it and sighed.

"What's changed?" he asked. "I mean I'm still successful and I don't plan on not being so."

I smiled, but it wasn't amusing. He wasn't going to make this easy on me at all and for the first time, I was willing to accept this and still persist.

"I did mean it, but there's not much we can do about that is there?" I asked, trying once again to lighten the mood however he was simply staring at me, expressionless, but his gaze was dark and unhappy. My shoulders slumped.

"You know how terrified I am right now."

"I *don't* know," he responded and I was taken aback. "Because at one point I thought I knew everything I needed to know about you, and it turned out I was wrong. That you could spring whatever you wanted on me at any time as far as you decided it was what was best for us."

My eyes misted, and although as usual my automatic reaction was to recoil away from him, I stood my ground and listened.

"I don't want to make the same mistake twice," he said. "So this time around I'm not going to assume anything. Whatever you say to me is what I will accept. As it is presented."

I sighed once again.

"Alright," I cleared my throat. "Well, what I'm saying... Xander, is that my ending our relationship in the past I know now was a mistake, and if it's possible, I'd like to rectify it. I don't know if you still regard me the same as back then, and if you don't I understand. But I just... for once I want to disregard the constraints and limitations I seem to always cook up in my head, and I want to try."

I lifted my gaze to his.

He watched me, and then my gaze lowered to his lips as they parted to speak.

"I don't regard you in the same way," he said, and the stab to my heart was instantaneous.

He watched me, and with all of my might I tried to remain calm.

"I understand-" I began, however he cut me off.

"I'm not finished." I remained seated.

"I don't regard you the same, and I don't know if I ever will. I still care about you, and I'm sure I always will but... you broke my heart. Into pieces that I don't know if I'll ever be able to regain."

I parted my lips to respond but then the delicious French toast I had been eating felt like lead in my stomach.

My gaze shot to his and something he saw had his hold loosened and he let go. I didn't think I could say anything else.

I ran from my seat, not able to wait a moment longer. I hurried into the bathroom and slammed the door shut falling over the toilet just in time to empty the contents of my stomach.

XANDER

I was quite stunned.

So much so that for a few seconds, all I could do was stare at where she had been sitting.

I however soon looked away as my heart began to soften towards her, and I realized I had posed this to her as a test, rather than anything else. Sure, I wanted her, more than I'd ever or would probably want anyone else but this time, I wanted her to fight for me and to earn my full love back, with the hope maybe this time around she wouldn't let it go as easily.

A sigh escaped me as I heard the bathroom door slam and not the front door.

Before I could think too much about it she was hiding from me again, Jessie came up to me with her bag in hand.

"Leaving?" I questioned though after last night I could guess the answer.

"Yeah," Jessie giggled. "It's been… interesting."

I gave a huff of a laugh and looked up at her.

"It's time to forgive her, you know. You two are obviously not over each other."

"How can you be so sure?" I asked, not sure I really wanted to hear the answer.

"Seriously? You showed her more emotion last night than you showed me the entire time we were together."

She sounded bitter and I couldn't help but feel a little guilty. It wasn't her fault my heart belonged to another.

"I'm sorry I couldn't be what you needed. You are an amazing woman and you will find someone perfect for you." I couldn't help but think if it wasn't for Olivia I may have been that person.

She gave me a small smile and kissed my cheek, then she turned and left.

I continued to sit at the counter to think and then remembered Olivia fleeing to the bathroom.

With a sigh I got up and headed that way. I stopped outside the door and listened but didn't hear anything.

I raised my hand to knock when the door swung open showing Olivia with red rimmed eyes and looking almost green.

"Are you alright," I was still trying to figure out if she had been hiding or maybe something else was wrong, she looked ill.

"I think I may be..." she took a deep breath, "coming down with something."

I looked into her eyes, almost imploring me to believe her.

I sighed, not sure what to do.

"Can you drive? Do you... want to stay here?" I honestly didn't know what to expect from her anymore.

"I can drive." she replied, her voice small.

"Okay." I realized I was still blocking her way out of the bathroom. So I moved out of her way and she walked past me heading to the foyer.

Before she reached the door, however, she turned to look back at me.

"I want to try... to try and put your heart back together. If you'll let me." With that she turned and walked out the door.

For a long time I just stood there staring unsure what to do with myself, but hopeful for the first time in a long time that we may have finally found a way back to each other. I was still going to guard myself and wait for her to make the next move.

"So…"

I looked up from the lesson notes I was preparing for the next day as Elise came into my classroom.

I was a bit taken aback by the excitement in her tone, and the wiggle of her eyebrows at me as though I was supposed to understand whatever was causing the spring in her step.

"So…" I repeated after her, perplexed.

At first she seemed certain I was joking, but when she realized I wasn't, her face fell.

"Did you forget?"

"Forget what?"

"Tonight… our date."

I had absolutely no idea what she was talking about.

"Derek's cousin? Jack."

And then I was reminded.

"Oh," I said, and she frowned.

"Oh? He's been so excited about it. It was all he could talk about as soon as he got into town last night."

"Oh," I said again, reminded of one of the major reasons why I hadn't bothered to even note the set up in my mind.

My lips parted. I didn't know what else to say so I returned my gaze to my notes.

"Olivia," she called, and I tried to hide my smile.

"You're looking for an excuse to come up with right? So you can get out of this?"

I returned my gaze to hers. "You know I'm trying to work things out with Xander."

Its Derek's cousin. So don't think of it as a date but an excuse to go let your hair down."

I sighed then, my mind going to the one man I wanted to see but for some fucking reason still hadn't contacted. I picked up my phone again and it had become my habit over the last two weeks, waiting... checking... contemplating over and over again.

What was happening? I had asked myself a thousand times.

Was he waiting for me to contact him again? I was hoping after our last talk that maybe he would reach out to me. I was interrupted from my musings with Elise not taking the hint.

"You're checking again to see if Xander has contacted you?" she asked dryly, and I lifted my gaze to hers.

She sighed. "Olivia, are you ever going to get over him? I thought you two were over?"

I figured he would contact me to at least ask if I was alright after leaving. Maybe he wasn't alright. I really should just call him… well maybe a text.

I returned my attention to the phone, and only when Elise exclaimed did I realize I had been about to put it down.

"Olivia!" she called, her tone quite alarmed.

"I'll come," I groaned. "Please leave me alone."

"No, you can't keep doing this to yourself. You've been so morose lately."

"Elise, honestly I just haven't been feeling very good," I said, and she forced herself to calm down.

"But you *are* coming?"

"I'll be there," I agreed much to her surprise, but hoped in my heart that perhaps tonight would be the night that Xander would contact me and I wouldn't have to.

Later that evening, I was nursing a virgin cocktail and seated at an Italian Restaurant downtown. The ambience was cozy, the meal pleasant and our conversation flowing.

Elise and her boyfriend were seated across from each other, just as I was from his cousin, Jack.

So far, the night had been pleasant. He was a junior partner at one of the highest ranked firms in Boston, brown thick mass of hair, grey eyes… strong nose. He was boisterous, humorous and knew how to hold a conversation and keep it going. Was even successful at pulling me out of my shell, making me forget temporarily about Xander. However as soon as things quieted down, my mind and heart went back to thoughts of Xander and how I wished he was the one sitting across from me.

Thankfully, I was able to curb my unpleasant habit of checking my phone frequently, however when I excused myself to go to the bathroom I couldn't help but do so, Elise walked in and I was caught.

"I knew it," she said, and with a sheepish smile I quickly put it away to focus on turning on the sink's tap.

"You didn't even wash your hands first, did you?" she asked.

I scowled at her through the reflection in the mirror. "You're hounding me."

"And?"

I shut the tap off, and went over to grab some paper towels.

"Elise," I called. "Enough. I'm not wrong or dumb for still trying to get things right with Xander. It's where my heart is right now and I don't want to have to defend myself or apologize for it."

At my words her gaze softened. "I know," she sighed. "I'm sorry. I guess I just feel sometimes if you'd just look elsewhere then maybe-" she shook her head then, and decided not to complete the sentence.

"Don't mind me," she said. "I understand. I know what this feels like... I'm sorry. I used to be a mess too over my ex before I met Derek."

"I'm not a mess," I couldn't help but complain, somewhat amused and she too smiled in response. But it was sad.

She headed over then and I was pulled reluctantly into a hug.

"We're about to order dessert and call it a night, but Jack suggested that we move the party to a club. They want to go dancing."

A wave of exhaustion came over me at the mere thought.

"Ugh," I made a sound and she laughed.

"It might be fun though, don't you think?"

"Maybe, but I'm exhausted. It's been a long day."

We began to head out of the bathroom together. "Me too, but there's one just down the street. An hour or two might not be too bad?"

I thought about it and when the suggestion was officially brought up at the table, I couldn't help but concede to it since I would have been the only one with an objection.

Perhaps it would be just what I needed to exhaust my mind off its focus on Xander.

OLIVIA

I t worked, because about an hour later we were throwing back what had to be our third shots of the night. Since we'd decided to take Ubers home so we could let loose, the limited alcohol intake rule had been lifted. As the tequila burned down my throat and chased away the chill I hadn't even realized had filled my insides, I couldn't help but smile at the resounding shouts all around. Derek made a joke in the distance that caused a laugh, but I didn't catch it so I simply set my glass down and attempted to clear my head.

We had gotten a booth to ourselves, and could barely see each other in the dimness of the corner we were lodged in, and all of this was to Elise's displeasure.

"Stop sulking," I leaned over to whisper into her ear and she scowled at me.

"Does Xander make you laugh? I bet Jack could."

I couldn't help my smile at this. "Absolutely not," I replied, as I leaned forward to pour myself another shot. "I make him laugh and I'm not hooking up with Jack."

I downed it with a wide smile on my face, and missed him even more. And so I couldn't help but lean over again to speak to Elise. "I love our arguments. I wouldn't even call them arguments, more like banter. Charged banter."

This however didn't sound right to me. "Actually, it's not banter. We used to banter when we were younger before we dated, but now we actually just fight and argue... and I fucking love it. Well I don't love it but I don't hate it either. I just think I'd enjoy doing anything with him. Even absolutely nothing. As long as it's with him."

I leaned away from her and wondered if she caught all I had just said. I felt as though I couldn't recall all I had just said. And so I cocked my head in thought and she laughed at me.

"Are you drunk?"

"No," I shook my head... but then I wasn't sure. Was I? My gaze was clear. I felt quite light headed but the deafening music and crowd was sure to do that to anyone. I turned once again at the sound of laughter, and met the guys seated across from us conversing and gazing out at something on the dance floor ahead.

Jack then turned to me, a kind smile on his face. I couldn't help but return it and then looked away.

"Do you want to dance?" Elise asked and I thought about it. My gaze lifted and I was reminded once again this wasn't the same club as there was no second floor VIP section. I thought of Xander, and couldn't help but recall how my first ever experience at a club had been with him.

He'd been so cautious about it, held onto my hand and basically guarded me like a mother hen all through the night.

And I'd had a blast, because thanks to him there had been no reason to be cautious about anything. He'd guided me and protected me and danced with me. I recalled grinding on him with abandon on the dance floor, and screaming my lungs off, much to his amusement, with Danny when a particular song we'd both loved at the time had come on. I couldn't even remember what it was, and thought for a moment that perhaps he would. That would be reason enough to text him wouldn't it? To ask.

He would probably ask me why I wasn't texting Danny instead for such an inquiry.

I scowled and picked up my phone and began to type out a message to Xander.

Something cautioned me that I was making a mistake but I didn't care... I could barely see the words. After I was done it seemed to make sense to me, but I wasn't quite certain because the words seemed to be bouncing around the screen so I nudged Elise and pushed the phone close for her to peruse.

She however turned too sharply from speaking to Derek and the phone fell from my hold.

"Shit," I cursed, as she quickly apologized.

"It's alright... it's uh..." I seemed to have forgotten what I wanted to say. But then I soon picked the phone up and was glad to see that the screen was still intact.

We laughed together about it, and then she asked me if I wanted to dance.

I looked towards the dance floor, and wanted to say yes but it seemed as though I was forgetting something. However I couldn't figure out what it was and since Elise rose to her feet I did the same.

We both downed one more shot for an extra boost of energy, and staggered towards the dance floor, hands held tightly to stabilize each other.

We were amused and in high spirits, but I had no idea why. And it absolutely didn't fucking matter.

XANDER

"*J dx what song Dann screamin cglo=bb? A few yearsss time*"

I was in the midst of a conference call when the text message arrived, and for the longest time I could only stare at it, absolutely confused.

What?

I couldn't help but feel alarmed. *Was she alright?* I should have checked on her after she left. I just didn't want to be the one to put in all the work.

"Sir?" I heard the sudden call, and looked up at the screen of four executives. I had absolutely no clue as to what I had missed them say.

And for a moment I almost didn't care. "Just a second," I said, and reread the message hoping to somehow understand or figure out what it was about.

It had to be something serious or she wouldn't have contacted me at all I was certain.

I lifted my gaze for a moment to think, but was unable to figure it out, so I put the phone aside with a sigh.

"Please carry on," I said, and the meeting resumed. However what was discussed only registered for a few seconds, before my mind was once again wandering off, trying to decipher what Olivia's text message had meant.

And then it hit me.

Was she drunk texting me?

Once again, I was alarmed so I picked up my phone to confirm. Did she not have anyone with her? Was she safe?

I couldn't help but recall how extremely vulnerable she became when intoxicated, and as a result I cursed under my breath.

My chest tightened anxiously as I quickly began to type out a response to her.

"What is this?" I asked, and set it down so I could return my focus to the call.

About five minutes later, I was tapping my foot against the floor.

I thought about calling, but if she picked up, I didn't have much to say. I didn't even need to clarify what the message was about. I just needed to know that she was okay.

However I had to wait until the meeting was over, and we still had about eight minutes to go.

Needless to say it felt like the most excruciating eight minutes I had to wait in as long as I could remember. I rose up the moment they wrapped up, turned my screen off, and headed towards the windows behind me. The city's night-time skyline was lit beautifully, but I barely took note of it even though it was right before my eyes. Her phone soon began to ring, however there was no answer.

I tried again... and again and again and still there was no response. I was certain then that she was at a club, and most definitely wouldn't hear it unless the phone was on her. But it should have been on her. I couldn't help but feel annoyed. Why the fuck wasn't it on her?

At the sudden surge of my temper, I forced myself to regain my calm and took deep soothing breaths. They helped, and soon enough I was able to talk myself into believing it was none of my business and she was fine. So I returned back to my seat and continued catching up with all the work I had to handle before the midnight hour so I could finally head home.

I succeeded, and soon enough my focus had returned back to my work. About twenty-five minutes later however, a call from her arrived.

I stared at it, unable to decide whether to respond to it or not. I was nervous, but didn't realize so until she called back again and my heart jumped into my throat.

I answered it and just listened before answering, "Hello?"

It was made clear to me I had been right, and she was definitely at a club of some sort. Now this was one clue to her cryptic message, but then what about the rest? The mention of Danny? And screaming?

"Are you there?" she asked, and I could barely hear her.

I cleared my throat. "Are you okay?"

She went silent, and once again all I could hear was the noise from the background. It was a bit quieter now I realized, so I presumed this meant she had headed to a less noisy place. This also meant that perhaps she was sober?

"You're an asshole," she said, her voice quiet, and I was so taken aback that for the first few seconds I had absolutely no idea what to say.

"Excuse me?"

"You heard me," she said, but it didn't sound like Olivia.

"You are a fucking asshole."

"Olivia… let me… I just… he's-"

I listened to the scuffle, and relaxed. My hand slid into my pocket to wait, as I listened carefully to what I could make out of all that was happening.

"Stop," I heard her say, exasperated and then her voice was clear once again.

I waited and listened.

"Are you there? Xander!" she said and I could finally hear the slight slur of her voice. I couldn't hold back my smile.

"Are you alright?" I repeated, and could only hope that my amusement was undetectable.

She heaved a sigh.

"Come pick me up," she said. "Now. I'm downtown. At Sinkhole. "

Once again I was stumped.

"And why should I do that?" I asked, my gaze looking out and now clearly seeing the lit skyline, although I could also clearly see her face in my mind.

She went quiet, and after a few seconds I had to check to make sure the line was still connected. It was.

"Xander, I'm waiting for you," she said and then the call came to an end.

I held the phone against my ear, and wondered how to respond, however I couldn't make up my mind. So I lowered my hand, and then stared up ahead at the night sky filled with stars.

The question was could I just ignore the demand? I didn't want to take advantage of her tipsy state and I didn't want her to have regrets in the morning. But tipsy Olivia was a fun one. Not that I had seen her tipsy all that often.

And just like that... the memories once again came pouring in.

OLIVIA

"I don't think he's going to come," Elise said behind me, and in her tone I could tell just how drowsy she was.

I felt bad she was out here... however my legs had thus far been unable to move from this very spot.

I didn't want her to be out here with me, waiting, but she had refused to leave, perhaps ready to rescue me in case I crumbled and broke down because he didn't come like she was sure he wouldn't.

I, on the other hand, wasn't sure what I was expecting. At the time I had placed the call to him, I was barely coherent, but then afterwards and at Elise's shocked look at me, I'd quickly regained my senses, like a bucket of cold water had been splashed on me. However I had refused to back down like she had suggested. To call him back and apologize, or at least send the message it had been a drunk call that he could ignore.

I was pretty sure he had figured that out, and I couldn't wait to see how he would react. But as the time ticked past, my heart was beginning to sink so low into the ground I wondered if I would ever be able to recover it. All around us there were other drunk party goers, or perhaps those who were waiting or just hanging around.

"Do you at least want to sit down?" she asked, and I turned to look at her perch on a flower bed. Her tone was drowsy, and her head sunken down, and I couldn't help but feel even worse as I looked around at the passing cars, wondering if he would truly come. I'd had no doubt I realized now at first that he would, even in my semi-sober state because he'd always shown up. *Always...* but this I guess was the clear reminder once again this wasn't the past.

I pulled my phone out to check the time, and could see thus far it had been about forty five minutes since I had spoken to him. We were currently downtown which was in the location of his office, so he should have been here within at least fifteen minutes. I sighed then, and turned around, slightly wobbly on my feet even though all I had on were comfortable flats. I was sober now... the cool evening wind and the pain of his rejection ensured this, so I was able to clear headedly go back to Elise.

"Let's go in," I said, and grabbed her arms to pull her up but she was too drowsy.

"I'm too old for this," she whined and I smiled. "You're only twenty-seven Elise."

"And you're a fetus," she mumbled. "So why are you tired?"

"I'm not tired," I said out loud, but said the truth to myself. *I'm heartbroken.*

"Hey!" I suddenly heard male voices, and looked up to see Derek and his cousin make their way through a loud group laughing and crowding the entrance.

"You both disappeared," Jack said, while Derek immediately headed over to his girlfriend. "Is she alright?"

"She is," I replied, and was happy when he was able to guide her to her feet so she could fall into his arms. "Alright time to go home," he said and his cousin came up to me.

"What were you two doing out here?" I looked at him, and for a moment wondered what to say.

I turned once again towards the road to look at the passing cars, and allow myself to hold onto hope for just a minute longer.

I glanced at my screen, and then turned around to watch as Derek began to guide his girlfriend back into the club with him.

"Ready to go in?" Jack asked, and I once again glanced behind him.

"Yeah," I replied. "I'm also ready to go home."

"So are we all," he said "I think Derekjust wants to use the bathroom first."

With a smile, I told myself to take a look at him. A good look because just maybe, he was the better alternative to Xander.

However the very idea of being emotionally involved made me so queasy, that I concluded the better alternative was to just be alone. So I turned and began to head back in.

Suddenly though there was a call to my phone, and I picked up as I tried to find my way through the group that was still noisily crowding the entrance.

The voice sounded immensely unfamiliar, so I immediately rejected it.

"Wrong number," I said, and brought the call to an end.

I soon returned inside with them, but the phone began to ring again.

I considered switching it off but then it occurred to me that perhaps... my heart leapt into my throat.

I stopped and answered it

"Miss Rose?" the caller said.

"Yeah?"

"I'm here to pick you up."

My heart nearly stopped in my chest.

"Did um... did Xander send you?" I asked.

His response came immediately. "Yes, Mr. King did. He told me to take you home."

"Thanks," I replied, but then I didn't know what to do.

"Where do you want me to wait for you?" he asked. "I'm out front."

My gaze lifted to my companions. "I'll call you back," I told him and ended the call.

"How are you all getting home?" I asked.

"I'll go with Derek," Elise said, lounging on a seat.

"I can take you," Jack said, and my gaze settled on his.

"Um, a car's here to pick me up. So I was wondering if any of you would need a ride."

"What about your car?" Elise asked.

"We came in an Uber," I reminded her.

"Oh yeah. Alright you can leave. See you next week."

I smiled at her cute exhausted tone.

"Wait, what? A car came to pick you up?"

"Bye," I gave her a knowing look as I grabbed my purse, waved to the others and was on my way.

After exiting the club, I found the driver who had arrived in a tinted town car, and after a quick greeting I was settled in the back seat.

He immediately started to drive without even asking me where we were headed, so I assumed Xander had informed him of my address.

However home was the last place I wanted to return to.

"Where's Mr. King?" I asked, and the chauffeur met my gaze through the rearview mirror.

"I don't know ma'am," he replied and I sighed.

I thought of calling him once again, to inquire but then I currently felt all sorts of confused about him and the way he was responding to me. For instance, rather than send a driver to me if he truly felt concerned, why didn't he come himself like I had asked him to?

Did he care about me or was this just out of some offhand moral obligation?

Unable to stomach these unanswered questions plaguing me, I picked up my phone and dialed his number.

"Do you mind if I roll the windows down?" I asked the chauffeur.

"Not at all ma'am," he said and I did so, needing the breeze to completely clear out my head. I was thirsty, I realized. Extremely.

"Hello?" his voice came over the receiver, and my breathing hitched in thy throat.

I swallowed. "Where are you?"

"Hasn't the car I sent to you arrived?"

I sighed. "It has," I replied. "He was told to take me home."

"Hmhmm"

"I didn't ask to be taken home. I asked you to come get me."

"And? I figured you just needed a ride home."

I scoffed. "Really? Well, I wanted you not the ride." Nothing quite like being full of liquid courage to spell this out for him.

At this he went quiet.

"Where are you?"

"I'm at work," he replied. "I have a lot to handle tonight."

"M'hay," I said to him and then ended the call.

Afterwards my gaze met the chauffeur's through the mirror. "You know Mr. King's office right?" I asked, and he nodded. "Please take me there."

He however seemed reluctant.

"You can call him if you wish," I said. "To confirm. Or you can just drop me off here and I'll find my way there myself."

XANDER

For the third time in the same night, she had me stumped and my phone left against my ear. Before I could lower my hand though another call came in and I didn't need to check to know who it was from.

"Sir," James's uncertain voice came through the receiver.

"Bring her over," I said.

"Yes sir."

The call was disconnected and I laid my phone down on my desk.

I was yet to resolve my internal conflicts about her. Regardless, I had to admit I couldn't wait to see her. It had been almost two weeks and in that time, not an hour had passed without me thinking about her.

However, a new merger with a hardware manufacturing company had kept me occupied and my impulses curbed, otherwise I had no doubt I would have sought her out.

Once again I found myself rising to my feet and heading towards the windows, and there, unexpectedly, I remained until the office intercom telephone rang.

I turned around to gaze at it with a sigh.

It was now past 9 PM, so the receptionists on my floor had left for the day, therefore I was certain the call was the security on the ground floor requesting my permission to let her in.

I returned back to my desk and gave the instruction for her to be escorted up, and then I sat back down and tried to get a bit more work in before she arrived.

Soon enough there was a knock to the door and my heart rate spiked.

"Come in," I said, and the door was pushed open.

I looked up, eager to watch her arrival, also somewhat concerned as to her state. She had sounded intoxicated on the phone at one point, and then clear headed in the next and I was unable to figure out which was currently the case.

I instantly met her gaze and watched her intently, till I was able to conclude her eyes were clear. She also moved quite stably so there didn't seem to be any cause for concern.

She was dressed in a skirt, high-waisted, riding past her knee and a matching blouse in the same checkered pattern. On her feet were the same thick heeled shoes I'd seen on her multiple times now, comfortable and stylish.

I admired how perfectly they adorned her small feet, and couldn't help wondering if they were the same size. In the past I'd gotten her at least three pairs of sneakers at varying times as they had been her go-to footwear of comfort. She could be stylish when she wanted to, but had always put the effort more into her outfit than her feet. I also remembered we used to joke that my present to her, if we ever got married, would be a pair of white sneakers she could change into at the reception for when her feet got tired from wearing heels around.

She'd responded with an attempt for me to get her the Converses back then so she could break them in ahead of time, rather than wait until we got married. I'd been amused at the time, and had truly intended to gift them to her at one celebratory occasion or the other but then our relationship had come to a screeching halt before I'd ever gotten the chance to fulfill this.

"I'm hungry," she said, forcing my gaze to lift up to hers. "Did you eat dinner yet?"

I sighed. "No, but I have a lot of work to get done. It's best if you went home."

At this she scoffed. "You have to eat."

"I'm not hungry." I replied, and she began to walk towards me, boldly… assured.

"For anything?" She almost purred.

"What do you think?" I asked and she smiled.

"I won't stay long," she said as she finally arrived before me.

We stared at each other and then couldn't help our smiles.

"What are you doing?" I asked, and she sent the question back to me. "What are you doing?"

"I'm working."

"Well…" she began but stopped.

"Well what?" I asked.

"I want to have sex with you, and then I'll leave."

I watched her, gave it a long thought, and then pushed away from my desk. "Alright."

Her eyes remained on mine, and I couldn't wait to see how she was going to maneuver her way into getting things done.

"Why do you keep making things difficult for me?" she asked, and my smile widened even further.

She released a deep breath, and grabbed the head of my chair in an attempt to turn it around, however I held onto her wrist and stopped her.

"Xander," she called, but I ignored her until suddenly she was lowering to duck under my arm.

"What the-"

She got stuck and thus my arm was pushed away, sending my mouse across the desk. Grabbing onto the handle of the chair she worked her way onto my lap and sent us both rolling backwards.

"Olivia!" I called out, amused as I tried to grab onto the edge of the desk to keep us both anchored. Soon she was on my lap and trying to settle in as much as she could.

"You're so fucking aggravating Xander," she said, and I couldn't help my amusement. However when she turned around to meet my gaze the smile disappeared from her face.

"What now?" I asked, and her gaze roved across my face. I had always automatically held my breath in the past when she did that, because it had always made me wonder what she saw and thought. Now, I realized I still cared to know this.

She leaned in then and my breathing stuttered. I got the whiff of alcohol on her which made me suspect perhaps she was still somewhat intoxicated. Maybe this was why she was acting the way she-

Her lips connected with mine and my eyes automatically slid shut. I was hesitant, but that soon melted away to the soft touch.

I was able to taste her but only slightly, and then she pulled away her eyes boring into mine. I wanted to lean forward once again, but I held myself back. Waiting until she did whatever she wanted, however all she did was watch me.

"How much did you drink?" I asked.

"Enough," she said "You weren't there."

"Was I supposed to be?" I asked and her gaze on me softened.

"I wanted you to be." She glared at me, and then leaned forward once again to kiss me. This time, I deepened it and for the next few seconds after, I lost cognizance of all else beyond the warmth and sweetness of her.

She tried to pull away once again but I stopped her, against my better judgement. My hand curved around her neck and my head was slanting to slide my tongue even deeper along hers.

She tasted like heaven.

Eventually though her slight struggle to pull away registered, as well as the hand around my wrist so I stopped and opened my eyes. My breathing was now labored and so was hers. We gazed at each other.

"Get up," I said, and she frowned. I felt my heart shift with contrition at the hurt in her eyes.

"You're fucking mean," she said, twisting slightly sideways on my lap and then cradling the side of my face so she could kiss me even harder. My chair began to roll away at the force, so my arms automatically went around her to keep us both in place.

I loved the sound of her moan, and then the feel of her fingers as they slid into my hair. I was content to continue this forever but then once again she was pulling away and I couldn't help my groan.

She laughed softly, especially as my lips latched on to her bottom lip refusing to let go.

She pulled her eyes open and up close I couldn't miss the sparkle in them.

How I loved her, I couldn't help but think, however the warmth was quickly followed by an equally poignant ache. She leaned slightly away and I held onto her so she wouldn't fall. And then her blouse was coming off. She pulled it over her head and my gaze couldn't help but lower to her full breasts, encased in a lacy white bra.

I swallowed, my larynx bobbing up and down my throat, and then her hand was curving around the back of my head once again. I loved the feel of her fingers as they slid into my hair, and couldn't help but do the same as I returned the kiss.

Unable to stop myself now from taking things even further, I began to kiss down her chin, eager to taste her skin. Her neck arched backwards in response, her moan breathless and the effect made me slightly woozy. In no time my hand was grabbing one of her breasts but my lips couldn't reach the full mounds easily until she lifted her arm and then I was pulling the lace down to suck onto the sides.

"Xander," she breathed, her frame once again collapsing onto mine. She turned even further towards me and then my lips were sucking on one of her nipples.

I couldn't get enough of her. She buried her face in my hair, and then was once again leaning downward to seek out my lips.

I rolled even further backwards so that she could rise, and then her skirt was being pulled up her thighs. In no time I'd rolled her panties down her legs, and the scrap of material was flung away. She turned towards me, her gaze heavy with lust and longing.

"Can we do this here?" I asked.

"Of course," I replied.

"Surveillance?"

"Not a problem."

With a beautiful smile on her face, she lowered to her knees and began to unbuckle my belt. I could do nothing but watch her. Her hair was down framing her face so as she leaned forward it obstructed my gaze and I couldn't bear it so I pulled it back into one hand so I could watch her.

"Do you have a hair tie," I asked, and her eyes lifted up to mine.

"Why?" she asked as she began to pull my zip down with what appeared to be only one thing on her mind. She leaned down and took the head of my cock in her mouth.

"*Ah*," my breathing shuddered, strength rapidly seeping out of my body. She sucked hard on the head, and pleasure coursed through my veins like liquid fire.

My eyes came open once again to see her lips wrapped around the head and glistening wet. I didn't need to ask for what I wanted any more so I leaned forward and then began to arrange her hair into a quick braid.

Her mouth bobbed up and down the length of my dick, but soon she realized what was happening and stopped, a smile spreading across her lips.

"You still remember how to do that?" she asked, however I was too turned on to respond. She leaned forward then to kiss me and my light grip on her hair was pulled away, nearly untangling all of my work.

"Livvy," I groaned, but the taste of her temporarily halted all further complaints from my lips.

"Why do you want a hair tie?" she asked again, and all I could do was stare at her for a moment.

"You want to see my face that badly?" she asked and I frowned.

"Your hair's in the way." A greedy smile curved her lips.

I could never get enough of looking at her especially in this state of being so intimate and exposed before me.

She kept smiling and then leaned away to reach into the pocket of her skirt. In no time a hair tie was retrieved and her hair secured in a ponytail, then she reached behind to unsnap her bra and her breasts were spilling out before me, full and weighty.

"Get up," I said to her, and she did as instructed. I turned her around and then palmed her slit with my fingers digging into the wetness of her folds. She writhed against me, restless and as my fingers slid into her, a small cry escaping her lips.

I sucked onto the skin of her back as I began to thrust in and out of her, my hand curving around her waist to keep her in place.

"*Xander*," she moaned out my name, her hand reaching out as she began to lower back down to slide down the girth of my cock.

So I pulled my fingers out, palmed her one more time and then clutched onto her waist to lower her onto me.

She teased the head of my dick through her slickness, and then I was impaled into her.

My head fell backwards as her warmth and tightness engulfed me, and for a few seconds all I could do was feel. Being this intimately joined with her felt like heaven. It soothed my soul to depths thus far I didn't think anything or anyone else had been able to reach.

"I want to move," she rasped out and I obliged, releasing my hold from around her. My hand flattened against her back and then her hips were grinding against me.

I shut my eyes, my vision flashing and my blood beginning to boil as her walls grated the satiny smoothness of my dick.

She set the pace, rocking solely into me at first, and then she grabbed onto the edge of the desk to get her pace up. The way she rode me was fervent... insistent, and so passionate I couldn't help but grab onto her once again needing to bury my face in her neck.

"*Fuck*," I breathed, and only then did it register just how loudly our panting was filling the office.

"Turn around," I said to her. "I want to see you," and once again I felt her smile.

She did as I asked, turning to settle astride me. I grabbed her ponytail and pulled, arching her neck back so I could lick up the slender column of her neck.

"Fucking perfect," I whispered over her lips.

Our fucking resumed, with her grinding her hips into mine over and over again.

XANDER

The rhythmic sounds of flesh slapping against each other, our gasps and breathy moans were the dominant sounds in the room and they registered to my ears as music.

It didn't take long or much for that matter, to push me over the edge. I attributed this to my exhaustion for the day, however I just couldn't hold back my feelings or need for her, and I felt this immense connection... this intimate joining of her body with mine to the core of my heart.

Seemingly sensing this, she fucked into me even harder and soon enough, even she was quaking all over.

"Xander," she cried out my name as I released into her. Her head fell onto my shoulders while her arms around me tightened even further, holding on for dear life. I felt the rush of her release as it spilled out onto my groin, and soon enough, we were both wrapped desperately in the other's embrace.

I didn't want to let her go, and neither did she seem willing to let me go either, so we remained in place, basking in each other's scent and warmth.

Eventually though, I completely regained my senses and shifted. That was all it took for her to also regain hers, and soon enough she was lifting off me. I watched as my dick slid out of her sex, and felt the painful strike of pleasure to my core at the wet and intimate sight.

"Do you have a bathroom?" she asked, and I rose to my feet along with her.

"It'll stain," she said, however I didn't care. I buttoned my trousers, pulled her skirt down just over her hips and then taking her hand in mine, brought her with me to wash up.

In the bathroom and before I could stop myself, I lifted her by the waist onto the counter.

She watched, and I wasn't quite able to meet her eyes. I simply focused on retrieving some paper towels, and wetting them with some warm water.

"I can do it myself," she said, but I didn't respond.

This was an ingrained habit I had cultivated over the years in my dealings with her. Whenever we were done with making love, it was a joy of mine to clean her up and then to kiss her. She watched me, and once again I didn't meet her eyes.

Soon I moved to the sink to rinse the towels. Then I unbuttoned my pants and also took care of myself and I turned to glance at her as I dumped the paper towels into the trash.

We were soon decent and I took her hand to lead her out of the bathroom and take her back to my office.

I released her hand when we were passing the lounge in my office and I returned to my chair, hoping to still finish a bit of work before I left.

"I'm still hungry," she said, and I couldn't help but smile.

"Can you order something in for me?"

I lifted my gaze to look at her. "Can't you do it yourself?"

"Well, I don't know what services are delivered here," she said. "This is your territory."

I gazed at her and truly, my heart fluttered, I knew I was falling more in love with her and getting so used to her presence I never wanted her to leave.

I lowered my gaze down to my screen, however she soon sought my attention again with a tap against the desk.

"Food," she said, and I sighed. "I don't usually make the orders," I said and her mouth opened in an 'oh'.

"Right, that's true. You're the boss here. But I'm sure we can figure it out."

She reached forward to grab her phone from her purse, and then she was coming around the desk towards me.

I tried to return my focus to the budget report I had been perusing through before she had come over, however and suddenly she was lifting herself onto my desk making it near impossible for me to concentrate. I tried my best to ignore her despite how difficult it was, and since she didn't speak I was beginning to accept that perhaps I would be able to get some work done, however she suddenly uncrossed her legs and then rested her feet on my crotch.

My gaze first went towards her feet, and then back to her, however her attention was still on her phone. The act was something mindless I could recall she had done countless times in the past. The both of us would be spending some quiet time in each other's presence, and her legs would rest on my lap. It had been the same for me towards her, and at this recollection, I couldn't help but smile.

I leaned into the chair then and gazed up at her.

She finally looked up, and then she offered her phone to me. Her feet pressed on ever so slightly against my already hardening dick, and the moment she noticed the effect, her eyebrows slightly raised.

"Oh," she blushed. "Order something in for me and maybe we can go for another round while we wait for it to get here."

At the proposition, I shook my head with a smile on my lips and reached for my own phone on the desk.

"I'll make the order," I said and opened the app.

His office was dimly lit.

It was such a sharp contrast to how bright it had been the last time I'd been here, but I wasn't surprised either. He'd always been able to concentrate best at night, and in dimly lit areas. And besides, it made it even easier to appreciate the magnificent downtown skyline behind him.

However I found I barely noticed it because I couldn't look away from him.

He was so handsome I could barely breathe, despite the fact I'd known him for so long, I couldn't get over how he seemed to only be aging like fine wine.

His hair was also slightly tousled from my hand running through it earlier, although I was certain he had tried to put it in order. I couldn't help but lean forward to try to smooth my hand through it, but automatically he leaned away and thus my hand was left hanging in midair.

"What are you doing?" he asked, and I smiled.

"Your hair," I said. "It's messy."

He frowned and looked back at his computer. I took the hint then and jumped off his desk.

"I'll wait for my food on the couch." I said.

And with that, I got down from his desk. He straightened to get back to work, but just as I rounded his chair, my arm curved around his shoulder, and before he could stop me I was pressing a kiss against his cheek.

I truly didn't mean to be a bother, but I couldn't resist it. He turned towards me, eyes heated. My heart skipped several beats at the close proximity of our eyes, to the extent our lashes could have touched. His gaze lowered to my lips then and I took it as the needed push to once again kiss him. My lips coaxed his opened, and in seconds the sweetest of warmth was coursing through my veins.

His hand curved around the side of my neck, and he deepened the kiss and thus it went on and on until eventually he came to his senses.

He broke it off with a soft smack, and once again our eyes came open to meet each other's. I couldn't breathe.

"Couch," he groaned, and I couldn't help but smile. I tried my best to hide it however and straightened.

"Yes sir," I replied and headed over to the lounge area of his office.

I felt quite pleased with myself because more than anything, I'd somewhat forgotten the effect that I could have on him when the constraint of time wasn't present, and we weren't at each other's throats.

I settled onto one of the couches, but could still feel the burn of his gaze on me. I wanted to look behind but resisted, until I'd picked up the remote to his television and found a reason to. I couldn't believe how comfortable I felt, and almost even entitled to his space, and for a moment I began to wonder if this was because I'd been somewhat intoxicated earlier in the night. There was no doubt I had been since I regained my senses, but a part of me still wondered if I was still drunk. Otherwise, I should have been quite nervous or hesitating in encroaching this much into his time and space.

I turned around just in time, and just as I had suspected met him watching me. His gaze was intense, the look in his eyes the exact kind that always caused a burn in my chest. In moments like this it felt as though his aim was to figure me out, and in the past it had flattered me so much that he'd been as intense as this even when I wasn't even watching.

I cleared my throat, and tried to remember why I'd even turned to him in the first place.

"I'm going to turn the TV on but I'll put it on mute so that it doesn't distract you. Okay?"

He watched me for a few more seconds, and then he looked away, returning his attention to his computer screen. I switched the channels, but couldn't exactly find something I could be engaged in enough but also wouldn't have any headlines so as not to distract him. Eventually, all I could settle on was the cartoon channel. This was suitable enough for me, so I moved towards the head of the couch and stretched out on it. I was exhausted, I realized as my eyes grew heavy, I tried my very best not to succumb and fall asleep, but being in his presence absolutely felt like home.

XANDER

I realized she had fallen asleep after her phone began to ring and she didn't budge.

She'd left it on my desk, and I was forced to rise to my feet and go around the table just so I could picl it up.

I leaned against the desk when I saw it was Elise, and debated going over to hand it to her. Eventually I did, but met her curled up in the fetal position on the leather couch, and couldn't bring myself to wake her up so I lowered my tone and answered it.

"Are you home yet?" A woman's voice came through the receiver, along with the rush of water in the background.

"Hello," I replied and she instantly went quiet.

"This is Xander King," I introduced myself.

"Ah," she said. "Right. Olivia's with you right?"

"Yes she is," I replied. "She fell asleep."

"Ah, got it. I'm aware she was coming to you. I hope she's feeling better."

I gazed across the room at the peacefully sleeping woman. "She is," I replied. "I have her."

"Alright," she said. "Please tell her I called and I got home safely as well."

"Sure," I replied, and was about to end the call when she spoke again.

"I'm her coworker at the school."

I'd figured as much.

"Okay," I replied, and the call came to an end. I was about to head over to her when my phone began to ring. I saw from across the table it was the meal I'd ordered for her. I went around the desk to answer it. Afterwards, I headed over to the lounge area and couldn't help but watch her sleep.

I looked at the cartoon she had settled on and it amused me. It was so typical of her and it felt like I'd known her all of my life.

A knock sounded on the door then, and with a sigh, I turned around to answer it.

Soon enough I had her meal in hand, and thought of waking her up so she could eat it. But then I thought of a better idea.

It didn't take much to wake her. In the past, I would wake her with a kiss but this time around, I lowered to my knee and settled on just brushing my finger gently across her lashes. It tickled and before long, her eyes were fluttering open.

It took her a few seconds to come to, and then I watched as recognition struck.

A soft smile curved her lips in response, but it almost immediately disappeared when it truly registered that I was right before her. She got up then, almost startled and thankfully, I rose to my feet just before she could knock her head against the underside of my chin.

I watched as she brushed her tousled hair out of her face. "What-um.. is.. i-s it here?"

I tried my best to control my smile.

"Your food is here," I said, and started to walk away. I returned back to my desk simply so I could watch her as she regained her wits and decided on her next course of action.

When I settled back in, I found however she was still slightly disoriented. "The food?" she asked. "And my phone?"

"All here," I replied, and she somewhat wobbled over.

I hid my smile behind the screen, and watched as she began to retrieve her belongings.

"I'll leave now," she said. "What about you?"

"In a bit," I answered, and she went quiet for a few seconds.

"Don't you need to eat?"

I looked at her. I gave it some thought and nodded my head, and decided it was time to call it a night.

Once again I rose to my feet. "I'll take you home. Get your things."

OLIVIA

"**D**o you want to come in?" I asked, and lifted my take out bag. "We can share, or I can make you something to eat." I asked as we arrived at my door.

He watched me intensely as I turned around to unlock my door.

I did it quickly and headed in first, then I turned around to hold the door open for him.

He walked in and I shut the door behind us. Then I headed straight to the kitchen to take out our food, and was glad I'd ordered the extra-large rice bowl. There would be just enough for the two of us as I usually kept half of it anyway to warm up the following day.

We ate at my counter, quietly and it was… pleasant.

I knew he was exhausted from the strain in the corners of his eyes, and although he didn't show it outwardly, I hoped I could soothe him.

The plausible route now was to put him to sleep, preferably with me, but I had no clue as to how this would happen.

Soon enough, he was done with the bowl and got off the stool.

My heart lurched, not ready for the night to end.

"Do you want some wine?" I asked, and he shook his head. I watched as he took the plate to the sink, and began to wash it.

My stomach warmed instantly as I realized he hadn't changed one bit.

"I'm driving, remember?" he said, and I rose up to my feet. I headed towards him and stood by his side, much to his surprise.

"Why don't you spend the night? I asked. "It's already so late."

He turned and watched me, the tap still running.

A long moment of silence followed, and then he shook his head, amused.

"Alright," he agreed, and I couldn't believe it.

After dinner, he asked for the bathroom so he could take a shower and I left him to it.

Then I decided after clubbing I needed a shower too. The thought of showering with him again greatly appealed to me so I went into the bedroom to follow him into the shower.

I looked around and saw that he had draped his clothes over the chair across the room.

Quickly, I took my own clothes off and realized we had left my underwear back at his office. Flung off and abandoned somewhere on the floor. It was tragic, but so amusing it took a little while to bring myself under control as I headed into the bathroom to clean up with him.

The steam was already coming out the top of the shower and I slowly peeled the curtain to peek inside. He was facing me with his head thrown back under the spray.

My mouth went dry as I watched his biceps bulge as he rinsed his hair. I let my eyes stray down his muscled chest to his tight abs to his hard cock resting against his belly button.

That was all it took for me to climb in and instantly fall to my knees to worship him. His thighs flexed and I steadied myself against him and licked up the vein of his shaft. When I reached the tip I slid my tongue around his head and looked up to see his heated eyes.

He reached up and redirected the spray and held my gaze as I took him into my mouth. His hands moved to hold my hair back and fisted it in a ponytail at the back of my head.

"Fuck Livvy," his groan spurring me on.

I cupped his sack and rolled his balls around my fingers while hollowing my cheeks and sucking his length to the back of my throat. I swallowed a few times and then slowly rose off and let him leave my mouth with a pop.

"I love the taste of your cock in my mouth," I moaned up at him.

He leaned down and pulled me up, turning me and my hands slapped against the tiles.

His fingers instantly found my slit and he slipped one in and started pumping into me.

"So wet... so ready for me," he growled in my ear.

"Yes... please, fuck me... I need you," the pleas dripped from my lips.

He didn't make me wait and removed his finger to slide his hands around my waist and then his dick was probing at my entrance.

I stood on tiptoes and widened my stance pushing back against him.

He entered my in one quick trust. His hips slapped against my ass and I moaned my need.

"Harder!" I commanded.

He didn't disappoint and started to piston into me. My pussy grasping and clenching, begging for more and more.

I rested my head against the cool tiles and reached down to toy with my clit.

I screamed as the orgasm ran through my whole body and Xander had to hold me up as my legs gave out under me.

He turned the water off and climbed with me out of the shower depositing me on the counter and sliding back into me.

My head fell back against the mirror and I was panting, unable to catch my breath.

"Look at me," he demanded and I pried them open to stare into his heated icy blue eyes.

"Xander," his name left my lips like a montra.

When his finger circled my clit with increasing pressure I felt myself clench his cock rhythmically as another orgasm ran through me. I felt his whole body tense as he lost his battle of control and I could feel the warmth of his cum hitting the deepest parts of me.

He pulled me into his arms and I laid with my ear pressed to his chest. Listening to the thumping of his heart.

When our breathing steadied he pulled away and used a towel to dry me and then himself. He threw the towel to the floor and then slid his hands under my thighs, picking me up.

I yelped and threw my hands around him and nuzzled into his neck.

He walked into the bedroom and threw me onto the bed. As I bounced I looked up to see the gleam in his eye as he chuckled and climbed into bed next to me.

With a sigh, I settled on my side, turning my face away from his and trying my best to rein in my excitement that the love of my life was going to be lying down next to me tonight.

It had happened several times in the past, but there was something especially wonderful about tonight.

I felt movement by my side and held my breath. I felt him come up close to me and then his arm was sliding around my waist. He pulled me closer towards him and I let him. He then buried his face in the crook of my neck and breathed me in.

"God, I love you so much it actually hurts." he moaned into my neck.

"Good," I whispered.

He laughed. "Aren't you supposed to say it back?"

"I love you, Xander King. So fucking much it hurts."

XANDER

Once again, I woke up to her.

It wasn't the first time and I doubted it would be the last, but something was different.

In previous times, it was simply because we'd both been too exhausted after fucking our brains out to move away from the other. However after I'd woken up the morning after, I'd always lingered, to watch her as she slept peacefully.

In such a state, she looked so soft and vulnerable the urge from our past together to protect her with all I had always returned.

But then I'd recall what she did, and my heart would crack open, sending me away from her once again, and unable to bear her presence.

This time around however, things had indeed changed because she had explained her cheating on me had been a lie. It hadn't exactly healed my wounds, but I now realized it had weakened the walls I'd earlier erected against her. And with our admission of love last night those walls were completely broken.

I couldn't bring myself to move away from her just yet. I just couldn't find a reason even with the sun high in the sky. There didn't seem to be anything more important than lying here with her wrapped in my arms.

About half an hour later, she too began to stir. I was hard, painfully so and it'd been steadily intensifying ever since I'd awakened to find her bare ass nestled against my groin.

She moved again, and the immediate jolt of pleasure straight to my core pulled a gasp out of me. She shifted again, as though she was trying to find a more comfortable position but I couldn't help but wonder if perhaps she was wide awake, aware of my presence just as I was of hers, and now intent on provoking me.

I didn't speak. There was no need to. Instead I moved my hand from around her waist and slipped it between her thighs. I wasn't surprised to see just how wet she was, and I also wasn't surprised to hear the little gasp that escaped her lips. I should have known.

I began with her clit, stroking against the bud and then slipped my finger into her heat. One leg raised slightly to give me deeper access, and soon my second finger joined in the sweet assault. She pushed her ass even further towards me, so I pulled my hand out and then palmed her from the front. I felt her hand close around my wrist, but didn't relent. Instead I resumed spreading the slickness all over, and then the pad of my middle finger was once again circling her clit.

"Xander," she breathed hard, over and over again and I wanted to look into her eyes. I began by kissing her neck, nibbling on her ear lobes and then placing the softest of kisses on her temple.

Our gazes connected just as her hand curved around the back of my neck, eager in her search for my lips.

And I obliged.

We kissed, sweetly and deeply and softly, and as the minutes ticked by so did the intensity of my fingers thrusting into her. Soon, neither of us could bear the sweet torment so I pulled my fingers out of her and slicked her wetness all over my dick.

"Fuck," she parted her legs even further, allowing me complete and absolute access to her. It made me quiver.

As the thick head of my cock began to push into her heat I paused.

"Say it," I need to hear those sweet words from her lips again.

"I fucking love you Xander." and I thrust until I had her tightly wrapped around me like a glove. I held on tightly, and fucked into her, relishing the sweet melody of her moans as they filled the room.

Waking up this way was a dream I'd had no choice but to recall during the years we'd been apart.

With the quick, brief relationships that had occurred after her, I'd never ran into anyone I'd wanted to wake up to in this way. Early morning love making, Olivia had long shown me was laced with love and fondness and intimacy, and I'd never been one to simply linger around the moment I'd found a stranger was in my bed.

But this was no stranger to me, and as her cries and whimpers rang softly in my ears, my motions slowed, thrusting even more deeply inside of her.

We twisted and ground together, my hand flattening against the base of her stomach to hold her in place as well as guide her hips.

Soon she was flat on her back and I was fucking even harder into her, the bed creaking from the intense exertion. She cried out my name over and over, her face buried into my shoulders until my release exploded into her.

I felt the fervent clenching of her walls around my cock, milking me relentlessly even as her release trickled down the space between our joining. Eventually I leaned away and began to pull out, needing to relax enough to catch my breath and the messy sight kept my blood boiling even further.

She followed me as I collapsed back onto the bed, and draped her body completely over mine.

"I love you Olivia Rose," I professed as I held onto her as we both recovered, until once again and to my amusement, I found she had drifted back into a soft, and sweet sleep.

I however couldn't go back to bed because as all of the euphoric sexual haze cleared out of my mind I remembered a team would be gathering at the office to finish up with the merger report we'd not been able to complete the previous day.

I had been side tracked by the gorgeous woman in my arms, so I needed to examine a few reports beforehand so my grasp of the situation for the call later that afternoon would be adequate. Therefore I needed to get up and get going.

It took a little more effort, but eventually, I found the strength and was soon back on my own two feet.

I'd tried to be gentle, but I was certain my movements had jolted her awake once again, since after all, her sleep had been light.

I felt guilty about this, and as I headed over to the bathroom to get cleaned up, I considered taking a warm cloth with me to her. But I decided to let her rest a bit further with my release both inside and all over her hole pulsing, and still greedy and eager.

Afterwards, I headed to the kitchen. I could've just simply left but once again, I wanted to see her before I left.

I busied myself with searching, and soon found the little jars where she kept her beverages. The following few minutes were spent with me taking in the soft, clean, neutral toned deco of her entire home.

Even though I'd been here in the past, I never really cared to admire the home she'd made for herself but now that I did, I couldn't help but feel impressed. We'd both come quite a long way from the teenagers we once were.

My coffee was soon ready, and I took it with me to one of the counters to take my seat. It was then she came hurrying into the space. I didn't turn to her, allowing her whatever privacy she needed to get over what I was certain was her surprise I was still here.

She headed towards the counter, and I could see she had thrown on some shorts and a loose, lacy camisole. I couldn't help but to picture the exact state we'd been in just a short while earlier.

XANDER

My dick thrusting in and out of her… her whimpers in my ears, and the taste of her on my tongue. I was instantly hard once again, and lowered calmly to sip from my coffee. When I lifted my gaze, I couldn't help but look across the counters in this space, realizing I'd never fucked her before on one of these. We'd done it everywhere else I was certain. In my car, just before I'd gone off to college and she'd been nearly heartbroken. On her mother's couch, in her childhood bedroom and even their guest bathroom because once, she'd come in there to help with something and then clicked the door shut.

A smile came to my face as I wondered what had led to that particular incident, as her mother I was certain had been present in the house at the time. Despite all of these, we'd never fucked completely on a kitchen counter with her legs spread apart, and my dick sheathed inside her.

"Xander," I suddenly heard her call, and realized I had zoned out for quite a little while.

"Are you alright?" she asked, her tone filled with sweet concern.

"I'm fine," I replied.

She turned towards the pot of coffee I'd just made. "Do you want some more from this?"

"No," I replied, instantly understanding why she was asking. "You can have it."

"Alright," she said, and poured herself a fresh cup.

I was content to just watch her even though I was aware it was time to head back to the office, but I couldn't get my legs to move. My eyes followed her as she headed towards the refrigerator, and then bending down to the freezer. The outline of her hips immediately caught my eye. She had the most perfect figure, but then again I'd always judged every part of her as perfect so perhaps I was once again just being biased on her account.

"I have some corn dogs," she said, and my gaze met hers.

"Do you want some? If not I can make you some eggs and toast. I have pancakes too."

I couldn't help my smile.

I hadn't really thought of eating, and neither did I want her slaving away making me breakfast so I just got to my feet and opted for the corn dogs.

"You don't have to get up, I can do it for you," she said, but I ignored her and went over because truly what I wanted was to be close enough to feel the warmth of her presence.

She handed over the box, so I grabbed two and returned them back to her.

Soon, mine were on a plate and being plopped into the microwave while she was rummaging through the fridge. I couldn't help but wonder if she and her mother specifically had the corn dogs out of habit because they were both aware that I liked them.

"Shit," she suddenly cursed.

"What is it?" I asked, and turned to see her looking disappointedly at the contents in the fridge.

"I don't have any kale," she said. "I wanted to make a smoothie."

I was briefly unable to look away, mesmerized by the soft smattering of hair along her temples and the nape of her neck. She had pulled her hair up into a ponytail before coming out here, and it made her look so soft my heart throbbed.

"What kind of smoothie would you have wanted to make with kale?" I asked and she smiled.

"I know it doesn't sound promising but it's so delicious. Its kale mixed with cashews and berries."

I started to head towards her as she spoke without even realizing it. My intent had been to return to the stool, but instead I stopped before her as she kept explaining how creamy and healthy the smoothie would be.

"I'll make it for you the next time you're here," she said, and it felt good to hear her talking about the next time.

"Sure," I replied, and then headed over to my stool. In no time, the corn dogs were ready but I didn't even realize it since I was too preoccupied with watching as she retrieved some fruits and brought them along to the counter.

"Your corn dogs are ready," she said. "Don't get up, I'll get them for you."

I listened, and soon enough she was bringing them over.

"You still like it with sour cream?" she asked, and I nodded.

"You're so consistent," she smiled as she arrived by my side, and placed it on the table. I couldn't help but wrap my hand around her neck and pull her to me.

We kissed once again, deeply, fervently. My tongue stroking and sucking passionately on hers, while her lips latched onto mine. I spread my legs even further apart to bring her closer to me while her arms wrapped around my waist.

I loved her breathlessness, and just how intimate this felt, so I cradled the undersides of her face and kissed her even more deeply.

Suddenly, she jerked away. "Be back," was all she said and ran from the room.

I went to get up to follow her, but there was a knock on the door.

I turned and headed to the door and flung it open wondering who would be coming to her house this early in the morning on a Saturday.

"Linda," I couldn't get anything else out.

She looked equally surprised to see me and a smile spread across her face.

"Xander, it's good to see you," she said.

I quickly looked down to inspect my appearance, and was thankful to see my shirt and pants were buttoned properly.

Her mother on the other hand was dressed in full hiking gear in bright colors that were quite a lot to take in.

Just then Olivia came back into the room looking pale and I walked back over to the counter concerned. Before I could say anything though Olivia addressed her mom.

"Mom, what are you doing here?" Olivia asked, and her mom gave her an incredulous look.

"We're supposed to go hiking this morning. I told you I'd pick you up rather than you coming over. I sent you a message."

Olivia glanced at me then, somewhat confused, and I didn't need to ask to know she hadn't even bothered to look at her phone from the moment we'd both gotten up.

"You can't just suddenly spring plans on me like this," she grumbled as she went back into the bedroom.

"Your plan for Saturdays is to be at my place anyway," her mother called after her. "What difference does it make that we're going hiking instead of you coming to my house."

Olivia groaned aloud and I couldn't help my smile.

"Young man," her mother called just as I sipped from my mug, so I set it down and gave her my attention.

"Why are you here?"

I didn't know what to say, so I just smiled instead and she returned it. She came over to me and placed a soft kiss on my cheek, and once again it brought me back to my high school days with Olivia. She hadn't done it frequently, but whenever she had, it was the only way she knew how to show gratitude to me. I cherished it and she took her seat on the stool next to me.

"She's feeding you just corn dogs?" she asked, as she gazed at the plate before me.

"It's what I asked for," I said, and she narrowed her gaze at me. "Mmn. You didn't want her to go all out to make breakfast for you did you?"

I smiled at how she was never truly subtle about anything.

"I'll make you some proper breakfast," she said, and I almost rose to my feet then.

"No..." I refused. "Thank you, but I have to leave for the office. This is all I have time for."

"Alright," she said, but still went ahead anyway to search through her daughter's cabinets. "I wonder if she still has-"

"Mom my phone is charging," Olivia said and we both turned to see her return.

"Do you still have that passion fruit tea?" her mother asked, and Olivia shook her head. "No, just chamomile. I'll make it for you."

"No need," her mother said, wrinkling her nose as she headed over to the refrigerator for her own stint of rummaging.

Olivia shared a look of fond exhaustion with me, and I smiled again. It felt just like old times.

"Olivia, can you please help me pack these to go? I have a meeting I want to get ready for in advance."

At first she seemed disappointed, but suddenly light came back into her eyes and then she was nodding in understanding.

"That's right, you didn't finish last-" she stopped as she remembered her mother was in the room.

She cleared her throat.

"I'll pack them up to go."

A few minutes later, I said goodbye to her mother, while Olivia escorted me to the door.

I didn't know how to say goodbye, so I simply didn't turn around. However at the last moment, she caught my arm and as I turned around, she kissed me, her tongue slipping in to stroke against the tip of mine.

Afterwards, she pulled away shyly.

"See you later?" she questioned and I nodded before she backed up and shut the door.

OLIVIA

I sighed as I twisted the lock then turned around to meet my mother as she repeated my words to Xander.

"See you later?"

I was in no state to respond, and neither did I particularly want to, so I simply headed into the kitchen and returned to the fruits I'd been rinsing in the sink for my smoothie. I felt woozy, and still slightly intoxicated as though the ground underneath my feet was unstable.

I couldn't believe I had to ruin the morning by running off to vomit. I guess I had more to drink than I thought. But it worked out because mom had showed up and who knows what kind of compromising position she may have found us in.

"So you're dating a billionaire?" she suddenly asked, and I was so taken aback that I had to stop momentarily.

"What?" I said and she laughed.

"Which part exactly seems more foreign to you? The fact that he's a billionaire or the part of you two dating?"

"Uhm," I didn't know what to say. Were we dating? I mean we said we loved each other but does that mean we're dating?

"Just sleeping together then? That doesn't sound like Xander."

I could feel heat beginning to burn my cheeks.

"So it sounds like me? Mom!"

"Oh please! Calm down. The two of you have been in love with each other for so long. How could it be that you two haven't been intimate yet? Plus I just met him here with his shirt barely buttoned and hanging out of his pants."

"It's Saturday morning," I complained.

"Exactly," she said. "What is he doing eating corn dogs at your house so early on a Saturday morning?"

I decided I wasn't going to engage, so I returned my attention to my fruit and brought it with me to the counter to begin my smoothie.

"Seriously though Olivia," she called.

I decided I needed to give her something. "We said we loved each other last night, but I think we are going to move slow-"

"I knew it!" she squealed.

I transferred the fruits into the blender and turned it on. The noise filled the room and for a few moments, allowed me to escape into my thoughts and forget she was still watching me.

Thankfully she took the hint and let it go. Instead she got busy with retrieving some eggs for herself and setting them on the stove to boil.

However as the seconds ticked by even further, I grew more restless.

I didn't find the courage to ask her the question I wanted to until we were midway through our trail route.

We stopped briefly on a rock off the path so that she could rest, and as she lifted her water bottle to her lips the words spilled out of me.

"I'm scared," I said to her.

My gaze lowered as I kicked a stone around, but then at her silence I lifted my eyes and found that she didn't look so good.

"Mom?" I called, suddenly alarmed.

She turned her gaze towards me then, and managed a smile. "I'm fine," she said. "I just feel quite tired."

"Well you're supposed to. Do you want to stop here?"

"Give me a few minutes," she said, and I waited, going over to her side so I could squat down and take her hand in mine. However she was too pale and it worried me.

Eventually she spoke. "It seems you still need my help in figuring a lot of things out," she said and I couldn't help but scowl, although her words were true.

I couldn't help but notice she sounded even more exhausted than normal.

"Are you alright?" I asked.

Her eyes bored into mine as she shook her head.

"No," she said calmly. "I think I'm a few minutes away from fainting."

My heart lurched into my throat.

"What?"

"Don't panic," she said, "I just have to get out of here. I can walk down. It's easier than climbing up. Let's just take it slowly."

"No!" I exclaimed and pulled my phone out. "We need an ambulance."

"You can't get reception here."

"I can, it's not that bad."

"Olivia," she rose to her feet. "I'm fine, or rather will be. I've just been plagued by this enough to notice certain symptoms beforehand. So let's just head down."

She rose to her feet then, and I caught her arm to stabilize her.

I didn't let go, and continued staring at my phone until service bars started to appear.

I placed the call for the ambulance then, much to her dissatisfaction.

"They'll be here soon," I said and she held onto my arm.

"Thanks," she said, and once again looked around for a rock to settle on. She couldn't find one and to my surprise she just collapsed to sit on the ground.

"Mom!" I exclaimed and she let out a somewhat breathy laugh.

"I'm fine. I'll just wait here."

"This was a bad idea."

"I guess," she said. "But I was feeling particularly weak. I just wanted to stretch out a bit more."

"Stop talking," I gazed at her worriedly, and then settled down by her side. "If you had felt weak then you should have said so. A simple walk would have sufficed rather than hiking up a –"

"Stop nagging me," she interrupted.

I realized I truly was, and out of remorse immediately stopped, my hand running up and down hers to soothe her.

"How exactly do you feel?" I asked.

However she didn't respond, and instead turned back to my own problems.

"You said earlier you were scared?"

"Yeah, but don't speak. Conserve your energy."

"I'll listen then," she said, and I nodded at her. Perhaps she needed this, to get her mind off her current discomfort. I kept my attention on her as I tried to speak but couldn't help but note how hard it seemed for her to keep her eyes open.

"Mom," I called and she turned towards me. "I'm fine. Tell me."

I wanted her to stay active as my hand tightened around her arm.

"About what?" I asked but she didn't respond right away.

"What are you scared about?" her gaze opened further and focused once more on me.

"I think I might be pregnant."

She kept looking at me, so in order to avoid her having to strain to ask any further questions I kept speaking.

"I keep getting sick in the morning and we haven't exactly been careful and… I don't know what to do."

"Have you taken a test?" she asked, and I couldn't help but worry at how breathless her voice had become.

"No," I replied softly. "I was going to get one later bu-"

"Mom?"

My heart slammed against the walls of my chest as her eyes shut closed.

"Mom!" I yelled just as she lost her balance and began to fall over.

Everything from then on for me happened in a blur of panic and fright as I tried to shake her awake.

"Mom!" I yelled over and over again, but she had lost consciousness I realized and we were out in the middle of nowhere.

"Help me!" I screamed over and over again as I held her in my arms and kissed her forehead. I dug out my phone then and once again called the ambulance.

"We're on our way to you," they told me as soon as it connected.

"When?" I fucking screamed.

"Please stay calm, please describe exactly where you are."

I stayed on the line with them and each minute that passed by became more excruciating than the next.

I tried my best to be coherent as I reported her medical history, my hands wiping the moisture of her frail face as my tears dropped on it.

"Mom," I called over and over again, but there was no response.

My heart broke over and over again as I watched her. "M*om*."

"*Mom, I need you.*"

XANDER

I received the call just as my meeting was about to start.

My default response was to reject it since the team was beginning, however I couldn't help but find it peculiar that she was calling me after I'd just left her home.

It disconnected as I was about to reach for it. I took my hand away, and tried to focus on the presentation.

Most of the staff present were working overtime, and the last thing I wanted was to make them feel under-appreciated for working into the weekend.

A few seconds later however, the phone's screen lit up again, notifying me of her call once again coming in, and I couldn't help but be worried.

I however didn't want to walk out of the meeting, so I simply answered it and said a quick, "hello."

The first thing I heard was sniffing, and instantly my nerves tightened in alarm.

"Olivia?" I called, not even realizing it when I rose to my feet.

"What's wrong?" I asked, and instantly began to walk out of the room.

"My mom," she said to me, and I stopped in my tracks.

"What? What happened?"

"She's in the ER."

"Sir?" I heard someone call around me, but I had already walked out of the conference room.

What gnawed at me the most was how recently I'd just seen both of them, and at how distraught Olivia would be.

"What happened?" I asked again, and for the first seconds as I returned to my office to grab my things, she was unable to speak.

I understood there was no need to further converse.

Grabbing my keys and jacket, I was out of the office in no time, and soon arrived at the ER.

I met her in the hallway. She was pacing... unable to remain still and I felt a deep hurt in my heart as I watched her.

I quickened my pace towards her, and she turned around to face me.

I watched the tears fill her eyes, then roll out as she began to head towards me. I quickened my pace to her just as she did to me and then she was in my arms. I embraced her hard and tightly, needing to assure her I would be here. She sobbed into my shoulders, and as her entire body quaked with emotion, it felt like I couldn't bear it.

I also needed to know what was happening.

"How is she?"

It took her a little while to respond. I didn't rush her because I knew she was trying to get herself together.

"She fainted," she finally answered. "Pain and fatigue. Her drugs have stopped working."

At the despondence in her gaze as though she couldn't stand a moment longer, I led her towards the chairs along the wall.

Thankfully she came with me. Once we were seated I guided her head to lean against my shoulder.

I waited for her to speak, to share only what she wanted to, and soon enough she did.

"She's been having severe shoulder pains. That was how they discovered the recurrence- the mass near her right rib. Her drugs were working, they started to shrink the tumor down but the doctor told her two weeks ago it was only able to reduce the tumor by 1 cm before the drugs became ineffective. That's why she came over to hike today. The pain was quite grave. She was exhausted, and so to distract herself, she thought it would be best to exercise and spend more time with me."

I looked up towards the closed door of her mother's room.

"What's the way forward?" I asked, and Olivia sighed.

She started to raise her head from my shoulder, but with a hand gently on the side of her face I stopped her, and she obliged. She rested back against me, and after a little while resumed speaking.

"She'll need surgery now. It's the last resort but she might lose her mobility."

I felt her begin to tremble, and held her even tighter to me. "Her doctor said this time around she'd have to have one rib and a part of her back muscle taken out."

I was a bit surprised to hear this. "The last resort?"

"Yeah," she breathed. "She's already had chemo, mastectomy, lymph nodes removed and radiation. She can't do it again. They've all reached their limit."

I completely understood then why she was so panicked, and I didn't know what to say to comfort her. I didn't even know if there was anything to say that could comfort her. I wasn't very useful in these kinds of situations so I just held onto her.

After a while I had to leave, as the calls from the office became insistent. I had put it on silent but they continued to gnaw at me. She seemed to sense the restlessness in me. She eventually lifted her head and stared into my eyes.

"You were at the office right?" she asked.

I nodded.

"Go back. I'll stay here a bit with my mom and then head home. The doctors want her to rest here overnight to be monitored, but she hates being here. She's always so anxious when she comes here even though she doesn't like to show it. I'll let you know what happens by the end of the day."

I was reluctant, and in response she worked up a smile. She then rose to her feet pulling me up with her. "Don't worry," she said. "And I'm sorry for calling you over. I was just mid-panic and all I could think was how much I needed you."

She had to turn to meet my gaze at my silence. "I will always come when you need me." I was surprised by how shaken I'd been at the initial scare that something devastating might have happened to her mother.

I'd been especially scared for Olivia, because beyond her mother, she didn't have anyone else. If anything truly unfortunate were to happen, she would be crushed, and it worried me immensely. I didn't know if I would be enough for the comfort that she needed.

I turned once again towards her mother's door, hoping and saying a silent prayer she would be fine. That she would find the strength to carry on despite the setback. I wanted to say goodbye before I left, but I didn't want to disturb her so I instead pulled Olivia into my arms.

"Call me if you need anything," I said, and pressed a kiss to her cheek. "If either of you need anything."

I felt her nod as she returned the hug, and then I turned around to take my leave. She and her mother felt like family to me. At some point along our journey, they'd been ingrained into my heart as family.

OLIVIA

"Are you still at the hospital?"

I received the message just as I settled into bed with my mother. The only standing lamp in the corner illuminated her room warmly, and in the air was the clean scent of a calming incense.

My hope was she would be able to sleep and rest peacefully, so the last thing I wanted was to cause her any interruptions, but as Xander's name flashed across my screen, I couldn't help but grab onto my phone to respond.

"No we're at home," I replied, after I'd adjusted the brightness. "She insisted that she didn't want to spend the night there."

"Isn't that risky? Are you both okay?" was his quick reply. I couldn't help the warmth that filled me as well as the smile that curved my lips at his concern.

"We're fine." I replied.

"I'll bring some soup over. You're at her house?"

"I am," I replied.

It was nearing past midnight, and I had no idea if I would truly be able to sleep tonight given her condition and the test I had taken before bringing her home. But at the prospect of having him here with me I couldn't refuse.

And so when I got another message informing me of his arrival a few minutes later, I tucked her in as properly as I could, and went to let him in.

We were both quiet as I ushered him into the house, a bag of what I assumed to be the soup he'd brought along with him.

I thanked him as he handed the bag over, but lingered in the fridge as I put it away. I was deep in thought, because since the two of us had already had our dinners, I couldn't exactly force him groundlessly to stay, but I needed him to.

Suddenly, I heard the scrape of a stool across the floor and panicked. I spun around, slamming the door shut to see he had risen to his feet.

"Do you want me to stay?"

My lashes lowered. "Yeah."

"Okay," he said and just like that we were heading up to my bedroom.

I watched him when we arrived, and couldn't help but think back to all the countless times in the past he'd come to me in this room.

We were younger then, but it slightly amused me I still felt exactly the same. It was as though no time whatsoever had passed, but we both knew very little was the same. I had never imagined it would be possible for him to be back here, but he was and for that I was immensely happy. I did start to feel concerned however, when a problem I'd overlooked came to mind, and it was on the matter of my bed size.

It was a single bed, and in the past it had never failed to accommodate either of us but looking at his stature now, taller and broader and more muscled, I doubted if things would be the same.

I couldn't help but turn to glance at him, my lips slightly trembling with amusement.

I could see ease dancing in his eyes so I didn't hesitate to make a joke.

"I don't think I've changed very much," I said. "In size, I mean. But I think you have." I smiled and perused his body. He did the same to mine and I didn't miss the fact that his gaze lingered on the swell of my breasts. Desire instantly pooled between my thighs, and it left me gazing at him, waiting until his eyes returned to mine.

Soon enough, they did and he smirked. He then headed over to the bed and without a word, began to unbutton his shirt. I watched, my mouth watering as the muscles underneath his skin rippled and shifted as the fabric came down his arms.

"I need to take a shower," he said to me as he draped it over the chair of my desk right next to the bed.

"Yeah," I startled, and glanced back at the door. "You know where the bathroom is right? I'll get you a fresh towel."

His pants were lowered down his legs by the time I returned to him, and underneath was the taut, softly curved ass I was now all too familiar with. There was no trace of reserve with him before me, and it was as it should be, but for some reason I couldn't help but feel quite flustered. Maybe it was because I was in my mother's house and she was just down the hall though exhausted and fast asleep.

He turned fully to face me, and my breathing caught in my throat. I had seen his body numerous times at this point, but somehow it never failed to astonish me. To leave me breathless and filled with images of the various ways we had been joined together. What I couldn't believe was even in my forlorn state or rather especially in my forlorn state, what I craved the most was him. The escape he was able to give me so easily and thoroughly. I was well aware of how difficult it had been to breathe all day, and how at ease I was now although still breathless, but for a completely different reason.

"Did you leave the towel in the bathroom?" he asked, and I was suddenly startled.

"Yeah," I replied. "Yeah, I did."

He then moved and as he walked past, I felt his presence charge mine with tiny sparks.

Perhaps suggesting this was a bad idea, or maybe it was just what I needed. We wouldn't be able to go too far anyway since we were in my mother's home, but the fact I got to spend the night in his arms was all I needed right now.

The fact he had come to the hospital when I had called earlier, and was ready and willing to show his consideration warmed my heart immensely. And then he did the same tonight. I lowered down onto the bed and felt my insides shake. I was so in love with him I couldn't breathe, and it made me terrified of what I needed to tell him.

With a sigh, I looked at the clothes he'd draped across my chair and couldn't help but smile at just how comfortable he seemed to be around my home. I picked them up to hang in my closet, and realized these were the exact same clothes he had worn the previous night.

I knew he had been engaged in the office, and coupled with coming over to the hospital to see me, he'd probably not had the chance to go home to change. My heart melted even further.

How exhausted he must be.

I debated whether to quickly run them through the washer and dryer or not, but had to consider he would prefer them dry-cleaned. The best choice seemed to be to wait for his return, but I decided it would be the perfect chance to head to the bathroom. I too also needed a shower but wasn't sure if it was wise to join him given my mom down the hall.

A little while later, I knocked on the bathroom door, not really expecting there to be a response.

After the second knock, I went in and saw he was in the stall. The bathroom was small, and for a moment I was struck by the fact it was at least eight times smaller than his. It amused me as I pictured it, and only when the door to the stall suddenly came open was I brought back to the present.

Steam billowed all around him as he wiped the moisture off his face, and then his gaze was on mine. At the question in his eyes I quickly regained my wits and explained.

"Can I run these through the washing machine for you? Or would you prefer to have them dry-cleaned?"

He shook his head, his hand once again lifting to brush his wet hair off his face. "There's no need," he replied. "I'll head home in the morning for a change."

I hesitated. "Um... what will you wear then? This is what you had on yesterday too, isn't it?"

"Is there a problem if I put it on again?" he asked, and I immediately wrinkled my nose in distaste. His immediate smile increased the warmth that was already simmering deep within me, and for the seconds that followed all I could do was stare at him. Until he spoke again.

"Don't you have any of my old t-shirts?" he asked, and the smile left my face.

I watched him, my throat suddenly closing up.

"You don't?" he asked again, and I cleared my throat.

"I uh- I'm not sure. I think I do."

I turned around to leave then, but he caught my hand and I was forced to return my attention to him.

"You don't?" he asked again, staring into my eyes. "You threw all my stuff away?"

"I didn't," I shook my head.

"You didn't throw all of it away?" he asked, and I noticed then the hint of hope and tenderness in his tone. Before I could stop myself my hand reached out to curve around his cheek

"I didn't throw any of it away," I repeated. "How could I?"

I could almost feel the tension on his face then dissipate. My eyes once again couldn't help but rove down his beautiful and exposed body. I sucked in my breath. "I don't think

343

they'll fit anymore. You've put on quite a bit of height and muscle."

"T-shirts stretch," he said, his breath washing warmly over my face.

My gaze returned to his entranced.

"You might not need it."

He cocked his head, eyes sparkling. "I thought you didn't want me wearing the old shirt?

"I'm referring to tonight," I said. "I don't think you'll need one since you'll be sleeping next to me."

XANDER

I couldn't remember ever being so eager to be done with showering.

As I worked the shampoo onto my scalp, and as the warm cascade fell on me, it almost felt as though I was in a dream.

It had never been my intention to stay over but at this point, I suspected I was no longer capable of saying no to her. I didn't want to, given what she'd gone through today with her mother, I was quite certain I was ready and willing to give her whatever she asked for just so she could be soothed.

Whenever Olivia was stressed out, she found it difficult to sleep, and I remembered this especially because during our period in high school together, her mother had been going through a painful and drawn out divorce with her step-father.

Back then I'd spent the nights with her, and her mother sometimes was none the wiser, but then it rapidly declined after we became intimate. Olivia was furious at this, but she'd understood my need to keep my outright disregard of her mother's trust to a minimum, especially because back then Olivia had quickly become hooked on us making love.

I couldn't help but smile now as I recalled my concern back then with trying to curb what was beginning to seem like her addiction to me, but soon enough, trying to get into college had properly engaged her and I was more or less left alone.

I hadn't loved it, but I couldn't complain either because I loved just how focused she had become.

With a sigh, I shut the faucet off, and got out of the stall. Perhaps I should have pulled her into the stall with me, given how turned on I was aware she'd been earlier. She'd outright been flirting with me, that unmistakable hunger clear in her eyes, but then she'd scurried away with my clothes before I could even think of taking advantage.

Maybe she too recalled her addiction to me from our earlier years together and how I'd tried to curb it. I'd given her the reason it was because I'd wanted her to focus on her studies, but I always knew she didn't completely believe me. Perhaps now she was trying to hold back so that just like back then, she wouldn't receive any complaints.

I sighed as I grabbed the towel she'd laid out for me, and picked it up. After slightly blowdrying my hair, and applying some of her lotion, I soon walked out of the bathroom with just the towel tied around my waist. I saw her seated on the bed, her hands in her lap and her gaze lost, making me wonder what was so immensely occupying her thoughts. Without a word, I sat beside her, and it was only then she realized my presence. She slightly startled, and then she turned to me, eyes widened and lips parted.

My gaze lowered to the unforgettable pale pink softness that never failed to make me weak.

"What are you thinking about?" I asked, and she shook her head.

Her eyes then roved across my face, and the affection behind that perusal made me feel as though I was the sole object of her adoration. It suddenly became just a bit harder to breathe. She reached out and my eyes fluttered closed. I could feel her fingers run through the strands of my wet hair.

"There's a blow dryer in the bathroom," she said. "It's plugged into the wall. You didn't see it?"

"I did," my eyes came open to respond to her. "I just got tired."

She smiled, her sliver of beautiful white teeth flashing at me. "You mean you got bored."

"Yeah," I nodded, "there's that too."

She turned away shaking her head. "There's always that."

"I'll go get it and dry it for you," she said and rose to her feet, but I automatically caught her hand.

"No need," I said, when she turned back questioningly. "It's dry enough. Will it bother you?"

"Of course not. I guess, I'd just like to do it for you. It's been a while. Plus I need to get ready for bed too. "

"I'll come with you," I said, and rose to my feet but both of her hands shot out to stop me.

"No."

I was a bit taken aback.

"I mean…" she tried to explain. "Being there together… I'll probably be seated on the vanity so I can reach your head."

"And?"

She sighs. "Your hips will be between mine."

I was amused.

"So?"

"Xander, that's a tiny, currently heated space and it's all too intimate. I'm really trying with my whole heart here to behave but you're not making it easy. So, you can come along if you can accept I may lose my mind halfway and force myself on you, or you can wait here while I take a shower and then come back to dry both our hair."

I considered this, and although the first option was the most exciting, I truly began to feel the deep exhaustion down to my bones. I wanted her, but we couldn't be careless and alert her mother. Plus there were other more quiet ways I could take her if my self-control eventually snapped. The bed was just small enough it could fit us, and we'd figured out earlier it was especially perfect when we were completely and intimately connected to each other's bodies. It wouldn't take long then, she'd be held tightly in my arms, her ass to my groin and I'd rock her silently to sleep. It was one of the best moments I'd missed about her during our time apart, and the prospect of possibly doing that again with her was quite enticing. I decided then to behave.

"Alright," I agreed and stood to my feet.

"I washed your briefs and put them in the dryer," she told me. "So you'll have to keep the towel on till I get back. They should be ready by then."

I smiled. "Thank you," and with that she was on her way.

OLIVIA

When I returned to the room, I saw him still sitting on the bed and wrapped in the towel. Somewhere at the back of my mind, I had naughtily expected to meet him naked but it turned out I was in over my head.

I turned around to shut the door so I could recollect my thoughts before finally facing him. His eyes roved down my sleeping attire of just a white T-shirt, and tight, grey, boy shorts that stuck to my body like a second skin and even rode up high on my ass, revealing the rounded curves beneath.

I headed over with his warm clean briefs and handed them over, but his gaze refused to lower to them.

With a smile, I set the briefs down on the table beside us, and then moved along to plug the dryer into the socket by the bed. The room was quite dim, with only the small lamp on my desk switched on. Despite the fact it gave the room a warm, cozy ambience, it made it a bit difficult for me to find the socket.

Eventually I did, but just before I could plug the dryer in, I felt his hand lift my shirt up my lowered back.

"Xander," I complained, but couldn't stop myself from remaining lowered and pretending to search for the holes to plug the dryer into.

"You're wearing this to bed?" I heard him ask.

"I'm covered up aren't I? Is there a problem?"

"You're really asking me that?" he teased. "I thought you wanted us to behave tonight."

"I don't live here," I reminded him. "They're a bit tight because I've had them for years. That's why I have the t-shirt on. Just ignore it."

I reached backwards to pull the tail of the t-shirt back away from his grip however he didn't budge.

Instead, and just as I had expected, his huge hand went between my legs and I nearly bumped my head into the wall from leaning over at the instant barrage of sensations.

"Xander!" I held onto the side of the desk, still refusing to straighten.

"They're grey," he pointed out. "I can see you're wet."

"Of course, I'm wet," I said to him then, and finally plugged in the dryer. I then straightened up to meet his hungry gaze. "I just took a shower."

"So you're saying you didn't dry off?"

"Of course, I did," I replied. "That's not water."

He smiled then, and my bones went limp. I kept my gaze fixed on his, and in no time I was standing between his thighs.

"Be good," I reminded him as I picked the dryer up, but then his arms cradled my waist. He then leaned forward to press his nose between my breasts, and my head tilted backwards.

"Xander," I was about to work up the will to push him away once again, but he turned his head and latched onto my hardened nipple through my tee.

"*Ah*," I moaned, and it was immediately too loud. My heart stuttered as I thought of my mother down the hall, so I couldn't help but grab onto his hair.

"*Xander*," I rasped out, but he didn't listen. His hands grabbed onto my ass from behind, which made me falter until I was almost falling on top of him. Laughter ensued as I tried to regain my balance, and he helped me until we were staring into each other's eyes.

I loved the way he held me, and the way my free hand cradled the back of his head.

"Your hair still curls up so beautifully," he said, as his eyes moved away from mine to admire the damp, clumped strands as they fell down my shoulders.

"Yours doesn't," I said, affectionately stroking his scalp.

And then I sighed, because once again I couldn't understand how I had thought it reasonable in any way to let him go.

"Alright, let's get your hair dried," I said, and after confirming the functionality of the dryer I turned it on.

I knew his eyes were on me, and he was watching me intently but I didn't bother meeting his gaze as it would make me too flustered.

I did however dislike he was looking up at me from underneath my chin, and I relayed my dissatisfaction to this.

He laughed.

"I'm serious. The bathroom would have been better."

"Well, you made the decision for us to do it here. You're in charge tonight."

"Thank you for being there for me today," I said, as I held the dryer to his hair, my fingers combing through it.

He however didn't hear me.

"What?" he asked, and I debated whether to repeat myself. I eventually decided to so I briefly shut it off.

"Thank you for being there for me today. Despite how busy you were. And I'm sorry for interrupting your day. I know it puts a strain on you."

He watched me, and his gaze was much too intense.

"Xander," I smiled, but he didn't say a word. He simply returned it, calmly, and my heart suddenly felt too big for my chest.

I had no choice but to turn the dryer back on, and return to the task. In no time, it was decently dried but when I tried to move away to get a brush so that I could comb through, his hold around my waist refused to budge.

"Xander," I complained half-heartedly, but then before a resolution could be decided on he was turning me around to take his place on the bed.

Then he took the dryer from me, and after putting his briefs on, to my surprise, reached towards the first drawer of my desk to retrieve a brush. My eyes widened in surprise.

"How did you know it was there?"

His response was an amused smile, while I was unable to contain a blush because how could he not know. I'd just thought he'd forgotten, but it seemed as though everything about us had remained in his mind.

Soon enough we were done, and he ran the brush down my hair. Then he tilted my face up to his and pressed the sweetest of kisses to my lips. It was soft, brief, wet and so perfect that I couldn't help the goofy smile that came to my lips. However, I quickly lowered my gaze from his and proceeded to move onto my side of the bed. I pulled the covers down and in no time he was joining me. I turned into his frame, ready to bury my face into the crook of his neck so I could be enveloped in his scent. However he still seemed to be busy.

He got up once again, and began to fiddle with something I'd ignored on the floor.

"What is that?" I asked, and when he didn't respond immediately I leaned over to check. My heart slammed into my chest.

"Oh my God," I exclaimed and he smiled. "Where did you find that?"

"On the floor in the corner," he said, referring to the dark corner between my desk and bed.

"Oh, yeah."

"You forgot you had it?"

"I think at some point I thought it was broken."

"It is broken," he said. "What did you do, smash it against the wall?"

I went silent then as my memory reminded me that was exactly what had happened. I recalled the night in the most vivid detail. It'd been about two months after I'd broken up with him, and I was still bleeding out from every pore in my body.

I'd returned home from college to visit my mother and out of habit, I'd grabbed onto the small projector that he'd gotten for me years before. I'd then turned off the lights expecting to see the stars that it'd reflect across my ceiling, the stars that every time we had spent the night together in this bed, we had fallen asleep to. It'd been breathtaking every time, but this time around, the tears hadn't stopped falling as I'd stared up at it. I'd cried until the tears had dried up, and just when I'd thought I could go to bed, it had begun all over again.

At the time I didn't think I deserved to be sad, so I'd denied myself the luxury as much as I could. I'd been the one to lie to him... the one to break up with him, so what right did I have to mourn over him? But that night, I couldn't stop and with my heart splitting in two I grabbed onto the machine and flung it across the room.

My original intention had been to smash it against the wall, but I couldn't bring myself to because I was aware it would be irreparably shattered, and at the moment, it wasn't something I could bear to have happened. But it had broken just enough for its possibly irreparable state to register in my mind.

"What happened to it?" he asked, and my heart lurched as I wondered about how to respond to him. Just as I was thinking about it, the device came on and my breath seized.

It had been four years since I'd seen this sight, and now, it seemed even more beautiful.

"It works," he said and rose up from the floor then, but I couldn't even follow his movement. All I could do was gaze up at the tiny stars spread all across the ceiling, but then suddenly I heard the lamp click off and it was even more stunning.

We were encased in darkness, but the lights up above were magical. I couldn't stop the tears from filling up my eyes. He returned to bed and I smiled, taking the chance of him settling in to wipe the tears away. I then laid down as he pulled the covers over us, and couldn't stop my eyes from turning misty again when I felt his arm go underneath my neck to wrap around me.

I didn't need any further invitation to snuggle in even closer, however as my leg bent across his, I realized just how aroused he was.

It made me laugh.

"You're hard," I said, as I lifted my gaze to meet his. He smiled and replied, although his gaze remained on the ceiling.

"Of course."

My hand on his chest started to inch downwards towards his groin but he suddenly reached out and stopped me. "If you start that now we're not going to stop until I come so just leave it alone to go away on its own."

I was amused.

"Who says we have to stop?" I asked, and he turned then to gaze at me.

"Didn't we decide to be good tonight?"

"Oh, yeah," I blushed. "Sure."

He smiled and my hand moved further up to rest against his chest. I tried my best to quiet down... we both did, and in no time I could feel the beating of his heart just under my touch.

"Meeting you was a gift," I eventually said to him, and he laughed.

I was curious then as to why. He felt my gaze on him and explained. "I was just remembering the first time we spoke to each other. That day in the locker room when you came to look for Danny."

I couldn't help but tense up slightly at the mention of Danny's name. But this was soon eased away as I recalled my shock and sputtering. "Yeah," I smiled. "It was so hard to believe you were talking to me that I think I turned back to look at the wall."

At this he laughed, and I loved the low rumble the sound made, and the corresponding shake of his body.

I loved everything about him.

He didn't comment any further on this, his gaze continuing to gaze up at the lights.

"What are you thinking about?" I couldn't help but ask, however he shrugged.

Instead his gaze lowered to mine.

"What are *you* thinking about?" he asked, and I decided to completely open myself up to him.

"I love myself," I told him. "I believe I'm alright. I'm content with who I am and what I'm doing but I've always thought I wasn't…" I hesitated but then at his rapt attention, I steeled my spine and went on.

"A part of me has always believed I just wasn't enough and you could do better."

At the furrow of his brows at my words I hurried on to explain. "I wanted you to have someone who was as ambitious as you were, and who was as attrac-" I stopped then and swallowed.

"You don't think you're attractive?"

"No," I replied. I couldn't make a joke of this by saying yes because every second of this was me baring my whole heart to him. "I know I'm attractive enough, but I always wanted someone better than I am for you. Someone more beautiful… someone… *more*."

He gazed at me for so long I suspected he wasn't going to respond. But then he spoke.

"What makes you think there's someone more?" he asked.

I couldn't respond so I smiled instead, but he didn't reciprocate. I knew he wasn't going to let us depart from this solemn and heartfelt path.

My voice was small as I spoke, but I meant it. "There's always someone more."

"And more is perfect?" he asked. "For me?"

I didn't dare respond to this.

"I wanted *you*. Not *more*. I don't know who the fuck more is."

I swallowed, however the lump in my throat seemed to never want to go down.

At the hurt in his eyes, unhidden for once and detectable, I couldn't help but try to explain myself just one more time.

"It was easier for me to believe there was someone else you were talking to behind me when we first met. Even though I was aware there was nothing else besides the wall."

He blinked, calmly and I was sure he could hear just how hard my heart was pounding in my chest. "Didn't I do enough?" he asked. "To show you just how much you meant to me?"

My fingers curled against him. "You did," I replied. "You did more than enough"

"But somehow you still believed I wanted more."

I shook my head. "No, I wanted you to have more. It was because you did more than enough that I could shake my belief that you deserved more." My voice was small. "You deserve the whole world."

At this, he no longer spoke and instead turned away, his gaze returning once again to the ceiling. I felt so heavy inside, and wished to God we could talk more.

The seconds ticked by and my eyes shut.

"Do you remember the day I got you this projector?" he asked, and my throat closed up. I knew exactly where he was going with this and I didn't think I could stand it. I wanted him to stop.

I cleared my throat, but found that I still couldn't speak so I nodded.

His gaze turned to mine.

He wasn't going to let me get away with not speaking.

"Yeah," I said.

"When?" he pressed further.

"My eighteenth birthday. You threw me a surprise party."

"And…"

I sighed again.

"We spent the night together."

"And…"

I turned then, as the tears poured down my face. It was a while later before I was able to get myself under control again and find my voice, and he didn't interrupt. I knew he was waiting. That this time around he wasn't coming to my rescue. And so I muttered against his neck just as he had done against mine on that night.

"You told me that you loved me."

He waited.

"For the first time."

A few more seconds ticked by, and then he said the most devastating statement of all. "I don't know how to make you believe this... and truly... I'm done trying anymore... and I think I'll start to hate myself. And then I'll start to hate you."

I was the one who couldn't figure out what to say after this. And so we both remained quiet, but I could barely hold back my grief at how much I had disappointed him... and at how much I had hurt him.

But I also had my own qualms, because although I hadn't expected him to put up a fight given the reason I'd given as the cause for our separation, I still hadn't expected him to give up so easily. He'd just walked away and as a result, I'd been able to convince myself I had done the right thing. I had set us both free where he otherwise wouldn't have.

I lifted my gaze to his, and wondered if I should bring this up. It sounded to me like I was just trying to find a defense, and regardless of if I believed I deserved this but, what would it solve in the long run? After all, he'd never done anything prior to betray or hurt me. I was the one who had caused our troubles.

I sighed, and decided against it. Instead I snuggled even closer towards him and stared up at the stars.

"I came back," he said. "After you told me, I was in shock. I thought you were joking. You had to be. It took me that day to process it, and then that night I couldn't fall asleep. So I went over to your apartment. And I saw you with Danny."

My heart slammed into my chest.

"You seemed fine," he said. "You both had grocery bags in hand, and you were laughing together. Like everything was the same. Like nothing had happened. You'd broken my heart and yet it was all as if nothing had happened."

I began to shake my head as the gravity of that sight dawned on me. No wonder he'd never called after that, no wonder he'd never shown up and no wonder he'd been unable to forgive me.

"Oh my God," I breathed, and he lowered his gaze to mine.

"He was just trying to cheer you up wasn't he?" he asked, and tears poured down my face again.

He smiled then. "Don't cry."

"He was," I nodded urgently as his hand came to pat the moisture off my cheeks, but I needed him to focus so my gaze chased his. "I swear it. He knew what happened and saw I didn't have any food. He was leaving for college that day so he forced me along with him. He made me laugh but it was so brief. I was devastated. I couldn't sleep for months."

He wiped the moisture off my face completely, his eyes lost in thought. Eventually and when he was done, he finally looked at me.

And then he gave a simple nod.

"You believe me right?" I asked, and he smiled.

"I do." And with this, he returned his gaze to the stars before turning back to face me.

"I love you so much Olivia."

I took a deep breath and decided to finish this night with another confession.

"Xander," I leaned up to look into his eyes.

"Hmm," his gaze held mine.

"I know the timing isn't the best... and it feels like we're finally in a good place..." I paused to fortify myself for his response and he tensed beneath me.

"I'm pregnant," I whispered and held my breath for his response.

For a while he just stared at me. "Please say something," I didn't want to start crying again but I felt the emotion well inside me at his continued silence.

Then his arms were wrapped tightly around me and I let the breath out I'd been holding.

"I didn't know my heart could be this full. I can't wait to see you round with my child. It's like a dream I never thought would come true."

"I love you, Xander King."

He captured my lips with his mouth. For a long time we simply luxuriated in the kiss.

Until we fell asleep, inseparably bound and in each other's arms.

EPILOGUE

OLIVIA

Eight Months Later

"Where's Xander?"

I sighed as my mom lowered into the car, but kept my eyes on her expression, watching for any signs of discomfort.

"You do know that asking about him has become your hello to me right?" I said, and she laughed.

"I'm serious," I said as she shut the passenger door, and began to put on her seatbelt.

"Oh c'mon, you're exaggerating."

"I'm not," I said as I pulled away from the hospital.

"You are," she insisted, and I sighed again, my gaze glancing once again at her.

She turned then and our eyes met. "How was your session?" I asked, and she groaned softly underneath her breath.

"I thought it would get easier but it just doesn't."

"Physiotherapy isn't working?"

"It is," she said. "My mobility is improving but it's still not getting easy. Being alive though sure beats out the pain so I can't complain too much. Did Xander get stuck at work again?" she asked, and I couldn't help my amusement.

"Mom."

"I'm just concerned about you. He's been the one picking me up, and when he can't make it he sends the car. Why are you the one driving? You should be resting."

"Mom, I'm pregnant, not an invalid. I can drive over to pick you up."

"But we have to go to the store after this. You can't walk around for too long."

"How long do you intend on spending there?" I asked, slightly alarmed.

"See what I mean?" she said. "I always take my time with him when we get groceries, and he's never worried that we might walk around too long. You on the other hand I'm sure will be ready to leave in ten minutes."

"Again, I'm pregnant," I said as I stopped at a light. "I'm allowed to not want to do things for too long."

She sighed. "I think it's because it's my birthday today," she said. "He couldn't come and decided to send the next best thing instead."

"Mom," I complained, and she laughed again… carefully, lightly, so as not to hurt herself.

"Sometimes I think you're his mom, not mine. You've always been so nice to him."

"He's always been kind to me," she replied. "Respectful, caring. I could sense it from the very first time you brought him home."

This warmed me all over, so rather than say anything else, I just basked in her appreciation of my dear husband.

"Do you have your list ready?" I asked, and she sighed. "I do but I'm not going to rush because of you. I'll find somewhere for you to take a seat when you get too tired, and you can rest there, okay."

"I can manage," I said just as the light turned green.

"Alright."

"I still don't understand why you're the one hosting us on your birthday." I said.

"Because I'm happy," she replied. "I get to see another birthday."

"That's too dark Mom," I said, my brows furrowing.

"Maybe, but I didn't think I would make it."

"But you did, so no recalling that time. It was excruciating."

"I know," she said. "It was excruciating for all of you, but you both have been so careful and sweet to me so this is my way of saying thank you. Rather than just eating out."

"Alright," I said and we continued on our way.

I was able to keep up with her for about thirty minutes, but then Xander called and I decided I was done. I found a chair to settle on, and left her to wander. She knew where everything was, but then grocery shopping had become her favorite pastime recently and none of us wanted to deny her that.

"Do you think it's because you've done that with her every Saturday for a long time?" Xander asked as we spoke.

"Who knows?" I replied. "Maybe. She didn't use to care but now she's hell bent on trying everything in this store. And since she can't eat that much she uses us as her guinea pigs."

"I'm not complaining," he said and I shook my head.

"Of course you aren't. You can work out after she's done stuffing you while I can't. I'm already having nightmares about all the work it'll take to shed this weight after the baby comes."

"I'll help you," he said and I couldn't help my smile because I knew he meant every word.

"As you should," I said. "You're partly responsible for this too."

He laughed, and it was such a hearty sound to hear. It also made me realize he hadn't been as chirpy as this for quite a while since things at work had become even more hectic for him.

"When will you be home?" I asked.

"I'm going straight to your mom's right?" he asked.

"No. She needs to use some of our baking equipment so we're having dinner at our house. You forgot? I told you last night."

"Slipped my mind," he said. "Remind me to call her before this call ends. I want her to pick up some grapes for me."

"I'll pick them up for you," I said and started to rise to my feet.

"Olivia, you waddle when you walk now. You need to remain seated."

I didn't listen. "You both need to stop lecturing me all the time on how to behave and what I can and cannot do."

"Yes ma'am," he said and I didn't miss the amusement in his tone.

"Do you want the seedless ones?" I asked. "Be clear now on if you want them. I'm not letting you have mine."

"I do, get me a bag please," he said, and soon I was done picking them up. "Call me an hour before the meal is ready so I can be there on time," he said.

"Alright, see you later babe," I said, and the call came to an end.

After this, I walked for a little bit around the store in search of her, before seeing that she was now at the baking section. The buttery, sweet scent was soothing, but it made me wonder all the more what she was making for us for the evening and why it involved something baked.

I placed the grapes in her cart and she turned to gaze at me.

"What are you making for us tonight?" I asked, and she smiled beautifully. "Top secret," she replied, and I couldn't help but rest my hand on my belly.

She noticed my motion.

"Are you consoling him?" she asked. "Don't even bother, he's not escaping his grandmother's cooking experiments."

"I'm looking forward to them," I laughed. "I'll just be by some corner watching you two. Since his mom doesn't like to cook, it's great that his grandma does."

Her nose slightly wrinkled, and I wasn't sure of what I had said wrong.

"We need to talk about what he'll call me. I don't like 'grandma.' I'm not even sixty yet."

I laughed again as I grabbed our cart and rolled it forward.

As we walked along, we discussed alternative titles until she began to settle for him just calling her by her name. I outright rejected this. "No first name basis, in our family," I said. "Everyone gets a title."

"Fine," she said. "Have you and Xander decided on his name yet?"

"We have." I replied, and we're keeping it to ourselves till he's born."

She became upset. "I don't understand why you both are keeping this away from me."

"Because you might influence us too much and insist we change it."

"So my opinion means that much to you two now?"

"Unfortunately, it does." I sighed. "At least until you're done with physiotherapy and our hearts are not as soft towards you. Can we leave now?"

"Nope," she said and began to walk ahead. "I need some spices."

I had no choice but to follow.

Xander

I couldn't wait to get home.

Especially since I knew that by the time I arrived, my wife and mother-in-law would have spent enough time together and clashed enough times to be bickering.

It was always amusing to watch and listen to, especially since both of them, though annoyed with the other, still tried their best to be sensitive to each other's feelings.

In little time I arrived home and in hand was the cake I had delivered to the office for her. The moment I walked out of the foyer, I didn't see anyone but could hear their voices in the kitchen.

So I headed over, and sure enough saw them both bent over the stove watching whatever she was stirring.

"Olivia," I called, and they both turned to me. Her mom looked excited to see me, while Olivia just looked exhausted. I couldn't help my amusement.

"Welcome home," her mom said, while I set the cake down and waited as Olivia came over.

My heart was full as I watched her, knowing what she needed beyond all else was a hug. I stretched out my arms to receive her and she melted into my embrace.

She held tightly onto me and for the next few moments we were solely lost in each other.

"Seesh, you two," her mom teased, but I was too busy rubbing Olivia's back.

I brushed the escaped tendrils from her ponytail away from her face so I could look into her eyes.

"You okay?" I asked. But all she did was groan in response so I lowered my head to kiss her.

"Mom, Olivia looks like she's been bullied," I accused.

"She's my daughter. I have the right to bully her," her mother said amused, I leaned down to kiss her again.

"See?" Olivia said, and I kissed her one more time before finally letting go.

"Sorry babe, she's right," I said and began to pull the cake box open so I could show Olivia the cake with our son's name on it.

"Nice," she said, but when her mother began to head over we closed it right back.

"You can't see it till dinner time," Olivia said.

"It's a cake," her mother replied. "There's nothing special about a cake."

"So wait then. You're not telling us yet what you're making so we're not showing you what the cake looks like."

With a sigh, she returned to the stove while I returned my attention to Olivia. "We don't know what's for dinner?"

"It's top secret apparently," she replied. "But I have my theories. C'mon let's go get you changed. Do you need water?"

"No," I replied, and held her hand in mine.

"We'll be right back," I told her mom and soon we were on our way.

We walked quietly together as we headed up the stairs and soon we arrived at our bedroom.

"How was work?" she asked, and I gave her the needed updates. She took her time in loosening my tie and then unbuttoning my shirt and I let her, knowing she loved to do this when the time allowed so we could slow down enough to catch up with each other.

Eventually, she pulled the shirt down my arms and I turned around to face her so I could cradle her belly once again. My heart raced in excitement.

"I can't wait till he gets here," I said.

"I need him to get here already, I'm tired of waddling around all day. And plus I've been so horny today I felt like I was losing my mind." At this I laughed, and began to lead her towards the bed.

"Well, thankfully I'm home."

"Thankfully you are," she said, and was happily led until she was seated on the bed with her elbows propping her up.

I pulled her dress up as we spoke and in no time I was peeling her panties down her legs.

Afterwards I spread her legs even further apart, and the words were stolen from her lips the second mine latched onto her sex.

"Ah," she moaned, her hand reaching forward to grab onto my hair.

"Xander."

It was just what she needed, and I made sure it was more than enough to take her through the rest of the evening until I could pour my full attention on her later that night.

"Keep your tone down or Mom will hear us," I warned her, but she could barely speak as my tongue speared into her.

"I don't care," she gasped and I couldn't help my smile. Soon enough, I wanted more than anything to watch her face so my fingers replaced my mouth as I came over her. I watched her endearing struggle to keep her eyes open so she could hold my gaze too, but it was too much of a feat especially as the thrust of my fingers in and out of her became harder and faster. In no time, she was grabbing onto me and spilling onto my hand, the sweetest cries falling from her lips.

"Oh God," she moaned and thrashed against the bed and I lowered to kiss her until she was fully sated. Afterwards, I held her in my arms as the exhaustion from the day finally came down on the both of us.

"We need to head back soon," I said.

"Yeah," she replied, and held me even more tightly.

"I love you," she said, warming my heart, and I leaned down to press a kiss to her forehead.

"I love you more babe."

The End

Chapter One
AVA

It's baffling how some people are born with a silver spoon while some of us are born with... well, nothing.

Sometimes I try to analyze life, but it just does not make sense to me. How can some people have the whole world in their palms while some of us can't even afford a place to live? Ok, I'm not saying I can't afford a place to live, but you know what I mean. It's just crazy how life kisses some people on the cheek and pats their back while it slaps some of us hard on the face and slams us against a rough wall. Don't get me wrong, of course, I am grateful for the little I have. I mean, look at me, working as an executive administrative assistant at the prestigious L.M. firm, a job some people out there would kill to have. It's amazing, and I would like to say a very big thank you to Miss Luck for sending a job like this my way. But let's talk about the owner of this great firm. Let's talk about his only spoiled son, who never shows up at the company and is unwilling to help his old father. He's one of the many reasons I think some people don't deserve this wealthy life that's given to them on a platter of gold.

Today marks my third year working in this firm and believe me when I tell you I have never set my eyes on Mr. Miller's son since I've been working here as his father's executive administrative assistant. I know it's rich people's business, and I might not understand it, but what type of son never shows up at his father's company?

I asked Betty once before, and she told me it's not a topic she'd love to talk about. Pfft, that's Betty, she's one of the most taciturn people I've known in my entire life. She's so confidential, never wanting to talk about anything. No wonder she has worked as Mr. Miller's secretary for almost forty years and still counting. Betty might be boring, but she's hard-working. Mr. Lawrence Miller hired me to help her with the overwhelming workload, and it has been great so far. However, I'm still very interested in knowing why his son isn't helping him when he needs it the most. Is he physically impaired? Or does he suffer from an illness that makes him unable to work?

I also asked Joanna from the Research and Development Unit, and she also hasn't met the CEO's son. Joanna is talkative, and she always says what she knows, so I'm certain she truly doesn't know who Mr. Miller's son is. Nobody knows what type of man doesn't like to show his old and trying father some support. He should at least...

"Ava!" Betty shouts my name, snapping her fingers in front of my face.

"Oh, my God." I blink several times, raising my head to face Betty, who looks like she's been standing in front of my desk for five or ten minutes. Oh, God, I need to stop zoning out. "Yeah?"

"What's going on in that big mind?" Betty questions sarcastically, folding her arms against her chest.

"Oh, nothing, just thinking about my neighbor's dog that gave birth yesterday," I lie. Grandma Jane is the only neighbor I have, and she doesn't even have a dog. But Betty sure doesn't know that.

"Tsk, it's lunchtime, and you only have fifteen minutes because you need to pick Lulu up from the vet clinic in..." Betty pauses to check her wristwatch. "In thirty minutes, so hurry up, there's no chit-chatting with Joanna today," she expresses, waving her warning finger in my face.

"I don't chit-chat with Joanna during lunch breaks," I smirk, pushing my chair back to stand up.

"You and I both know you do," Betty speaks as she walks back to her seat.

She's right. I chit-chat with Joanna every lunch break because she's the only person in this company that knows all the company's business and the latest gossip. It's fun talking to her, unlike Betty.

"How about you? Aren't you going to get lunch?" I ask her, wondering why she's sitting instead of preparing to head out.

"Should I?" she raises her left brow. "Would you sit here in case Mr. Miller needs anything while I go grab lunch?"

"Oh, um…," I shake my head in disagreement. "I'll be back in five min –" a sound intrudes on my speech, and I pause. "What was that?" I wonder, turning to face Betty. We pause to listen carefully, and the sound is coming from Mr. Miller's office.

I quickly rush to pull his office door open. My eyes first hit some scattered files across the floor, then the disorganized desk. "Mr. Miller, are you ok?" I question, walking towards his desk to check why he placed his head on it. "Mr. Miller?" I tap him gently, but he doesn't respond. "Mr. Miller?" I call to him again, trying to lift his head gently, and that's when I realize he's unconscious. "Oh, my God!" I scream in fear, and Betty rushes inside the office.

"Ava, what's going on?" she implores as she hurries to meet me. "Mr. Miller? Jesus, he's unconscious!" her eyes widen in fear. "Wait here. I'll get my phone and call 911."

"Please hurry up," I plead, watching Betty as she hurries out to get her phone. I can't believe this is happening. Mr. Miller was all fine this morning. He even had a meeting with the shareholders earlier, and he looked fine. Why is this happening all of a sudden?

Betty, Anthony, and Jake rush inside the office a few minutes later with concern drawn across their faces.

"My God, what happened?" Anthony questions as he hurries towards Mr. Miller's desk.

"Have you called 911?" I turn to face Betty.

"Yes, I have, I…"

"The paramedics are here," Cecilia announces, leading two paramedics inside the office with her. "He's over there," she points in our direction.

The paramedics rush to lift Mr. Miller and gently place him on the gurney. Anthony and Jake run ahead of them as they push the stretcher to their ambulance while Betty, Cecilia, and I follow them outside the building and watch as Mr. Miller is taken away by the ambulance. Anthony and Jake volunteer to follow the paramedics while we wait behind to cancel the rest of Mr. Miller's plans for the day.

"Oh my," Betty breaks down in tears as we watch the ambulance drive away. "I hope he's ok,"

"He'll be fine, I promise," I assure her, patting her back, but deep inside, I'm scared too. I am so scared.

"Let's go inside," Cecilia suggests, and we all walk back inside the company and straight back to the office.

I can't believe the turn today is taking.

I comb my fingers through my blonde hair roughly, trying to think. Betty is still crying, and Cecilia is trying to get her to stop while trying so hard not to break down as well.

"We should inform Mrs. Miller," I suggest, walking to pick up the office phone. Mr. Miller's wife was here yesterday morning. It feels weird that I have to call her now to tell her that her husband was just rushed to the hospital, but I have to.

I dial her number and impatiently wait for her to answer the phone. She does not. "Come on, answer... answer, please," I redial her number, praying in my head that she answers, and this time she does.

"Hello?" her calm voice hits my ear from the other end of the phone.

I let out a sharp sigh. "Mr. Miller was just rushed to the hospital. He was unconscious and…"

"What!? Which hospital?" she implores, and I can hear the fear in her voice.

"I'll text you the hospital's address–"

"Please do," she responds before cutting the call.

I sharply pull the phone away from my ear and decide to call Anthony to ask for the hospital's address. God, why are my hands shaking?

"Hey, Anthony, how's he doing?"

"We just arrived at the hospital and are still waiting to hear anything."

"Please text me the hospital's address for Mrs. Miller."

"Ok, I will."

"Thank you."

The phone beeps, and it's a message from Anthony. I quickly forward it to Mr. Miller's wife. I know how worried she must be. Honestly, Mr. Miller has been overworking himself lately. I'm sure the stress took a toll on his health. Throughout last week, he was up and everywhere, traveling from one state to another, all for the company's betterment. He's hard-working and diligent, and I think he needs a break from this stress, a long break. Well, if I'm asked to share my opinion, I'd suggest getting his spoiled son over here to help his father. From what I've heard, Mr. Miller's son is in his early thirties, so why can't he help his father run the company?

Chapter Two
MAX

You want to know what sucks? Being thirty and being a billionaire's heir.

I know some of you might say, 'oh, how does being a billionaire's heir suck?' Yes, you can say that, but, let me tell you something, it does suck, at least to me. It's annoying that children aren't allowed to choose the family they wish to be born into. I would have preferred a simple family where I can be myself, and not much would be expected of me, but this family? Not so much.

My father is the owner of L.M. Multinational Retail Corporation. I am his only son, and I hate to talk about the weight of responsibilities that are resting on my shoulders. Honestly, I have thought about it so many times, thought about embracing those responsibilities and owning up to them, but I can't. It's not what I want for myself. I hate to be at the forefront, having my lifestyle on everybody's tongue. It's how rich people live their lives, their daily activities become topics in magazines and blogs. I've realized I am not about that life. Call me weird if you want, but I don't even have a social media account, and I hate the camera.

My mom told me she was worried about me when I was younger. I had no friends. I was just this smart boy in class that hated to associate with anyone. Well, I still am, just now, I've grown into a man. I still hate associating with people. It's hard to explain it, but I love my space. I don't see myself doing well as the CEO of my father's company, and I'm not even contemplating that idea. Working from home is easier and calmer for me. I like the peace it brings, and I don't think I'll get this peace being the acting CEO of my dad's company. I can't.

The CEO life does not entice me, not even a little bit. I love what I do now as a freelance illustrator. No, it's not a super lucrative job, but does it give me the peace of mind I crave? Yes, it does and that's why I chose to do this instead of taking over my dad's position in the company. My parents hate that I chose to be a freelance illustrator when I could be sitting in a well-furnished office, commanding hundreds of people. I can't count how many times my mom has tried to talk me into changing and helping my father with the company. It's hard to explain it to her. It's like she just wouldn't get it. She doesn't understand it's little things like this that give me joy, things like winning a project, sitting in front of my computer in this small cozy office, drawing, sketching, painting, and getting creative.

Switching on my computer, I decided to start working on the recent children's book project that I won. I've sketched out my plan for the book already, and I can't wait to get started. I crack my knuckles in preparation, but my phone rings as I attempt to start working.

"Damn it!" I groan, wondering who's calling me. I pick my phone up from the desk, and my face falls when I see the caller. It's my mom. I bet she's calling to rant about how I need to assist my dad. That's the only reason she calls me these days. She no longer calls to ask if I'm fine. It's always about the family's company.

Breathe in, breathe out. I coach myself before deciding to answer the phone.

"Hey, mom."

"Max…" my mom halts her speech, and a loud outburst of tears follows.

"Mom? What's wrong?" I ask with concern in my tone.

"Your dad, he's… he's… oh God! He's sick, and we are at the hospital. The doctor said his condition is critical, but…" she starts crying again.

"Mom, calm down, ok? Calm down, just text me the address of the hospital. I'll come there now,"

"Ok, I'll text you the address, Max, I–"

"Mom, it's going to be ok. Please try and calm down and text me the address."

"Ok," she says before ending the call.

Fear draws across my face as I push my chair back and stand up to pick up my jacket. Dad, sick? I saw him this weekend, and he was fine. What happened?

I rush out of my office and hurry inside my room to get my car fob. My phone beeps in my pocket, and I quickly pull it out to read the text message from my mom. After reading it, I dash out of my apartment to drive down there.

…

A whiff of pungent smell hits my nose as I step inside the hospital's cardiac intensive care unit. I'm still wondering where to turn when I see my mom flagging me down with a wave.

I hurry to meet her, and the first thing she says is. "You, Max, are going to take over the company. You are the reason your father's laying in that bed. You have to…"

I sigh before holding her hands. "Mom, calm down and talk to me. What exactly is going on?" A doctor steps inside the waiting room before Mom can speak.

My mom releases her hand from my grip and hurries to meet the doctor. "Doctor, how is my husband doing?"

"He had a heart attack and will need to undergo coronary bypass surgery," the doctor explains.

"Oh dear," Mom collapses in my arms, crying and hitting her hands against my chest simultaneously. "You should have listened to me. You should have agreed to assist your father,"

I stand there in a daze, not knowing how to feel. How did this happen? Coronary bypass surgery?

"What will you do now? What will you do? Are you going to keep sitting in that little office of yours, drawing and painting irrelevant things while your old father works himself to death? Is that what you want?" Mom panics, hitting her hands against my chest as she cries.

"Mom, calm down, please," I walk her to a chair and sit. "Dad will be fine, I promise,"

"Yes, he will be, and you are going to take over the company," she insists.

I sigh, burying my face in my palms. I hope my dad survives this, or I'll never be able to forgive myself. Maybe my mom is right. Perhaps it's time I face my responsibilities. I'll have to sacrifice my interest for the family business, after all, isn't that what billionaire heirs are born to do? I wanted to change the whole concept and thought I could be a billionaire heir living his dreams, but I guess not.

Five hours and some tension later, the doctor walks into the waiting room. "The operation was successful," he announces.

"Oh, thank goodness," Mom heaves a sigh of relief, and I pull her into a tight hug.

"You may go in to see him now," the doctor says before walking away.

We walk inside my dad's room, and what I see breaks my heart. "Dad," I walk to the side of his bed, staring at his unconscious body as he lays there lifeless. There are tubes and wires hooked up everywhere. Machines line the one side of his bed.

"Oh, my dear Lawrence," Mom moves to sit on the chair next to Dad's bed, crying as she watches him.

The doctor walks back inside the room. "He will be fine," he starts. "However, he will need a few weeks to rest before he can fully recover. Also, I noticed stress is the major factor that led to his heart attack. Once he recovers, he will have to stay away from any stressful activity to avoid this from reoccurring,"

"Thank you, Doctor," I nod before sighing.

"It's your fault," my mom rants again. "Take a good look at your father because you are the reason he's laying here lifeless like this," she sniffs, wiping off the tears on her cheeks. "If only you had listened to us."

My mom is right, and I feel guilty too. I pull a chair over to sit beside her and take my dad's hand. "Dad, I'm sorry for not listening to you," I sigh, shutting my eyes. "I promise to be a better son from now on. Just wake up, please," tears threaten to crawl out of my eyes, but I sniff them back.

"You heard what the Doctor said, your father cannot resume being the CEO of that company even after he recovers," Mom expresses.

"Yes, I did. I will start this afternoon and take over Dad's position as the CEO."

The days of freelancing as an illustrator are over. I'm left with no other option than to step in as the CEO of L.M. Corporations, and I will.

Chapter Three
AVA

I still can't wrap my head around everything that's happening. It feels so surreal. Like why do bad things happen to good people? Mr. Miller is one, if not the nicest person I've known in my entire life. He's calm, easy to work with, friendly, and has an amazing personality. He's the last person something like this should happen to. Well, isn't this what life is – a bitch. It gives people what they don't deserve. I just hope Mr. Miller wins life on this one and gets well soon.

Betty has been pacing up and down the office, and I don't even know what to say to calm her down. I'm on the verge of losing my calm too. We are waiting for Anthony and Jake to return and let us know what exactly is happening.

"Anthony and Jake are back!" Cecilia announces.

"Are they?" Betty and I hurry out of our office and straight down to the accounting department to confirm.

Anthony stood in the middle of the room, Jake standing next to him. The expressions on their faces burned through my heart. It was nothing close to relief or 'everything-will-be-fine.' It was sadness and anxiety. Exhaling, I walk to meet Anthony. "Hey, how is he doing?" I ask, knowing I won't like his reply.

He sighs, shaking his head from left to right. "It seems serious. We didn't wait to hear what the doctor said. Mrs. Miller arrived and told us we should leave."

"He will be fine, right?" Betty asks, and tears have gathered in her eyes again.

"Hopefully," Jake plugs in sadly. "We can't say yet."

"I need to go out for some fresh air," Betty says, trying so hard not to cry as she rushes out of the department.

Sighing, I walk back inside our office, and this time, I can't help the tears from crawling out of my eyes. Why is this happening?

As I sit, my mind returned to the day I came here for this job interview. It was a Monday morning three years ago, I didn't think I could get the job. In truth, there were people with better qualifications. I had nothing but decided to try my luck. That year, my life had hit rock bottom, and getting a job was the only way out, not just any job, but a great one because I was drowning in piles of debt. I had applied to many jobs, and this one was the last. I was surprised when I got an email that I had been shortlisted. It was the best news I'd got that morning, and on the scheduled day, which was the next Monday, I dressed up and came here for the interview.

I sat outside with other candidates who looked way better than I did. I remember rocking a thrift pencil skirt and a shirt I've had for a long time. There was no finesse to how I dressed compared to the other ladies I met here. I didn't even sleep the night before coming for the interview because I worked weekends at a bar, and I couldn't miss a day. So, coming here on a Monday morning with no sleep the night before, I don't think I have to tell you what I looked like – super exhausted. Unlike me, the other candidates I met here looked ready for the job, who looked desperate to get the job. I knew there was no way I'd get the job.

All the candidates went in for their interview, and I was called in last. I stepped inside the room that morning with pessimism and the little luck people used to tell me I had. Mr. Lawrence Miller, Betty, and Mr. Alex Brown (you don't know him, but he works here too. He has a crush on me, but ew, no, I don't like him.) So, the three of them were in the room that morning and seeing them, I thought, *'Girl, there's no way you're getting this job.'*

"Good morning. Are you…" Betty started, and she paused to read my name from the file she held. "Ava Roberts?"

"Yes, I am," I nodded.

"Please, have a seat." Mr. Miller told me calmly.

I sat, and the interview started. I was asked various questions. I can't remember what the questions were, but I remember I didn't answer any correctly. I wasn't even prepared for the interview. I didn't read anything before coming here, and I failed all the questions they asked me about the company. I just knew this job was not for me.

The interview ended, and I went home knowing I had failed. When I got home, I struck this job off of my list and hoped that the other companies would reach out to me.

Two weeks later, no company had reached out to me, but a miracle happened, I got an email from L.M. Corporations. I couldn't believe the email when it mentioned that I had got the job. I saw the email late – on the morning of the day I was supposed to start the job. Well, that was because I stopped checking my emails, as it affected my mental health.

I hurried out of bed, got dressed, and started work here. It felt like a miracle. After working here for a while, I decided to ask Betty why I was hired because I saw better candidates here on the interview day. Betty told me Mr. Lawrence Miller picked me for reasons she too couldn't wrap her head around. She told me her choice was the red-haired lady that sat next to me on the interview day. But Mr. Miller, he was my guardian angel, and that's why he has to survive whatever this is.

I wipe the tears from my face and sniff sharply. If there's anything I can do to help Mr. Miller, I'd be willing to do it.

"Good morning?" a bass voice breaks in, causing me to raise my head. "Is this…" he pauses and reads something from his phone. "Betty and Eva's office?"

"Ava, yes," I respond, wondering who he is and why he's here. "I'm sorry if you are here to meet with Mr. Miller, he's currently not in the office today, and…" I halt my speech, and my eyes drop on his broad chest, then move to the defined arms. According to the stadiometer, in my eyes, the man is heavily built and 6'5 or 6'6? He's casually dressed in jeans and a short-sleeved collarless pullover shirt, and he looks like someone that lives in the gym. Oh, wait. "Are you Mr. Miller's physical therapist? Please sit over there, and…" I switch on my computer, remembering Mr. Miller talked about meeting with his physical therapist later today. I don't think I canceled that appointment.

Instead of obeying, the burly man moves to walk inside Mr. Miller's office. I stand up and block him, frowning, I say. "I'm not in a great mood today, so, please, don't make me mad. When you are asked to sit, you sit. You don't just walk inside like you own this place, young man," I clear my throat sharply, rethinking the 'young man' I just called him. "Burly man," I correct myself, gesturing at the whole muscly look he's got going on.

"Ava?" Betty calls as she steps inside the office. "What's going on?"

"This man just walks in here and won't listen to me," I size him up with my eyes, but that's just a return of how he's been looking at me – with a frown and inspective eyes. I could punch him, but I won't.

"You must be Betty?" the man speaks, turning around and extending his hand in Betty's direction.

Oh, wow, he can treat Betty with that type of courtesy, but he won't even answer my questions? How ridiculous!

"Yes, I am," Betty accepts the handshake respectfully. "Welcome, please go inside," she gestures towards Mr. Miller's office.

My face breaks into confusion, and I stand in the way, frowning at Betty, I say. "Why are you allowing a stranger into Mr. Miller's office?" I turn my eyes in the burly annoying man's direction.

"Ava," Betty calls me, casting me warning eyes.

"Betty?" I question, not understanding what's happening right now.

"I'm Max Miller, the CEO's son,"

I blink several times, and my shoulders drop. No, I don't believe it.

"Say again?"

The man sizes me up with his eyes again as I move out of the way, creating space for him to walk inside.

I stand there, confused, and trying to think about what I'll do with my life when I get fired from this place.

Wait, how can he be Mr. Miller's son? This man looks super healthy, and from what I saw, he's not handicapped in any form.

"Betty, he's kidding, right?" I ask in a low tone, following Betty to her seat as she walks. "He's not Mr. Miller's son, is he?"

"Yes, he is," Betty replies sharply.

"Are you kidding me right now?" I pull a short nervous laugh. "That man can't be–" I stop talking after observing the look on Betty's face. "No way, oh, my God," I throw my hand over my mouth, wondering what I had just done. "I need to see Joanna," I say, running my hand through my blonde hair.

"Joanna? Why?"

"She told me about a job vacancy last week. I want to ask her if it's still available," I respond.

"Ava, is this the time to…"

"The two of you should see me now," the man's voice breaks in as he peeks through Mr. Miller's office's door.

I know what this is. I've seen these things in movies. As I predicted, he's probably taking over, and guess who is getting fired?

Pre-order here:
CEO GRUMP

ABOUT THE AUTHOR

Thank you so much for reading!
If you have enjoyed the book and would like to leave a
precious review for me, please kindly do so here:

On His Terms

Please click on the link below to receive info about my latest
releases and giveaways.
NEVER MISS A THING

Or
come and say hello here: